PRAISE FOR *ROSIE COLORED GLASSES*

"Without so much as dipping a toe into cliche territory, Wolfson's heady descriptions of love will curl into readers' souls. With a simplistic elegance to her prose, the author delivers a treasure of a read."

—*The Washington Post*

"Takes the reader into the heart...[and] demonstrates the power and limitations of love and the ability of family to heal."

—*Library Journal*

"Behind the beautiful language, the idea that children see their parents through rose-colored glasses will resonate with readers beyond the last page."

—*Booklist*

"Tender and bright, a compelling novel of a young girl (who completely owned my heart) and the mother she adores and fears and needs so badly."

—Luanne Rice, *New York Times* bestselling author

"Brianna Wolfson has done a marvelous thing. I followed Willow with a hopeful, breaking heart, reminded how all of us are different in so many ways, and yet so absolutely deserving of love."

—Nancy Thayer, *New York Times* bestselling author

"A bittersweet, tender exploration of many kinds of love. This compelling novel, with unpredictable turns, reveals what love can save—and what it can't."

—Helen Klein Ross, award-winning author of *What Was Mine*

"Sparkling, insightful and honest, the Thorpe family's powerful story will stay in my thoughts for a long time."

—Phaedra Patrick, author of *The Library of Lost and Found*

"What a wonderful, emotional ride! It's like the *Ordinary People* for the 21st century.... Such an achievement!"

—Robyn Carr, #1 *New York Times* bestselling author

Also by Brianna Wolfson
Rosie Colored Glasses

That Summer in Maine

BRIANNA WOLFSON

mira

ISBN-13: 978-0-7783-5123-8

That Summer in Maine

Mira
22 Adelaide St. West, 40th Floor
Toronto, Ontario M5H 4E3, Canada
BookClubbish.com

Printed in U.S.A.

For Lana, Michael, Trevor and Kate.
Home wouldn't have been home without you.

That Summer in Maine

PROLOGUE

ONE YEAR AGO

All mothers wish a perfect love story upon their daughters. The wish that their daughters will grow up wrapped in love and that one day they will go on to wrap others in love. They wish for their love to be simple and pure and uncomplicated.

As a single mother, Jane did everything she could to uphold that perfect love for her daughter, Hazel. At least, she'd tried.

Today, Jane gave birth to twin boys with a man she had recently fallen in love with and married. In the postbirthing haze, Jane could taste the salt on her upper lip where her sweat was now dried. The fiery heat deep within her body was starting to subside and her spine still felt sore and twisted. Jane held one twin against her bare chest while the other was tucked into the crease of her husband Cam's arm. Jane motioned for him to come closer and embrace the start of their family. "I love you," she said and kissed him and then the two babies gently. She looked up to see if she could find her daughter. The back of Hazel's shoulder was just visible in the doorway as she stood cross-armed, looking away from the room. Hazel, at fourteen years old, looked both young and old for her age all at once standing there.

"Come in, honey, and meet your brothers," Jane said gently.

Hazel turned around slowly, her black hair like a veil in front of her eyes. She shuffled toward her mother without lifting her feet and leaned over her bed. Jane brought her free arm up toward Hazel's face and tucked her daughter's hair behind her ear, revealing her eyes of different colors. Her lashes were damp, and her eyes—one green and one hazel—were clear and dewy. A mother can always tell when her child has been crying. Jane leaned over to kiss Hazel's cheek, but her sudden movement startled her newborn, who let out a brief wail that ended when Jane returned her body to its original position.

Hazel's shoulders fell. Hazel wanted that kiss. Perhaps needed it.

"Meet your brother Griffin," Jane whispered to Hazel, tilting her arm ever so slightly so that her daughter could see her brother's face. "And that's Trevor over there." Cam took a few steps toward Hazel and smiled with pride.

"I thought we were going to name him August," Hazel challenged.

Jane chuckled.

"Last-minute change. Give them both a big kiss, big sis."

Hazel rolled her eyes and placed her lips on each baby

and then huffed out of the room without another word. To Jane, her family finally felt full. But she could tell that for Hazel, something had emptied.

In her happiness of sharing this moment with Cam and welcoming her two new healthy babies, Jane had neglected to consider the impact on Hazel's perfect love story. Cam came over and kissed her forehead.

"I love this family," he said.

Jane let that sink in. Deep. And then wondered if he was including Hazel in his definition of *family*. And couldn't deny a shift within her own heart. It had expanded and made room for two more babies. And these two new sons deserved their own pure, simple, uncomplicated love story. And Jane would give it to them wholeheartedly. She felt resolute and focused about it.

Indeed, she forgot to wonder what it would mean for Hazel's happiness. For her sense of family and her sense of self.

PART I

Home

1

HAZEL

Hazel Box had been feeling self-conscious about the blackness of her hair lately. She had long gotten over having a different last name than her mom. She had even come to enjoy telling the tale about how her hazel eye came from her mother and her green eye came from her father, whoever he was, wherever he was. But the blackness of her hair was really beginning to get to her now. Every other member of her family was blond. The blond of Marilyn Monroe and stock photos of Midwestern families. The blond that could look white depending on how the light hit it.

Lately, sitting down at the dinner table had become an exercise in holding back tears.

"Food's ready, honey!" her mother shouted from the other room.

Hazel flinched. She considered staying locked in her room and declaring she had too much homework, but her tummy grumbled. So she dragged her feet along the hallway and into the kitchen. She was disappointed to see Cam there, though she should expect it by now. Cam always tried to be home from work early enough to share these moments with the family. Still, Hazel couldn't help but wish and wish there was a single day, any day, he'd have to work late and miss dinner.

As soon as Hazel slid onto her chair and tucked her knees under the table, all those gurgling feelings of disgust and resentment and faraway-ness began stirring around in her belly again.

"How was school?" Cam asked Hazel without looking her way as he finished setting the table. Hazel felt like she was too old to be getting this question but sensed that it was a thing Cam thought fathers were supposed to ask their children. A thing he was practicing for when the twins grew up.

"Fine," Hazel responded, barely audibly.

Cam continued to shuffle plates and cups and forks and knives from their cabinets and drawers onto the table. Hazel paused. There was an effortless rhythm to Cam's sound in the kitchen. It was different than the syncopated clanking that used to ensue—dish knocking against dish, cabinets opening and closing precariously.

Hazel tried to recall when Cam started moving so naturally through space. When his movements became so automatic, rehearsed. Cam pulled a glass out of the cabinet, filled it up with water from the sink and leaned against the countertop as he took a slow, casual drink. There was so much comfort there, she thought. Like that glass, that water, that countertop was his. Like this space was his. Like this whole home was his.

Her thoughts were interrupted by the twins chattering in food-stained T-shirts despite their bibs. Her mother ran over to give all of her children kisses. Hazel was last.

As far as Hazel was concerned, the day her mother married Cam was the day she lost a mother to a wife. And the day the twins were born was the same day she had become an orphan. It was only a year ago but it felt like so, so much longer. The day a family was created in her own home without any regard for the family that had already been living there. The family of Hazel and Jane. Mother and daughter. Just the two of them. Watching all the thin, delicate blond locks swaying as they reached for a plate or turned their heads to the side was only a reminder of the new family that existed that she was no longer a part of.

Cam sat down and carefully scooped a large spoonful of pasta onto Jane's plate and then his own and smiled through closed lips. Jane rubbed Cam's shoulder tenderly as he reached for the next bowl, and Hazel's tummy did another flip.

Jane divided her pasta into small bits with her fingers and placed the pasta in front of the twins on each of their high chair trays. Griffin pinched his index finger and thumb precariously around one and brought it to his mouth. "Mmm," he said, looking back at his mother for approval. Trevor smiled and then reached over into Griffin's pile of pasta, eager for his own slice of the attention.

"Mmm," he said, too, slightly louder than Griffin had.

Hazel was grateful that something had finally interrupted the awkward silence at the table.

Hazel served herself a spoonful of pasta and looked over at Cam.

"So-o-o, how was everyone's day?" Cam said transparently as he tried to start some kind of conversation. His eyebrows were raised like two exclamation marks on his forehead.

Hazel considered rolling her eyes but instead turned her gaze down toward her plate and listlessly stirred her food with her fork. She was more nauseous than she was hungry now.

"Great, darling," Jane responded after just a bit too long. "Just great." She shoved a forkful of pasta into her mouth and began chewing as if that were the thing stopping her from extending her response.

Still, Cam smiled broadly as if someone had just told him something significant. Hazel rolled her eyes as discreetly as she could. She didn't trust people that were so easily charmed.

Hazel looked toward her mother and wondered if she, too, had been charmed by absolutely nothing. And it appeared she was. She had her eyes locked on her husband and both her feet resting casually on his chair. What could she possibly be so impressed by?

Hazel rested her fork down on the table and continued to stare her mother's way, wondering if she would look back. Willing her to look back.

And finally her mother did, as if snapping out of a trance.

"And how was your day, Hazel?" her mother asked sweetly.

Hazel was about to utter her usual response, "Terrible," but then the twins started their nightly performance.

Griffin dropped a piece of pasta from his high chair and watched intently as it fell to the floor. He stared down at the falling thing, first quietly, curiously, at its failure to return. And then his legs began to squirm as he became increasingly agitated that the pasta remained on the floor. Ignoring the remaining dozen bits of pasta on the table, Griffin began to cry. At this point, Trevor had become enraptured by the scene. Cam sprang into motion and restored the single piece of pasta to its position among the other pieces of pasta. The crying stopped, and Cam assumed his position back in his chair.

Hazel rolled her eyes at how easy it was for Griffin to get even the tiniest attention he wanted. And then she rolled her eyes again as Griffin and Trevor each began to curl his tiny, still-glitchy fingers around another piece of pasta and threw it down to the floor with a gummy smile. The excitement of throwing the pasta was as delightful to them as the consequences were alarming. The crying began again. This time doubled. First Griffin and then Trevor wailed in his high chair.

No matter how many times Hazel had observed this scene, it always surprised her that the response to this chain of events was to start it up once again. As soon as the object—this time a piece of pasta, other times a pacifier or a toy—was returned to their hands, they would drop it once more. They would fill with joy as they watched the object fall and then become devastated when it stayed there. With each repetition, neither delight of the thing falling nor the distress of the thing remaining on the floor ever lessened. Surely they would have realized by now that their heartbreak could be avoided. But they never seemed to. As Cam bent over and picked up the pasta, returned it to the table for the second time, and both boys became elated once more, it occurred to Hazel that she had been misinterpreting the scene the whole time.

Their distress, suffering, their tears, created magic for them. It caused the chaos that then allowed order to be restored. It enabled the delight in dropping those things to become possible again. It proved their father to be a healing force in this world.

This was something she wished she understood, and felt, about Cam, too.

Suddenly, the whole idea of being at the dinner table seemed too pathetic to participate in; the act of raising a fork to your mouth and saying "mmm" even before the taste hit your lips. Or passing a pitcher filled with cold water extravagantly decorated with sliced lemons. Or placing a small bit of each part of the meal in front of the twins, only to have them slap their palms into it or throw it onto the floor. It was all so elaborate, so superficially charming, but ultimately meaningless. A ceremony with no purpose. It was as if they were following the script written about the meal of the loveliest, happiest family. But Hazel felt a gurgling refusal to participate in the show of it all.

"I have some homework to finish," Hazel lied. "Is it okay if I go back to my room?"

Hazel's mom reached her arms across the table and opened her palms. And Hazel put her hands in her mother's, leaving her fingers and wrists limp. Her mother gave them a tight, tight squeeze and then brought Hazel's hands to her lips and kissed them loudly.

Trevor and Griffin pressed their own tiny palms, messy from dinner, to their lips and smacked their lips clumsily together in a kissing motion.

"Mwa, mwa," they said.

"You've trained them well, Mom," Hazel said, smirking and rolling her eyes.

Jane relinquished Hazel's hands.

"My children will never be able to give me too many kisses."

Hazel slid her chair out from under the table and walked back to her room. She shut her bedroom door behind her and pressed her back up against it as if she had been chased in there. Her chest was rising and falling and she noticed that her hands had curled up into tight fists.

She slid her back down the door, the grooves in it providing a comforting massage, until she was seated on the carpet. She closed her eyes and tried to escape to somewhere else. Somewhere she felt part of something again. And just as she began to dream, her mother's voice rang through the air.

"Hazel, honey. Give the twins a bath, won't you?"

Hazel dropped her chin into her chest and left a brief moment of silence hanging in the air. Just long enough to let the slightest tension build.

"Of course, Mother," Hazel shouted back, too emphatically through clenched teeth, and then dragged her legs along the same hallway she had just walked down and turned into the living room.

Hazel continued to the kitchen and scooped each twin up into her arms.

"Okay, you two, bath time."

Hazel rested Griffin and then Trevor down onto the bath mat and turned the faucet to the right. Water poured out, first cold and soon just the right amount of warm. The twins chattered in near unison at the sound of rushing water.

Hazel picked up Griffin to undress him. First his little pants, and then his little shirt. His legs kicked and body squirmed in anticipation. A drool-laden smile spread across his face. The diaper always looked so big on that tiny body. Hazel smiled and then pressed her face into his soft, protruding belly. Griffin giggled, which made Trevor giggle, too.

She carefully removed their diapers and placed Griffin, and then Trevor, into the water and scooped water over their fine whorls of hair as they wobbled in place. She plunged the duck-shaped sponge into the bath and watched it expand with warm soapy water before pulling it out from under the water. Griffin and Trevor smiled in anticipation of the dripping sponge meeting their bodies. Hazel supported Trevor's chest with one hand and then pressed the saturated sponge into his back and rubbed it around. He giggled some more and waved his arms jerkily into the water. Griffin played along, slapping his palms onto the water's surface. Hazel applied the soapy sponge to each fold in their soft, drooping skin. The creases of their wrists were her favorite—where arms met hands in a formless puff of delicate flesh.

Then Hazel dumped a bucket of floating animal figurines into the tub. They bobbed awkwardly, some on their sides, some right side up, some with their feet peeking above the water. Griffin and Trevor splashed some more at the excitement. Hazel picked out the lion from the bunch and held it up.

"What does a lion say, boys?"

They looked at her inquisitively. Then Griffin opened his mouth to make a scratching, grumbling noise.

"Yeah! Ro-ooaa-ar," Hazel said playfully as she walked the lion shape along the ledge of the tub. "Ro-ooa-rr."

Griffin reached out for the figurine and Hazel placed it in his hand. Trevor picked out the hippopotamus shape out from the bunch and mimicked Griffin's scratching, grumbling sound with his own screeching twist.

"Sure, that works," Hazel said and watched them enter their shared trance of play. It was so intimate the way their worlds became entangled in an imaginary space that was as real to them alone as it was invisible to everyone else. They played and chattered and traded snacks and toys together from the moment they opened their eyes in the morning until the moment they closed them together at night. The bath was always transformed into a magical realm that Hazel could merely observe. Her participation was nothing but superficial. She wondered what it would be like to feel siblinghood as deeply as this. For each item in this bath to become a shared and sacred prop in some sort of make-believe narrative. She wondered what it would be like to cross a threshold with another person that no one else could see into. It used to feel like that with her mother, but things were different now. Now her mother had Cam. The twins had each other. And Hazel was left with hollowness. A world she wanted to escape from but no world to escape into.

Still, Hazel couldn't help but feel a warmth inside her as she watched the twins enjoy each other so wholly. So gently. So effortlessly.

They were so quick to enjoy their life together. So open to joy. It was refreshing to see the world through their eyes at times.

Hazel bent over the edge of the tub and brought Trevor's hand to her face. She pressed his palm to her lips for a long kiss and held it there. His fingers curled sweetly around her face. They were pruned and wrinkled from his time in the bath.

Hazel pulled each small body from the bath and wrapped it in a towel before scooping each up once again into her arms. They smelled so sweet and pure and innocent. Then Hazel brought the twins to her mother, who was still in the same position on the couch. She nestled each one on either side of her body. Her mother pulled the boys in close and gently kissed each one on the forehead and inhaled.

"It's so sad to think that one day they'll lose this smell," Jane said.

Hazel turned around without responding and walked back toward her room.

She had certainly lost that freshly-bathed-baby smell a long, long time ago.

2
JANE

Jane rocked her little boys, one in each arm, and inhaled. They smelled so sweet after their bath. One by one, as she rocked them, their eyelids fell heavy. She placed them in their single crib. She remembered that Cam was originally surprised when she returned home from the store with just one crib.

"Saving the other crib for your next trip?" he asked genuinely.

She smiled at the thought as she watched the boys lying peacefully. She had read that one twin could disturb the other's sleep if they were in the same space, but she'd willfully neglected it. And, as usual for Jane, her intuition was right. The boys had always been able to soothe each other, at times even more than she could. When she woke up in the middle of the night to feed them as infants, they would have already hooked their tiny little fingers into each other's. Even as she watched them falling into their slumber before her, they were naturally wiggling their little bodies over toward each other until they felt the comfort of their brother alongside them.

Jane traced Trevor's tender, wrinkled feet gently with her finger. He flinched and Jane pulled her finger away quickly, as if it had never risked waking him. But he swiftly went back to sleep. When she was sure he was still, Jane brought her same finger along the wisps of Griffin's hair where they met the soft nape of his neck. Griffin, too, flinched and then returned to slumber without any more stirring. It was a mother's right to enjoy the smooth, buttery yet vulnerable skin of her children whenever she so pleased.

Griffin and Trevor were everything anyone would want babies to be—soft and cherubic, petal-soft hair smelling of something sweet and powdery. They absorbed love without the slightest hesitation. They smiled when you tickled their belly. They laughed when you stuck your tongue out during a game of peekaboo. They stared into your eyes curiously and unwaveringly. They reached their arms out longingly for you. They had even slept soundly from the beginning. And with Hazel old enough to help, Jane could put aside many of the empirical realities that typically accompanied the birth of a child, or two. Hazel was so supportive and helpful with the care and maintenance of the babies—bath time, night feedings, sodden diapers, spilled milk, unexpected tears and soiled clothes. Jane was left with the spiritual bliss of her still-new-feeling babies and her still-new-feeling marriage.

As the baby brothers lay next to each other, silent, Jane crept out of their room and closed the door quietly behind her. She pressed her ear against the other side of the wall to listen for any signs of stirring but heard nothing. Just the peaceful and heartwarming scenario of two freshly bathed little boys asleep.

Jane felt a warm smile spread across her lips and a light flutter in her heart. She was so lucky. It was almost as if all the pain in her past life didn't exist anymore.

Before joining Cam in the bedroom, she made her way into the kitchen and filled two big bowls with two heaping scoops of ice cream. She dashed back down the hallway, past the twins' room, past Hazel's room, into her own. They were always retiring to their bedroom as early as possible to get their alone time. Cam was already under the covers with his glasses on, reading a magazine. He lifted his head and smiled at Jane. She made her way toward the bed, with her hands and bowls of ice cream behind her back. She kissed him on the forehead, leaving her lips there for an extra moment, and then whipped the bowls out from behind her back.

"This one's for you," Jane declared and then joined her husband under the covers. "It has more cookie dough pieces."

Cam deliberately spooned a chunk of his ice cream from the bowl. Jane could see on the spoon that there was a large piece of cookie dough embedded in the vanilla ice cream. She looked down at the spoon and raised one eyebrow. And then Cam brought the spoon to her lips.

"Open wide."

Jane ate the cookie dough–filled spoonful in one quick bite.

3

HAZEL

After bringing her brothers to her mother, Hazel returned to her bedroom and cracked the door just slightly ajar. She couldn't help but remain acutely aware of the sounds of her home, even though they pained her. Aware of the ways in which everyone puttered around the house. The way they moved from one space to the next. It was comforting to know where everyone was, even if out of sight. She had come to familiarize herself with the delicate sweep of her mother's steps, the heavy shuffle of Cam's, or the fumbling patter of Griffin or Trevor.

She could tell by the vacant crackle of the baby monitor that the twins were asleep now. She heard her mother rummaging around the kitchen. She heard the strained whoosh of the freezer opening. Then, the slight clanking of silverware rustling as a drawer opened, and then the click of it shutting.

Hazel knew it was ice cream time. Hazel's mom said

Hazel couldn't call it a tradition, because she never knew when it would come.

"A sweet surprise for my sweet," she would say as she revealed two bowls of ice cream from behind her back and then sat down on the bed.

Each bowl would contain two scoops of vanilla and nothing else. "I'm a vanilla purist," her mother would say as she scooped spoonful after spoonful into her mouth. "None of that chocolate chip, cookie dough, brownie bite, peanut butter swirl, caramel, nut nonsense."

They would tuck themselves under the sheets and eat until their bellies were full. And then they would put the empty bowls on the bedside table and lie there quietly, usually until they fell asleep.

Hazel heard the click of one spoon, and then another, hit the edge of the bowl. Yes, she knew it. Hazel's spine uncurled itself from its hunched position over the puzzle and zipped straight up, ready for her sweet surprise. She heard the weightless sweep of her mother's feet moving across the floor of the kitchen, and then onto the carpet of the hallway. Hazel could already feel the coldness in her cheeks and the sweetness on her tongue.

Out of the crack in her door, she saw her mother appear one moment, and then move swiftly out of sight the next moment. The sounds of her mother's feet continued to move gingerly down the hallway.

Hazel tiptoed toward her door and peeked her head out into the hallway. Her mother stood in front of her own bedroom at the end of the hall, two bowls of ice cream behind her back. The top of a scoop of ice cream poked out over the edge of the bowl. She could see the brown globs of cookie dough mixed into the creamy white vanilla. And then she felt the familiar tingle in her fingertips and toes. She accepted that this was her life now. That this would always be her life.

She scooted back across the carpet. The tingling had now spread up through her cheeks and to the top of her head. She closed her eyes and pressed her palms into the carpet, reminding herself that gravity was still available to her. But then she let her palms float right back up. If this was what her life would be like here, perhaps she could go somewhere else. Anywhere else. Anywhere else out of Verona, New York, out of this house, with these people. She was invigorated anew at the idea of floating away to that anywhere place.

It wasn't that Hazel was longing for a more magnificent, more spectacular life. It wasn't that she needed ice cream in bed or to fall asleep next to her mother. It was just that she wanted to feel a connection. To anything. Anywhere.

Hazel looked over at the photo of her and her mother tacked up on the wall. She yanked it off and held it up close, looking into the eyes of her younger self and then her mother's younger self. She remembered this day well. It was the first chilly day of the year and they had bundled up in big puffy jackets and scarves. In the photo, both of their noses were pink from a day at the carnival. They'd played games and eaten cotton candy and fried dough and laughed and shouted on the rides until their bellies ached. Hazel looked down at the corner of the photo and observed how her mother's hand was wrapped tightly around her waist, squeezing the down jacket tight. Her eyes welled up a little bit. It was a different time. A time they would never get back.

Hazel threw the picture on the floor. It fell facedown on her carpet, revealing an inscription on the back of the photo that she never knew was there, and read it to herself.

Sleep little baby, clean as a nut,
Your fingers uncurl and your eyes are shut.
Your life was ours, which is with you.
Go on your journey. We go too.

The bat is flying round the house
Like an umbrella turned into a mouse.
The moon is astonished and so are the sheep:
Their bells have come to send you to sleep.

Oh be our rest, our hopeful start.
Turn your head to my beating heart.
Sleep little baby, clean as a nut,
Your fingers uncurl and your eyes are shut.

It was the poem her mother used to read to her before bed each night. "Lullaby" by John Fuller. Hazel could nearly recite the words from memory as she read them. She liked that it wasn't a simple nursery rhyme. She had never thought to contemplate the meaning before, but for some reason it seemed important now.

Hazel had the paradoxical sense that she was in the center of her story and yet entirely left out of it.

She was lonely. There was no other word for it. And she remembered the moment when that feeling had become a permanent fixture in her gut. The shift in feeling itself was sharp and harsh and solidified her position as an outsider in her own home. An outsider in her own family.

She couldn't help but replay the moment in her mind.

It was about a month before the twins were born and Hazel was coming back from school. She had just stepped off the pavement of the walkway into the front door and opened her mouth to shout "Hello," as she always had. But before she could get the word out, she heard her mother say something. She couldn't quite make out the words of what she had said, but she could clearly make out Cam's hearty laughter in response. Thinking the exchange was finished, Hazel closed the door behind her, and shouted, "Hello." There was no response.

She walked into the kitchen, thirsting to be noticed, but her mother and Cam were keeled over in laughter. She felt truly alone in their presence. Hazel understood that her mother now belonged to Cam and he belonged to her. When her mother was getting to know Cam, the three of them had spent time together and it had felt back then like that was how things would always be. But Hazel now knew that it had been an act. The twins were just another thing binding them together and leaving her out. This loneliness was her life now, until she could find a way out. She was sure of it. And the sight of her mother's large, extended belly bouncing up and down only reinforced her deep, incisive sadness. She knew her mother would soon belong to those boys growing inside of her, too. That she would be outnumbered by others. That the size of their family would be much greater than the size of her and her mother. That she had lost the battle. That she was nearly no longer a member of the family.

A sense of dislocation came over her and Hazel brought her hand to the doorframe to brace herself. The feeling of dizziness passed, but the loneliness did not. The next morning, and the next morning after that, and the next morning after that, it was still there. It only deepened and twisted even tighter when the twins came into the picture.

And now she was left with the feeling that she was watching her life, her family, her home from the outside, instead of participating in it. Some days, there seemed to be a promise of a resolution, but it never came. Some days she wanted desperately to get back on the inside of things. To join, really join, the dinners and conversations and happiness, but she couldn't. She just couldn't.

The permutations of loneliness were an endless development with each passing day. And the more intricate and specific Hazel's interpretation of her loneliness became, the bigger and more real those feelings grew. Hazel sometimes considered that her mother possessed an inkling of awareness, albeit never expressed in words, that things had changed between them. She would interpret a reach of her arms out across the dinner table to touch hands or the pulling of Hazel in unusually tight for a hug or kiss as an attempt to make it better. But right afterward, she would just flit away back into her other life centered around Cam or the twins. It solidified for Hazel the reality that there was no longer a shared understanding of what it meant to be mother and daughter. They would often end up in a room together, with little to say to one another. It would have been better if that silence between them was thick and heavy with sadness or regret, but it had become light and comfortable now.

Hazel and her mother were now connected by only the loosest stitch.

As these thoughts began to swirl into a vortex, Hazel sought the distraction of logging on to Wassup?, a social platform for tracking what your friends were up to. Joanna Jackson's photos were the first to appear in Hazel's feed; she had a party over the weekend that Hazel had uncharacteristically attended. Hazel was surprised when she received the invitation on Wassup?, but upon clicking around the page further, realized that Joanne had invited nearly the entire grade. It also could have been that Hazel's mother and Joanna's mother took the same pottery class. Hazel wasn't certain what compelled her to go, but she had.

She clicked into the photo album to see what had been captured from the evening. A small flutter emerged in her belly. She was excited to see herself in the middle of something. Excited to see herself connected and present. Perhaps someone would have captured her in the background. Or in line for the bathroom. She remembered feeling prettier than usual that day. Her mother had let her borrow one of her shirts and then, with a smile, applied blush to her cheeks and mascara to her lashes. Perhaps someone had captured a picture of her feeling that feeling, of being that person that she wanted to be far more often than she could ever be that person. She clicked from one photo to the next, but there wasn't a single trace of her. There were pictures from the kitchen and the living room and the yard. There were pictures of friends and decorations and even the Jackson family dog. But Hazel was nowhere to be found. Once again, she was a ghost.

As Hazel moved her cursor to look at the final photo, a message popped up in the bottom corner of the screen that said simply Hey.

It was curious that she was receiving a message at all, but the origin of the message was even more curious—Eve Warrington. Someone she didn't even know.

She clicked into Eve's profile page to investigate.

Eve Warrington lived in Connecticut and went to Wintor High School. She was in an open relationship with a girl named Abby Wasser, presumably her best friend. Cool. Hazel and Eve were also born just a few months apart.

In her profile photo, Eve was seated on top of a brick wall with her arms long at her sides and head tilted to one side, sending her full, sun-kissed hair tumbling across one side of her face and over one shoulder. Her long legs were crossed in front of her. She was smiling, though not a lot. It was just enough to accentuate the pinkness of her lips. She had two bracelets on her right wrist. Hazel could tell it was the real stuff, nothing like the plastic jewelry she had. Eve was wearing a leather jacket that looked new and expensive and a shirt that was lacey and a little bit see-through at the top. The picture was taken from far away, but still Hazel could tell that Eve's skin was clear and shining and her eyes were bold.

Hazel clicked through the next set of photos. Everything about Eve's life looked elegant and effortlessly curated. Her hair fell into any style with a messy grace. Her favorite style appeared to be a big sloppy bun tilted to one side. Eve was looking away from the camera in nearly every photo, which added to her cool confidence. Every picture made her look smart and just the right amount careless. Her gestures were big and daring and interesting and her limbs were long and tan. Through her loose-fitting clothes, Hazel could tell that the slope of her breasts and her butt were the perfect amount of round to contrast with the rest of her angular look. She appeared to be a person of extremes. A person without fear. It was mesmerizing for Hazel to behold.

Next, Hazel came across a selfie of Eve. The camera was right up close to her face and the picture showed every feature big and prominent on the computer screen.

Hazel gasped. It looked like her own face, only prettier. It looked like her own eyebrows, though fuller.

The base of her throat suddenly felt hollow.

The message box blinked again.

I think we're sisters.

Hazel swallowed. It took effort.

Well, half sisters.

Hazel turned her attention back to the big photo.

Her instinct led her to shout out. "Mom! Mo-om!" As she yelled, Hazel realized that she was out of breath. She clicked back through the photos, still panting a bit. "Mo-oo-om!"

This time, she felt a deep sense of knowing. She knew Eve like she knew her own hands. It was intoxicating.

Hey, Hazel responded to the message on the screen.

She let the silence sit for a moment.

Ha ha, yeah, it looks like it! she added nervously.

Ha ha, yeah, Eve responded. Well, kinda looks like it.

Hazel's mother popped her head into the room. Her sense of urgency didn't appear to match Hazel's or her desperate yelps. "What, honey?" She seemed exasperated, in fact. "I was just about to go to bed," her mother added.

Hazel gestured for her mother to join her at the screen, and as soon as she did, her mother brought her hands to her mouth. Finally her mother's reaction was appropriate in scale.

Another message popped up on the screen, and Hazel's eyes and body lit up even more.

Our dad lives in Maine and I'm going to go visit him.

Hazel watched her mother as she pressed her palms even harder into her mouth. The news appeared to surprise her mother as much as it surprised Hazel. She considered for a fleeting moment whether to ask her mother what she knew, but she let the feeling pass. Hazel wanted to keep this whole occurrence and all the feelings wrapped up in it to herself.

I went for the first time last year and will be going back again this summer. Do you want to come with me?

Hazel's heart and body filled with a surprising longing she had never experienced before. She felt new and bold and optimistic. She felt light enough to float right out of the room.

Definitely, Hazel replied before her mother could protest, and then tilted back in her chair and let the extraordinary possibility of her new life wash over her.

"I have a sister," Hazel muttered to herself.

"I have a sister," she said quietly again.

She inhaled.

"I have a sister," she exhaled.

Hazel was breathing this new information in. Breathing this new life in. Integrating it into her experience. Her very being.

"I have a sister!" she shouted with so much glee and life Eve might have heard her just a few hours from Verona into Connecticut.

4

JANE

Jane sat in shock next to Hazel as her daughter gave in so quickly, so effortlessly, so thoughtlessly to the possibility of going away. To another life. Another family even. At least temporarily.

Jane had had no idea that Hazel's biological father, Silas, had any other children. She felt stupid for not recognizing that possibility. But even if she considered that Silas could have other children, or even other girlfriends, what she failed to consider until now was that they would share some DNA. They would share flesh and blood in a way that connected one person biologically to another in the deepest of ways. In ways that could not be denied or overlooked or underestimated.

When Jane had left Silas, that was her choice. She had disconnected and untethered herself from him. She had shut his world out and welcomed a new one: first with Hazel and then with Cam and then with the twins.

But she knew it well from Hazel's single green eye that Silas was in her daughter. That genes mattered. That they connected people. And that had to include this Eve person, whoever she was.

Jane felt her breath escaping her.

She nearly surrendered to the inevitability that blood was blood and nothing could replace that connection, but then she stopped herself. Certainly other factors were at play here. After all, Jane was blood, too.

She thought back to all of those days and nights and nights and days alone when she soothed Hazel as a crying baby. When she fed her milk from her breast. All those times over the last fifteen years that she gave Hazel deep hugs and deep kisses and a bed to sleep in. Surely that counted for something. Surely passively sharing your DNA was not an equal trade for years and years of love and nurture and showing up every day. But maybe it was. Maybe it counted.

Would Silas and this Eve share more with her daughter than Jane did? What else was there beyond the green eyes and brown hair? Was there temperament and personality and quirks and ways of thinking or moving that they all shared without even having spent any of that bonding time together? How would it change Hazel's life to know these people? Would it change Jane's own life for Hazel to know these people? Wouldn't it ruin everything Jane had created? Or would it bring it to new life?

How could she know? *Could* she know? Did she *need* to know? Or was this type of exploration something that young women had to do? Was this something all young people had a right to? Did she go through a similar quest when she was Hazel's age?

If Jane was being honest with herself, her confusion and pain wasn't only directed at the thought of Hazel sharing that familial connection with someone Jane didn't know. It was her own thought of not being good enough as a mother. It suddenly dawned on her just how reluctant she had been to believe that Hazel would one day become independent. But in so many ways, Hazel had already. How had Jane missed the signs?

She suddenly was seeing her only daughter as a new person. Her own person.

Until this moment, Jane had felt that Hazel was an extension of her. When she talked to Hazel, she felt she had been talking to herself. When she felt warm and loving and happy with Hazel, she felt warm and loving and happy with herself. And when she felt anxious or angry or annoyed with Hazel, she felt anxious or angry or annoyed at herself. She felt all these things without realizing it.

But now, sitting in front of this computer, seeing Hazel as someone who wanted to be anywhere else than with her, made her realize that something had changed. Hazel had become her own person with her own hopes and dreams and desires and wants and visions for her life.

Jane didn't know whether to mourn or embrace that truth. To stop Hazel or push her toward more.

Even today, Jane still thought of her fifteen-year-old daughter as the six-year-old with ice cream caked across her cheeks, smiling up at Jane with a missing tooth and her unmatched eyes. Jane hadn't acknowledged that her little girl was no longer a little girl.

Should she allow Hazel to begin on this journey to find more of herself? Allow Hazel to discover things about herself that Jane didn't even know? Should she enable Hazel with the freedom to see a new world? A new world that she couldn't control? What kind of mother would her decision make her?

Jane felt an overwhelming urge to keep Hazel closer. To ask her to stay. To tell her to stay. To bring her close into her arms and rock her and fall asleep next to her again. After all, she hadn't even spoken to Silas in all these years.

"Let me, uh, think about it, honey" was all she could muster. She knew it was inadequate, but she couldn't fully put her thoughts, let alone words, together.

"And, honey," Jane continued through staccato breath and a swirling mind. "I'm here if you have any questions."

"About what?" Hazel inquired with more snark than Jane thought she deserved.

"About your father. Who he is. Who he was."

"I want to find out on my own, Mom."

Jane turned to walk away without a response. There were times when she'd imagined how this conversation would go, and this wasn't it.

"Oh, wait," Hazel jumped back in with a hint of desperation in her voice. "What's his first name again?"

Jane exhaled, disappointed. "It's Silas… And it's where you got your green eye."

Jane turned back around and retreated to her bedroom to collect her thoughts, but also to prevent herself from reaching her arms around Hazel's body and never letting her go. And to stop the room from spinning. She lay down in her bed atop the sheets, interlaced her fingers and pressed her connected palms across her eyes. Just as her back sank into the mattress and her thoughts began to slow, she heard Cam turn the page of his book. He looked up.

"What's up, honey?" he asked sweetly.

All of these words and feelings and ideas and reactions rushed through Jane's mind. They ricocheted around her skull, and just when one would make it toward her mouth, another one would zip in front of it to take its place.

The only thing that came out was "Oh, nothing."

"Doesn't look like nothing," he replied and put his hand on hers.

"Just a headache," Jane replied.

She wasn't really one for keeping secrets, but this felt like something between her and Hazel. Something for them to work through together. Just the two of them. Like the old days.

5

HAZEL

It had been only a few weeks since first hearing from Eve, and the possibility of leaving was all Hazel could think about now. Her father was all she could think about. At school, at home, in her room, with the twins, at the dinner table, all of it. She couldn't help it from oozing out of her at every moment. She thought about asking for more from her mother, but she enjoyed finally having ownership over the story of her life.

Hazel had a sister! A sister! There was so much to learn about her. And it didn't hurt that she looked so cool with her messy hair and thick eyeliner and perfect clothes and perfect body and all kinds of friends. And Hazel had a father! A real father! One that shared her flesh and blood and, from what she knew, at least one green eye. He would be so different from her stepfather, Cam. He would understand her. Really, really get her. He might even be just like her. This could be the family she was meant to have.

With every spare moment, Hazel would return to Eve's Wassup? page and click through her photos. She would inspect Eve's face in every single one of them. Her eyes, her hair, her cheeks, her chin, her nose. There was no denying that Hazel carried some of those features, too. Hazel would stand in front of the mirror and tilt her head as Eve did in her photo. Squint her eyes as Eve did in her photo. Curl her lips like Eve did in her photo. Pop her hip out to the side like Eve did in her photo.

And with every spare moment in between that, Hazel would search Silas's name on the internet and click around his website. She found pictures of markets where he was standing all tall and sturdy next to his furniture. The pictures were mostly small and blurry and it was hard to discern his features. His eyes, his hair, his cheeks, his chin, his nose. She wondered what she got from him, aside from that one green eye. She thought about asking her mom if she had any more photos of her father, but Hazel also wanted to wait to see him for the first time through her own eyes. She wondered why her mother never talked about him more often. But Hazel would claim that story for herself soon enough, she hoped. She would take control of her relationship, her bond, with her father.

Hazel thought about how she would ask Eve and Silas all sorts of questions about themselves. Favorite songs. Favorite movies. Whether they were right- or left-handed. Whether they slept on their backs or their bellies. Whether they also hated bananas but loved banana taffy. They would have weeks and weeks of getting to know each other in Maine, she hoped. And she hoped they'd find many, many, many things they shared. And sure, they all grew up in different homes with different people, but those were only things on the outside. Hazel was looking to share the things on the inside. Looking at Eve's and Silas's photos and trying to piece the person behind each profile together, Hazel couldn't be sure. But she hoped. She hoped for all of it.

These were the things she had to hold on to. To connect with. But she wanted more. She was so thirsty for more. She had had this feeling in a vague sense for quite some time. She knew there was something missing from her life. She knew there were gaps to close. An emptiness to fill. But now she had a solution. Now she had a way. And it had long full hair just like hers.

Did you talk to your mom yet? Eve's message popped up at the bottom of the screen.

Hazel's belly fluttered with the feeling that someone cared.

Hazel typed and deleted just about a dozen responses before landing on I'm working on it.

Okay, cool, Eve replied.

Hazel began crafting the next response back, but before she could pick one, Eve replied again.

My mom said you and your mom and dad should come by for dinner, if you want.

Good idea, Hazel responded, this time without needing much thought.

Anything she could do to layer on the requests and concessions to her mother, to increase her chances of going.

I'll tell you what she says, Hazel typed and ran out of the room to set it into motion.

"Mo-ooooo-om," Hazel yelled out and walked toward her mother. "Eve says we can all go and have dinner at their house." She finished her sentence just as she arrived at her mother's feet with two great stomps.

"That's very nice of them," her mother replied. "Why don't you and Eve schedule a day for us to go? It would be great to meet them before the end of the school year."

But this was only a small step toward the thing she really wanted. She was focused on getting to Maine and nothing else. Perhaps this was a move in the right direction, but the final outcome hadn't been realized yet.

Hazel didn't even have to verbally pester her mother with the question of whether Maine was part of the plan. Hazel had been asking hour after hour, day after day. All she had to do was look at her mother up close, right into her eyes, and her mother knew the question she wanted answered.

"I'm thinking about it," her mother would say.

And Hazel would storm off and sulk.

It happened for days until one day something in Hazel really erupted when her mother said, "I'm thinking about it."

"Are you serious?" Hazel challenged.

When her mother didn't respond, she asked again, this time louder and with more heat behind it. "I said, are you serious?"

"I'll think about it," Jane replied, just as seemingly nonchalant as the first time she said it. But how could she be so casual about Hazel's entire sense of identity? Her ticket out?

"I'm going, Mom. I don't care what you say."

"Honey, just let me think about it, okay?" Hazel detected a quiver in her mother's voice this time and decided to pounce. She wasn't going to let her mother ruin something else for her.

"There's a lot to do first," her mother replied.

"What are you even talking about?" Hazel wasn't prepared to let anything come between her and her new life.

"Look, Hazel. These people are strangers to us. They may not feel like it to you right now, but they are."

Hazel could tell Jane was trying to say calm, but Hazel wasn't having any of it.

"Well, call them, talk to them. Go visit them. I don't care. I have to go and you have to find a way to let me, Mom."

Her words were coming out more desperate now, but she didn't care.

"You don't want me here and you don't want me to go! What do you want from me, Mom?!"

Her mother's shoulders fell limp and her eyes went soft.

"Oh, honey," she said and reached out to hug Hazel.

With her mother's arms around her, Hazel's voice and energy went back to calmness. "Please let me go, Mom. Please. I want to go. I *need* to go." She felt a salty tear drip down her cheek. "The school year is ending soon, and when it does, I'll have nothing! Nothing, Mom! Please let me have this thing!"

Hazel's mother wrapped her arms around her tightly. "I understand," she whispered. "I understand."

Hazel could feel, by the weight of her mother's arms and the tone in her voice, that perhaps she was starting to.

6

JANE

Jane's hands were shaking as she picked up the phone to call Silas. She had kept his cell phone number all these years even though she'd never really used it. It was not that she meant to never call, or never have Hazel call; there just didn't seem to be a need for it. And he hadn't called them. But today, that changed. Jane knew she had to call him even though she didn't want to.

She had spent all these years in some ways so far away from Silas; but in other ways he was close. He was in her daughter's eyes all the time. But he certainly was not in her home, or her life, or her heart. And Jane had never expected that Silas would, at any time, become part of any of those things. For her or for her daughter. She had built her recent life around that premise.

As she heard Silas's phone ringing, Jane still wasn't sure she wanted him to pick up. She wasn't sure that he deserved her Hazel. But actually, she was sure that he didn't.

The phone continued to ring on the other end. After all this time, no outreach—not a single phone call or letter or question or even the slightest indication of interest or curiosity. Silas didn't deserve to look at their daughter or share space with her or have her in his presence at all. It was scary having to make a decision when Jane didn't know what anyone deserved. When she didn't know how everyone would be changed. But she knew she had to make that decision. And she knew what the decision had to be.

Suddenly, a voice interrupted the rhythm of the ringing. "Hello?"

She was surprised how familiar the voice felt to her. That deep and grumbling and sexy, scratchy voice. But still, his voice sounded far away. Almost as if he was speaking from a place of exile Jane had relegated him to after weeks, months, even years of waiting to hear from him.

"Hey." Jane had to take a moment to catch her breath. "Silas." She exhaled. "This is Jane."

There was quiet from the other side of the line.

"Hazel's mom," she added.

There was another brief moment of quiet before the beginning of a tailspin.

"Well, I suppose we haven't broached the whole Hazel topic directly, but I think you'd remember me. We met sixteen years ago at the Grandor Fair. Had a whole summer thing, and, uh, back to Hazel. Hazel's your daughter. Mostly my daughter, but I guess she's got your genes. Actually, she definitely does. She has your eyes. Well, eye. What am I even talking about? Oh, god. Well, I guess you know about Hazel now, being that you're in touch with Eve and all. And I, uh, just wanted to call and talk about the visit for a minute. Being that I am Hazel's mom."

More quiet on the line.

Even more quiet on the line.

"Yup. That's all. This is Jane. Hazel's mom."

"Jane!" Silas replied with feeling and knowing and something like joy. It was an enthusiasm she remembered in Silas from before, back when they spent that summer together. His eyes and cheeks would light up when she would walk through the door of his place or meet him at their go-to spot, Rosco's, for dinner. But Jane had always sensed he used the act to camouflage his pain or indifference or awkwardness, or something else entirely.

"It's been a while! How ya been? Still doing your beadwork? Man, I always loved that beadwork."

Just like all those years ago, no matter what it was disguising, Jane felt a tingling warmth as she let his enthusiasm wash over her.

It was quiet for a moment again as she smiled from her end of the line, and could sense that he was smiling, too. But then Jane felt an inexplicable hollowness. It would have been better if his words, his tone, were filled with sadness or regret or longing, but she could hear how happy he was that he was there and she was here. That he was there and Hazel was here. Jane snapped back into the moment.

"You know, I haven't been doing much beadwork lately," Jane replied, now matching his upbeat energy. "I've been kind of busy raising a kid. Three of them actually." She made sure to keep a levity in her sarcasm, but she hoped it stung Silas at least a little.

"Mmm, right."

Jane could feel Silas slinking back, and she felt pleased.

"But listen. I'm not going to bullshit you, and I don't have much to say. I just want this visit of Hazel's to be a good experience for her, okay? I need it to be. And I need you to help make that happen. Can you do that?"

"Yeah," Silas replied. His reply was sincere. She could feel that he wanted to be good to her. And to Hazel, too.

"And then there's this Eve character. Have you had much contact with her over the years? Do you know more about her than I do? I'm pretty surprised she exists. Were you? Don't answer that. I just want to know if you know whether she'll be kind to my Hazel?"

"Uh…" Silas instinctively replied, not yet realizing that these questions from Jane were largely rhetorical.

"I mean, what kinds of things do you even do up there with a fifteen-year-old girl? If I'm accurately remembering my time in Grandor, it isn't very teenager-friendly," Jane inquired.

"It depends what you think of as being teenager-friendly. Eve told me she got the best summer tan she's ever gotten in her life after spending time here last summer, so there's that at least."

"Very funny, Silas."

"I'm not kidding! Eve just lay out in the sun and found pockets of cell phone service so she could text her friends. I got to spend some time in the shop working on a few projects. We cooked meals together. Went out on the boat a few times. The days were pretty simple. It was just…nice."

"Well, nice seems pretty okay to me," Jane responded,

finding herself more comfortable more quickly than she expected. It was simple up in Grandor. That was why she had gone there in the first place. Simple and nice was something Jane could get behind. She, of course, had some doubts about Silas's ability to care for her daughter, but even though he had never been a responsible man, Jane felt sure he could be a good man.

It was quiet on the line.

"I have some more questions."

"I hope I'll have more answers."

"Where will they sleep?"

"In beds."

"Very funny. Where."

"Upstairs. Together in their own room."

"And what if one of them gets sick?"

"Then I will bring them to the hospit—"

"And what if they get homesick?"

"Then I will have them—"

"What will they have for breakfast? And dinner? And lunch? Are you going to tell them stories about me? I sure hope not. And what will you do if they're bored? And what if the girls aren't getting along?"

The words and questions were all just slipping out of her mouth. But this was just minutiae. It wasn't answering the big questions about what it would mean for the rest of Hazel's life. About Hazel's love story. And those were the questions that could not be answered yet.

Jane knew it.

Silas knew it.

"Then, I'll... Listen, Jane. I know this is a big deal. I know it is."

"It *is* a big deal. It's a huge deal!"

"I'll try not to fuck it up," Silas added with a little more lightness now. Jane could feel him smiling on the other side of the line.

"You better not!" Jane said, now smiling, too, then disconnected and placed the phone facedown into her lap.

"That's my little girl," Jane said aloud but quietly, even though the call was ended and the room was empty. "She's my little girl more than she's anyone else's."

Jane exhaled and brought her hands to her heart and fell backward onto her bed.

She felt she knew what she needed to do, what she wanted to do, but couldn't help the feeling of rubber-banding back to keeping her daughter close.

She called Cam into their room, and without removing her hands from her eyes or moving her body an inch, Jane said plainly, "I'm thinking of letting Hazel go to meet her biological father."

Cam was silent. And then she felt the weight of his body sit down on the mattress next to her. His arm grazed her tummy as he placed his palm gently on her hip.

"Apparently she's got a half sister, too, who goes to visit him in the summers. I think I know what to do, and I want to do it, but she is my baby, Cam. She belongs with me."

Lying motionless, with her hands still on her eyes, Jane said, "I can't just let her go."

She then sat up abruptly and slapped her hands onto the

bed. She explained the whole scenario in panicked and dis-jointed detail.

"This whole thing could ruin her life. It really could." Jane could feel her hysteria begin to ooze out of her. She could feel it beginning to fill up the entire room.

"Her biological father isn't exactly the most responsible or fatherlike, you know! He's the one who let me do this on my own. He's the one who didn't call or write or help or anything. He's a lone wolf. And he's scarred. Really, deeply scarred in ways even I can only begin to compre-hend. He's been through a lot in his life, more than most men should go through, but the outcome is still the same. He didn't want me and I felt so sure then that he wouldn't want Hazel. I didn't want to put *her* through discovering that. And now look what I get. He's the beacon of parent-hood in Hazel's eyes."

She looked straight into Cam's eyes. They were kind eyes. Always calm. She loved that about him.

Jane opened her eyes wider and lurched forward a bit to-ward Cam. She wanted something from him. Something big enough to match this big moment. But still he just sat there calmly, a gentle smile across his lips.

"After all, I am her mother," she said.

There was another brief moment of silence that Jane opened her mouth to fill, but then Cam claimed it instead.

"Honey, do you really think you are that important?"

Jane lay back, stunned.

"I am afraid you are terribly mistaken if you think you are. I haven't been a parent as long as you have, but there is something I have always known about our children, all children. And it's that their lives are eventually their own. You are here at the beginning, and to usher them through it from time to time, but their lives are ultimately their own."

Jane's shoulders lowered and her cheeks perked up and her heart opened and she listened. Really listened.

"Somehow parents convince themselves that every little thing we do, every little choice we make, every little word we say, marks our children forever. But that's ridiculous. They are independent beings."

Jane slid her hand onto Cam's thigh. It was not often he was so convincing. Not often he said things so profound. But it was always a thing Jane knew he had in him. She wanted to hear more. She wanted him to say more. She gave his leg a little squeeze.

"I love our babies. And I love Hazel. And I want to do everything for them. I want to make their lives good and perfect every day with every decision we make. And I know you do, too. But those are our ideas of perfection, not theirs. Those things we do are fulfilling our desires as parents, not theirs as children. They will pursue their own perfect lives full of their own desires. Hazel is a beautiful, smart, strong, capable girl."

Jane didn't realize it until Cam had stopped talking, but she had been nodding her head up and down.

"She can do this, honey. And so can you."

Jane reached her arms around Cam's neck and pulled him close.

"She is becoming her own young woman, just like you once did."

"Okay," Jane said, her voice catching in her throat on her own nervousness.

"Okay," she said again, this time with more conviction. It was for herself more than it was for Cam.

Jane pulled her body away, her arms outstretched with a hand on each of Cam's shoulders.

"Well, fine, then," Jane said.

It was now a question of how it was all going to work, more than it was a question of if Hazel was going at all.

7
HAZEL

Hazel was sitting quietly in her room when she heard her mother call, "Hazel?"

Hazel expected she was about to be asked to do some favor or chore involving the twins, and she skulked over toward her mother's room. "Yeah?" she asked listlessly.

"I've decided, you can go to visit Silas," her mother said matter-of-factly.

Hazel's eyes lit up and she sprung up onto her toes and tackled her mother over onto the bed she was sitting on.

"Thank you. Thank you. Thank you," she yelled wildly. "Thank you!"

Hazel nestled the crown of her head into the nook of her mother's neck and slowed down to stillness. "Thank you," she said again calmly and warmly.

Hazel's mother sat up and looked into her eyes. Her lips curled up a bit.

"But first, before you go we're going to meet Eve and her

parents, and then when you get to Maine, you are going to text me every day, and you are never going to forget who your mother is!"

"You're such a loser, Ma." Hazel sprang up to give her mom a big, sprawling, tight hug and then ran out of the room with a lightness in her stride her mother hadn't seen in her daughter for a long time.

Hazel raced to the computer and opened the app to message Eve.

It's happening! she typed. It's really happening, sis.

Immediately, even though they weren't leaving for another few weeks, Hazel packed up a duffel and left it in the corner of her room. And from that moment on, every subsequent message that Hazel received from Eve was a supernova. Each text blew everything that once was, wide-open. Started life anew. Illuminated every fiber of her being. And it was all happening in Hazel's own personal universe.

For so long, Hazel had felt that her life was duller than it ought to be. Inside she felt alive and dynamic and energized. But outside she was forgotten and lonely and bored. She felt that there was something deep within her that was better than her life allowed for. Her days were thick and sticky with kids at school who knew nothing about her real life. Her evenings were clogged with taking care of the twins and trying to ignore the fact that Cam had become a fixture in her home.

She was ready for things to flow free and wild. She was ready for the exciting, magnificent life she deserved. She was ready for more family and more love. This was the start of her new life.

Hazel lay on her bed with her eyes closed, but not trying to sleep. She just let her excitement flow through her. She let the reel of vignettes of her life play in her mind's eye. Finally, she was on the outside looking in and smiling. It felt as if she were finally part of the real story. And they would hold their hands to their hearts as she fumbled and groped her way there, but they would rejoice when everything gave way to the beautiful ending. She could finally feel the inevitability of her happiness.

Eve and Silas were her freedom. She felt a warmth emanate at the very thought of them.

She imagined what real sisterhood and daughterhood and fatherhood would look like.

She imagined what the cabin and the lake would feel like. What their room would smell like. What they would talk about and eat for dinner. How they would fill their days. How they would fill their bellies and their spirits. She imagined where they would go. The places they would explore. The feelings that would bloom.

Hazel considered that she didn't even have to know Silas and Eve to know them. They were a part of her. She carried them with her every day. She clutched onto her pillow, love and excitement oozing out of her.

Hazel heard the gentle creak of her door opening. And then the slow pressing of feet into carpet. Hazel knew these sounds well from all those evenings of her mother slipping into her room with ice cream. But she wasn't in the mood today. She kept her eyes shut and rolled over onto her side so that her back faced her mother as she approached.

The door clicked shut and without saying a word, Jane

crawled into bed with Hazel. She slipped her legs under the covers, curled her body around Hazel's in perfect contour, and tossed her arm over the flesh of her daughter's hips. Hazel stayed still and kept her eyes shut. She recognized that this was more for her mother's comfort than it was for hers. Perhaps it was even an apology. But she wasn't looking for those things from her mother anymore. It was true that she had been starved of them, but now she had been fueled again from a force that was not inside this house.

"I love you, Hazel. You know that, right?" Jane said softly into Hazel's ear, her hot breath cascading over the side of her face.

Hazel felt her body turn rigid.

"I know you're excited to go. I'm excited for you. I just love you so much. It's hard to imagine you away from home." Jane gave Hazel a tight squeeze.

But the words were lost on Hazel. Hazel curled herself into a tighter ball, holding on to her own flesh and her day-dreams of life away from here for comfort.

In perfect timing, Hazel's phone buzzed and lit up. And Hazel popped her eyes wide open to check her phone. Of course, it was Eve. It was a picture she had taken of herself. One eye was pressed closed; the other one was big and wide and swirling and lined with dark black makeup underneath a perfectly curved eyebrow. She was sticking her tongue out the side of mouth, and her hair, although messy, looked shiny and perfect.

Hazel chuckled and considered which silly face she could send in return. She wiggled out from under her mother's arm, and without turning over just said, "A little privacy please, Ma."

And without saying a word, Jane uncurled herself from around Hazel's body, slipped out of the covers and then slipped out of the room.

Hazel turned over just as the door was closing.

But before it shut, Hazel caught a sliver of her mother's sunken shoulders. And then she rolled over and held her phone up in front of her face for a photo.

Hazel held the phone in her hands, waiting for a response from Eve. And when she got it, everything inside of her body went wobbly again.

8

JANE

The ninety-minute drive from their house to the Warringtons in Connecticut was silent. Just a few days before, Jane had asked Hazel to get Eve's mother's phone number. Then Jane made an awkward call to this stranger with whom she unwittingly had something in common.

Susie sounded warm on the phone. She said she had recently learned about Hazel—and Jane—from her daughter. She immediately invited them all over for a visit.

When Jane, Hazel and Cam arrived, Jane didn't even have to knock on the door of the house before it came swinging open. Susie and Parker Warrington came out immaculately dressed. Susie smoothed her skirt over her thighs before pulling Jane, Hazel and then Cam in for hugs in quick succession.

"Welcome to our home! It's so lovely to have you."

Susie was a lithe, slim-bodied woman with surprisingly pert breasts accentuated by her periwinkle sweater and her sparkling necklace. Parker had his hand soldered to Susie's back. For such a strapping, handsome man, his eyes were surprisingly timid.

Susie and Parker had matching vacant smiles. There was a moment of quiet awkwardness.

"Come in, come in, please," Susie urged, bulldozing any space for tension.

Jane locked eyes with her daughter as soon as they stepped through the doorway and into the foyer. It was the nicest home either of them had ever seen. The order of the place was immediately palpable. A home well run. A life predictable. Something Jane never strove for—perhaps even feared as a cherished principle. Jane couldn't remember if she had yet uttered a single word.

"You have a beautiful home," Cam said earnestly, sparing Jane from having to talk first. "Thank you for having us."

Jane instinctively removed her shoes, and Hazel followed suit.

"Oh, you don't have to do that," Susie said through a chuckle and a dramatic wave of the arm before bending down to align them properly against the shoe rack. "The dining room is this way. Dinner is just about ready."

Parker patted his stomach. "I don't know about you, but I'm starving," he said as if his words were scripted. A caricature of a dinner party host. "I'll take you to the dining room while Susie finishes up."

Parker removed his hand from Susie's back for the first time. "Follow me."

They moved first through a living room. A modern print—surely straight from the MoMA gift shop, or per-

haps the real thing, judging by the signature at the bottom—
hung on the wall, strategically aligned behind a modern
cuboid sofa. The coffee table sat atop an animal pelt rug and
was made of glass. The glass was pristine and didn't have a
single smudge on it, just a neatly stacked pile of coffee table
books—*Chanel, The Elements of Style, Modern Treehouses.* It
was the perfect juxtaposition of modern and bucolic. Chic
and homespun. The magic of an interior designer's touch.
The reality of not having two babies with drooling mouths
and crusty hands to touch the pristine glass-surfaced touch
of an interior decorator.

Jane smiled at the thought of her boys. She imagined
them crawling around that room, knocking the *Chanel* coffee table book right from its stack and then moving to the
next lamp or vase or other delicate thing without pause. She
loved those little imps. And their cheeks and their hands and
their drooling mouths. Jane turned to look toward Hazel.

Hazel appeared to be in awe, but still comfortable in the
space as she glided through it, her head swiveling around,
her mouth the slightest bit agape.

"Susie loves this room. We barely even come in here—
don't want anything to fall out of place, now!" Parker said
through a nervous chuckle and then continued. "The dining room is right through here. Have a seat. I'll go get Eve."

As she took her seat at the table, Jane caught a glimpse of
the kitchen to the left. She could tell it was well equipped
but sufficiently untouched, assuring her that no one spent
much time in there. Without much more than a split second's view, Jane could tell it was a kitchen with a cabinet
of unused single-use appliances—pasta makers and fondue

sets. A kitchen with a drawer for pens and pads, a drawer for take-out menus ordered alphabetically, a drawer for first aid, and one for tape and scissors and glue. All things in their correct places, and complete. A far cry from the kind of home, and life, she'd created for her family.

From her chair, Jane searched for any evidence of chaos or enigma. But there was none. Until Eve entered the room.

Eve ran toward Hazel with excitement and threw her arms around her half sister. Her hair was piled messily atop her head in such a way that revealed her long neck—surprisingly elegant for a fifteen-year-old.

"Hey, sis!" Eve exploded, placing extra emphasis on the word *sis*.

Jane replayed the inflection of greeting back to herself in her head. What was it there underneath those words? Was it sarcasm? Earnestness? Just a teenager's way?

"That's my mom," Hazel declared nonchalantly. Jane said a warm hello, and Eve smiled back. "And, uh, my dad. I guess. That's weird." Hazel blushed a bit and Cam smiled through closed lips and waved.

Jane placed her hand on Cam's leg and it immediately relaxed her.

Eve sat herself next to Hazel and pulled her chair and place mat closer, disrupting the uniformity of the place settings. "I can't believe you're here!" Eve declared and rested her head onto her half sister's shoulder, as if they'd known each other their whole lives.

That inflection again. But Hazel seemed at peace. Happy even. As if it were only the two of them in the room.

Susie swiftly moved back and forth from the dining room,

laying large bowls of salad, then vegetables, then pasta, and then a large plate of steak in perfect orientation on the table. Jane tried offering to help, but Susie seemed insulted by the inquiry.

"Go ahead and start without me," Susie said, near short of breath.

"No, no," Parker protested, one hand already curled around his fork and the other around his knife.

Susie returned to her seat with an exhale. "You really shouldn't have waited," she murmured to her husband. Susie's long fingers fluttered rhythmically from the napkin on her lap, to her dress, and then to her hair, smoothing them compulsively. It was as if she was reassuring herself that structure and tidiness were available to her at any moment.

Everyone else at the table began passing dishes and scooping mounds of food onto their plates, but Jane found herself too absorbed by this woman to move. She wondered who exactly she was. There was a sense of drama about Susie. She seemed to be on the verge of tears that her overexpressive smile across a freshly lipsticked mouth could not counterbalance. Even though this absorption seemed arduous, Jane couldn't stop it. Something about the way Susie's eyes darted anxiously between the two girls, something about the way she rigidly forked her salad, something about her unease made Jane realize exactly who this woman was.

This was the woman that had ended her relationship with Silas. The woman Silas had slept with that night Jane was waiting to tell him about the baby in her belly. It had to have been her. And he must have gotten her pregnant, too. These girls must have been conceived within weeks of each other. There were so many questions, but none Jane could address now, in this moment. The words of the conversation swirled around her and then turned into nothing but a hum. Everything in the scene blurred except for Susie's perfect face and hair and neck.

Susie looked up from her plate and met Jane's eyes—Jane hadn't realized she was staring, or that her grip had tightened on Cam's pant leg under the table.

Jane wondered if Susie knew what she had done. She must have understood it now with the two girls in front of her—their faces so alike. It was impossible to ignore. You'd see one in the corner of your eye and mistake her for the other. The same thin shoulders. The same playful cheeks and rounded, delicate nose. The same shining hair. Eve's lips were glossed and compelling, and her eyes were traced and retraced around the edges with thick eyeliner.

Jane's Hazel looked so young next to this girl. Her makeup-less face and lips. The dimple on the right cheek. The nearly invisible scar above the right eyebrow from the time Hazel had fallen into the coffee table when she was just learning to walk. The barely discernible breasts and mismatched eyes.

But still, these two girls were related. There was no mistaking it.

Jane could tell that Susie had preempted any silence by leaning the conversation toward logistics. She detailed packing lists and itineraries. Jane could tell Susie wanted to maintain appearances. That she would never appear to acknowledge the awkwardness of things. Or want to discuss any intimate details.

"The bus is really the most efficient way for the girls to get up to Maine," Susie said with confidence. It was clear she had done this before and optimized each step of the journey. "I think the nine-thirty bus in the morning would be best. They will still arrive at a reasonable hour." She'd prepared packing lists for both the girls and read them out to the table. "Can't forget bathing suits! Or sunblock. Eve would go for the tanning oil if she could but I insist on SPF10." Eve rolled her eyes as her mother spoke.

"I *do* prefer tanning oil, and last summer I got the best tan that I've ever had even with the SPF10," Eve boasted, crossing her arms.

Jane couldn't help but grin. She brought her napkin over her face and pretended to wipe something from her mouth so that no one would catch her chuckling to herself. Silas wasn't kidding about Eve's tan after all.

To Jane's relief, the conversation moved on quickly and Susie described her arrangements for Silas to pick the girls up at the bus station. She'd ensured he had a car she believed to be safe enough for her daughter to sit in the back seat of. "And I think that's that," Susie declared, clapping her palms together and then returning them to her lap.

Jane smiled and said, "You girls are going to have such a nice time over those couple of weeks."

Jane spotted the corners of Susie's mouth turn down. Both Parker and Cam were staring down into their food. Eve and Hazel were snickering as they looked onto the same cell phone sitting in Eve's lap.

There was a weight, a thickness, a sense of loss in the room for all four parents. And the two girls were impervious to it. They had formed their own world now. And they were living in it.

Jane remembered back to when she was this way. Young and carefree. Energized about the life ahead. Happy and present. It felt long ago now. Long before she got the news about her parents. Long before she veered off course. Long before she made the choices she made to become a mother and then a wife and then a mother again.

She smiled seeing Hazel this way. She realized she had never seen her like this before. The Hazel she knew lately was using a fork to push her vegetables around her dinner plate or off helping to get the twins dressed or locked away in her bedroom quietly.

Jane's heart lifted and sank at the same time. Her heart lifted looking at her daughter enjoying herself. Seeking new friendship. Sisterhood. Ready for adventure. But her heart sank realizing that she didn't know this version of Hazel. She didn't know this girl who got excited by other girls with messy buns and eyeliner. She didn't know this girl who wanted to pore over a cell phone while dinner was on the table.

It was so clear to Jane now. Hazel's journey to becoming her own woman was underway now.

The journey was underway for all of them now. There was no stopping it.

Oh, what a mess she had made. Silas had made. Susie had made. They all had made. And now their daughters would carry the burden of it all the way up to Maine.

Hazel was ready to go and Jane was just along for the ride.

★ ★ ★

After making it through another hour of dinner, Jane thanked the Warringtons for the meal with the biggest smile she could muster as Susie held the door open for their exit. Cam and Hazel made their way through the doorway. But before Jane could do the same, she felt Susie's long fingertips curl around her elbow.

"I just wanted to say that I know what you're going through," Susie said. She kept her eyes locked on Jane's.

Jane tried to interpret the look in her eyes. Was it sadness? Empathy? Pity?

Whatever it was, it wasn't enough to open up any friendship or understanding of this woman.

"I've been here before. It was only a year ago that this was happening to me for the first time. It was just last summer that Eve told me she had found Silas online and wanted to go see him. So I understand what you're going through," Susie repeated, apparently ignorant of Jane's inner resistance.

Jane decided to make it more clear where she stood and pulled her elbow out from Susie's grip. "I'm not sure you do, Susie," Jane said, still not breaking their eye contact. "Our stories may be intertwined, but that doesn't mean they are the same."

"All mothers' stories are the same," Susie responded. "I know you think you messed everything up, I messed up, that we all messed up. But it's going to be okay. Our girls are going to be okay."

"Mom! Come on!" Hazel shouted from the car, breaking the thick tension of the moment.

"Well. That's my cue," Jane said through a closed-lipped

smile and raised eyebrows and began to turn and walk toward the car.

"Wait!" Susie said, a little more frantically than Jane would. "I want you to have something"

Jane rolled her eyes a little, but something kept her in place, wanting to receive whatever it was. Susie crouched down in a way that restored her air of elegance and pulled a beautiful leather-bound notebook out from a wooden bureau next to the door. "Read it when you find yourself lonely this summer."

Susie flattened her skirt and pushed her shoulders back as she stood up. Jane motioned to open it, but Susie pressed down on Jane's hands and nodded knowingly.

"Mom! Let's go!" Hazel shouted again, louder this time.

Jane took the book and walked briskly out toward the car, then took her place in the passenger seat.

"What was that about?" Cam asked innocently, like he was indifferent about the answer anyway, and reached over to put his hand on Jane's thigh.

"Nothing," Jane responded and propped her knee up so that the leather notebook was out of Cam and Hazel's line of sight. She gingerly opened the cover and peeked onto the first page.

The Mess Your Mother Made, it read in big black carefully written script letters. *Letters to my daughter I may never send.*

Jane's heartbeat came into focus. She could hear her own pulse. She didn't know if she wanted to read all of it immediately or none of it ever.

"Doesn't look like nothing!" Cam said with a smirk and squeezed Jane's thigh.

With a tickle running up her leg, Jane burst out with laughter at him tickling her leg. She slammed the notebook shut and shoved it into the passenger-side door.

As they pulled out of the driveway, Jane's eyes met Susie's through the window. Perhaps there was something to learn from this woman after all.

9

HAZEL

A few days later, as Hazel left her mother's car and approached the bus station to meet Eve so the girls could ride together, she prepared for her legs and arms and lungs and heart to float away from her and straight into the ether. For Hazel, sitting next to other girls on the bus to school was usually an act in self-vanishing. Just the simple truth that every single piece of her body could evaporate into the air without a single person noticing was enough to set the feeling off.

She forgot it would be different with Eve. With her sister. As she walked up to the bus, she prepared to be quiet and invisible.

But then there was a moment of eye contact with Eve, who was at the other end of the parking lot. It pulled Hazel back into her body. Into full, visceral presence, as she remembered she was no longer invisible to her world. She was the sister of Eve. The daughter of Silas. On the way to begin her new life. It emboldened her. Took over her. She waved wildly, excitedly in Eve's direction, hand swaying vigorously back and forth, eyebrows raised.

She stopped her arms abruptly. How desperately uncool she must have seemed there for a moment. She pulled her lips together into a much more tempered smile and stood calmly in place even though her heart was beating wildly. She waited for Eve to approach her and resisted the nagging pull to look toward her mother. And then Eve started running. Her backpack bounced on her shoulders. Her strides were constricted and awkward as the weight of her cumbersome luggage swung recklessly from its precarious hinge on her thin shoulder. As soon as she made it to Hazel, Eve dropped her bags dramatically onto the asphalt and threw her long arms around Hazel's ribs.

"We're going, we're going, we're going!" Eve celebrated. She jumped up and down, arms still locked around Hazel's torso.

"Come on, Hazel. Jump!" Eve whispered into Hazel's ear. And Hazel joined in. She jumped and shouted and smiled in excitement she still wasn't sure was real. Hazel could see what others would see from the outside. Two girls, two sisters, two best friends embracing. She liked the way it probably looked. And jumped and shouted once more.

Eve released her arms, picked up her bags and marched confidently onto the bus. Hazel remained in place, still stunned. Before she knew it, her mother's arms were now around her ribs. They felt much gentler. And suddenly, Hazel was a puddle of nerves, scared and unsure. She was disarmed. Over her mother's shoulder, Hazel spied Susie lingering in the back corner of the parking lot. She was clutching the straps of her bag with both hands. Her body was rigid and vigilant. Her thin face was enveloped by large, dark sunglasses. She could see what Susie saw from the outside. Two young women, mother and daughter, in an embrace Susie longed for. Hazel liked the way it probably looked. And no matter how much she didn't want it to, she liked the way it felt.

"Have fun, honey," Jane said warmly into the side of Hazel's face. Her voice rumbled below the surface. "I'll miss you."

Eve poked her head out the window. "Let's go already, Hazel! I saved you a seat!"

Hazel could tell that Eve had done this before.

And just like that, Hazel snapped back into her reality. Or nonreality. Or something else entirely. Hazel wiggled out of her mother's embrace.

"Mom! It's just a couple weeks!" Hazel declared loudly enough to make sure Eve heard. She picked up her bag slowly and pressed her lips into her mother's cheek decidedly. "I love you, Mama," Hazel affirmed before springing onto the bus.

"Bye, Mom!" Eve yelled acrimoniously and clicked the window shut as Hazel made her way down the aisle of the bus and into the seat next to Eve.

Eve rested her head onto Hazel's shoulder. And Hazel braced herself for more than just a bus ride.

PART II

Jane at Home

10

Jane's car ride home from the bus stop was lonely. There was no other word for it. Jane felt emptier than she expected to feel as she watched her baby go head out on a journey that was all her own.

As she got off the highway and drove down the familiar streets with an unfamiliar quiet in the car, Jane thought about Hazel and the last couple of years. She realized that she and Hazel had been drifting apart for months now. It could have even been years. Was it years?

It was less of a conscious choice than a series of unconscious ones, but the outcome was clear. Things were different than they used to be.

Some of that was to be expected with Cam and the twins entering their lives. But Jane realized that she had inadvertently assumed that it would fill Hazel's life with as much joy as it filled hers. For the first time, she realized that it hadn't. In fact, it was probably the opposite. Her daughter must be feeling so lonely in this new family setup. Cam and the twins were taking up so much space, so much time, in what was once their home. And there were certainly changes in her daughter, changes in her relationship she hadn't interpreted as clues until now.

How had she missed this? There were so many signs. She played them through her mind on a reel, but now the memories were playing through a prism.

There were Hazel's sudden announcements of "having too much homework" to join the rest of the family for dinner or a walk or a trip to the store. In the morning she was gone early. Sometimes Jane would catch Hazel walking out of the house with as much confidence as she could muster to take on her day. She never sat for breakfast or said goodbye. And when Hazel returned from school, Jane would offer up hugs and kisses, and promptly request help with the babies. Jane didn't want to exhaust herself with her boys like she had with Hazel all those years ago, but now she wished that she had spent more time with just Hazel on the couch. She had to admit dinners seemed quieter than they should have been for a home with love in it. The twins would coo and babble, but there wasn't much talking about real things. Cam was sweet, he always tried, but Hazel would eat quickly and return to her room. And when she did, she would always leave the door ajar—never open, never closed.

Jane wondered why she never pressed that door wide open and hopped right onto the bed where Hazel was usually perched. Sure, teenagers needed their privacy, their space. But they also needed their mothers.

Jane had always interpreted Hazel's behavior as evidence

of her coming into her independence. Jane was proud and excited about this prospect—but she could see now that Hazel's separating from them was something different than a need for independence. She realized now it was more of a loneliness. A cry for more attention, more love from her mother. Jane was sure of it now. And so sad she hadn't thought to give more of herself to Hazel.

Why hadn't she seen it sooner?

What a mess she had made.

When was the last time she and Hazel shared a bowl of surprise ice cream tucked under the covers together? When was the last time they found their bodies entangled after lying together and talking and laughing?

Jane wasn't sure if teenage hormones or Cam came first, but the touching had become so much less intimate, so much more careless, so much less genuine now. There could be a peck on the cheek or a half-hearted hug, or the occasional instance of a heavy head tilted over onto her shoulder, but there was never much more. Even when Jane would try to pull her daughter in close, her daughter pulled away. And Jane just let it happen. She let it all go so easily.

She wished now she had held her closer longer. She wished she had snuck into her room more often. She wished, more than anything, that she could pull Hazel toward her and press her so tightly to her body that they would be fused forever.

But now Hazel was on a bus. Now she was going away.

Jane squeezed her hands around the steering wheel tightly and shut her eyelids for just a few seconds. She had always felt that loving Hazel as much as she did would be enough. That Hazel would just simply know the scale and intensity of Jane's feelings. That Hazel would hold that knowledge inside her heart at all times. Even as Jane filled their home with new people. Even as she became a mother again, after it was just Hazel for so many years. But those expectations were unfair. She should have shown Hazel more love. With her whole heart and with her whole body and with all her words.

But now, she knew, she had to let her go. But only for a little while. Then, she hoped with all her might, Hazel would be all hers again.

But how? How could she do it?

She ached to know the answer. She needed to know the answer.

Jane pulled the car into the driveway and let her forehead fall against the steering wheel.

She needed to figure out a way to get her daughter back.

And right at that moment, right at that thought, Susie's book called to her from the passenger-side door.

The journal felt heavier in her hands as she lifted it up than she remembered it feeling when Susie gave it to her.

Jane pulled her fingertips over the leather and opened the cover to reveal the first page. She read the words again.

The Mess Your Mother Made.

Letters to my daughter I may never send.

There was a gravitas to it. Jane flipped through the pages and picked out a paragraph at random from the middle of the book. Susie's words were so earnest. So raw. So reflective. So human. So feminine. So motherly.

Jane understood every word. But not in a superficial sense.

She felt them right down into her very bones. Right in her heart.

This was the answer. Jane wanted to, needed to share her story with Hazel. Jane would describe her journey to independence and womanhood, just as Hazel was embarking on hers.

This was how they both would heal. Herself and Hazel, as individuals, and collectively.

This was the answer.

She closed the book Susie had given her and pressed it into her heart. She felt so much love for Hazel in that moment. And for Susie and Eve, too. Their stories were so similar. They were almost mirrored.

Jane would write her thoughts down, just as Susie had. Letter by letter. Moment by moment.

She pulled the car back out of the driveway and went to purchase a leather notebook of her own. Then she drove back home and, after putting the twins down for a nap, turned to the first page and inscribed it herself:

The Mess Your Mother Made.

Letters to my daughter I wonder if she'd ever want to read.

Then, before she composed her own first letter, she read Susie's.

11

LETTER 1
MEETING YOUR FATHER
SUSIE

Dear Eve,

I always enjoyed the life of an interior designer. I loved working with things I could touch and feel and connect with. I loved that the colors and textures of the furniture, and flooring, and tiles, and light fixtures, and accent pieces, and art could create the colors and textures of moods. Sometimes soft, sometimes sturdy, sometimes uneven, sometimes sharp, sometimes brilliant, sometimes harmonized, sometimes mismatched, sometimes calm. But it was always dynamic.

I loved walking into a new space and seeing potential. I loved closing my eyes, inhaling, and reopening them to a vision of a whole new space. I loved turning that vision into something real right before my eyes. I loved working toward a goal of creating beauty in spaces. And, I have to say, my clients loved it, too.

It was so much fun to source things to bring to their spaces. I could get into the crannies of the world and pull out something gorgeous. From time to time, when I needed inspiration, I could go to new cities or new countries to shops I'd never seen before and antiques fairs at the end of long roads my GPS could barely navigate to. I loved caressing the edge of a piece of furniture. I loved admiring a piece of art and imagining the perfect wall for it. I loved examining the quality of a side table and handling a piece of fabric between my fingertips.

About a year before you were born, I found myself particularly excited about the freedom and the newness to just go search. Your father never minded when I left and I really needed it because I was longing and aching for something my life so far would never bring.

Your father and I had learned that we couldn't have a child. Many, many tests had confirmed it.

I wasn't sure a childless life was a life that I wanted. But then I would look at your father and feel that just he would be enough. Every night when he came home from work, he would take me by the chin and kiss me so lightly on the mouth, and I would fall in love with him all over again. Sure, there were moments when I looked at him and saw nothing but shriveled vas deferens, clumsy sperm—some with death wishes—but those moments were becoming fewer and further between over time.

Still, I couldn't just kick the longing for a little baby—

and getting into my car and driving far away from my life distracted me. I searched for opportunities for those distractions constantly. And driving to little antiques fairs for work was the perfect one.

I came across the website for Box Designs at the end of a long meandering morning of clicking around the internet. I think you can guess who this website belonged to…

The webpage was plain and unembellished, but every single piece of furniture was stunning. I clicked through several pieces, inspecting the photos of each angle. Many designers photographed their goods in perfect lighting, with the perfect context. Nightstands with full bouquets on top. Tables adorned with full place settings of plates and forks and knives and spoons. But these were different. Just plain, straightforward, practical photos.

Every piece was made with rich, sturdy wood. Some had delicate carvings into the sides. The details had been placed such that you had to look close to notice. Nothing garish, but everything unique. I felt a magnetic pull to those tables and chairs and bed frames, and I clicked the Contact Me icon at the bottom of the page. I wrote with a directness of intention that I thought the person behind the work, a craftsman named Silas Box, would appreciate.

I said that my name was Susie Warrington and that I would like to see his furniture and asked where and when I could do that.

I didn't fumble over a single word as I typed. I jammed down on the mouse and clicked on Send.

I paused briefly and stared at my screen.

Nearly immediately, a return message popped up in my inbox.

He told me he would be at the Grandor Fair in Grandor, Maine, over the weekend and told me to text him when I arrived.

The clarity and confidence of the note compelled me even more to go. Grandor was a five-and-a-half-hour drive without traffic. Doable in one day. So I marked the date and the location in my calendar and found myself smiling as I texted your father about my plans. It was just such a rush to get out of my own head.

The town of Grandor was familiar, though I had never been there. I searched for the phone number for Box Designs and pulled out my phone to send a text.

When I arrived, I texted him that I was ready to see his furniture.

I placed my phone in my lap and waited for the buzz of a response from Silas. I rolled down the car window and felt a surge of happiness as I inhaled the clear air of Grandor. I observed the sights and sounds of the market. All the white tents propped up and people moving in between them. The gentle buzz of voices meeting. The piles of brightly colored fruits and vegetables. I looked at my phone again, but it was still blank. So I got out of the car and slowly joined the crowd. I looked left and right for the furniture I had seen on the website. Those sturdy masculine lines. Those smooth and durable surfaces.

A tent filled with honey sticks caught my eye. You know how much I love honey sticks. You probably remember me bringing you some when you were little. A row of clear jars filled with sticks of all different colors and flavors lined the rickety white foldout table. I traded a nickel for a root beer–flavored stick. I have to admit, I considered the calories in a single stick, but quickly dismissed the thought and nibbled on the edge to open it.

What was a little indulgence? My body filled with a warmth as soon as the sweet honey hit my tongue. These were a favorite treat ever since I was a little girl. I pinched my index finger and thumb at the bottom of the plastic, pressing more delicious honey onto my tongue. I closed my eyes to savor the taste.

At that very moment, my phone buzzed.

Silas told me where his booth was at the market, and then I'll never forget what he followed up with. He said he was six foot two with black curly hair and very good-looking.

On the basis of no evidence at all, I interpreted the text to be an expression of Silas's typical boldness.

If I am being honest, as soon as I received that text, I felt my cheeks get just a little warm. It was the kind of flirting that almost certainly should have seemed outrageous. I was a married woman, after all.

I tucked my phone into my back pocket, smoothed my shirt out so I'd look professional and walked in the direction of his booth.

Now, flash forward to the evening. The first time that night that I looked down at my phone to check the hour, it was already well after midnight. The edges of the numbers on the digital clock appeared blurry. I brought the back of my hand up to rub my eye. I wasn't inebriated enough to break my rule of touching my own face with oily fingertips.

I smiled delicately in celebration of myself, how truly I had stuck to my values even in this seedy bar in a town I had never heard of with a man I had never met before. Admittedly, I hoped the shape of my smile appeared sexy. Sultry. Mysterious, maybe. I had probably never been mysterious to anybody in my entire life, not even your father, but I felt I could be anyone here on this adventure of mine.

I brought my eyes to meet Silas's across the table. Those churning, passionate green eyes drew me in. I could smell his musty, sylvan scent from here. His thick fingers with dirty nails were clutching his beer as his forearm lay heavy against the wooden table. He was strong and tall and sexy, with his torn flannel shirt and work boots.

I was surprised to find myself attracted to this kind of man, but my heart could not lie. It was exciting. I considered whether it was just the tequila, or perhaps the classic rock crackling through the barely functioning speakers on the jukebox. But it was equally likely my own body aching for another man. Aching for another life. Longing for another man that would bring with it another life.

I felt an impulse to curl my fingers around his wrist, but instead my hand instinctively moved back to check that all my hair was still in place, wrapped in a tight little bun at the nape of my neck, but it wasn't. I could feel chunks of hair spewing out every which way and I thought for a moment about whether I should care. Usually I would excuse myself at the slightest stray lock, but I couldn't pass up the moment of trying a new life on temporarily. I brought my fingertips to the tip of my hair clip and tugged it loose to release the rest of my hair. I couldn't remember the last time I had felt so much hair across my cheeks. It felt so wonderful.

Silas chuckled and mocked me just a little bit. He said something like, "Really letting loose, aren't you?"

I didn't like that I was so easily identified for what I was behind the guise of my tequila buzz and my newly unleashed hair. But it was true I was not accustomed either to letting loose or to places with sticky floors and cheap decor. I had always been rewarded in my life for keeping things together. I had never before considered that beauty didn't mean pristine.

I considered showing my annoyance, but when Silas smiled, the deep seductive green of his eyes ignited. He sat back and pressed the chair onto its two back legs, the toes of his work boots gently hovering over the floor.

I gasped and lunged over the table, trying to make sure he didn't fall.

Silas laughed as he brought the chair back to its stable position on the ground.

He brought his hand onto my hand.

He told me to relax, through his charming smile. The feeling of another man's hand on my hand was so stingingly exciting. No one in my life had ever been so freely affectionate like that. Everyone had been nice and polite and thoughtful, but not affectionate. Not my parents. Not Parker. Not anyone. It surprised me that someone could just touch me at any moment. That someone could pick up my hand as thoughtlessly as picking up a shoelace to tie it. It set my entire existence on fire.

I sank back into my own chair, embarrassed by my own

histrionics and the buzz in my veins, which I was sure was apparent to anyone within miles. I felt determined to push the conversation back onto Silas. I crossed my arms over my chest and looked down to make sure my arms pressed my breasts up. I think by this time I knew where I wanted the night to go. I hope you don't think any less of me, or your father, because of this.

I asked what Silas was doing building a life up in Grandor. He stared down into his beer and told me that it was "nice living up here." I could tell he didn't want to say much more.

It was as if he had some kind of invisible boundary surrounding him. Protecting him. A line not meant to be crossed. Not by anyone. But the tequila and the bits of chest hair peeking out from Silas's shirt had me emboldened.

I asked him what he meant by "nice." A lot of places were nice and he didn't live in them.

It felt exciting to be so sassy, so outspoken, so bold. I was a different woman that night in Grandor. It really felt like that.

I brought my elbows down to the table, sure to reveal my cleavage this time. (I've seen you employ this trick yourself from time to time, my dear!) I wanted to keep it light, and sexy, but I still wanted to know more about him. I had never before felt a boundary so palpable in another man. Silas was so excruciatingly hard to please. He just looked back into my eyes, not even for a moment looking down at my chest. It was impressive.

He confirmed that he wasn't going to go any further than nice. He told me the woods and the lake and the solitude were nice.

That word, *solitude*, was my chance to probe. I asked him if he had a young woman to keep him company.

His eyes dimmed and his shoulders slunk a bit, although I could tell he would have been very upset to know that I noticed. There was a sense that trying to get at Silas's story would be a violation of everything he stood for. He was a man so deeply in possession of his truth. He held it close and it was for no one else to see.

There was a moment of thick silence.

And then I just leaned over the table, spilling the remainder of Silas's beer, and pressed my lips as fast and as decidedly as I could into his lips. And, before I realized I had said anything at all, I had invited Silas to my hotel room.

This is how your story begins.

I'm sorry if it made a mess of things,

Mom.

12

As Jane read Susie's words, her insides twirled. Susie's story was different from her own, but the feelings behind them were so similar. The outcome was so similar. Perhaps Susie was right that all mothers' stories were the same in one way or another. Jane felt an urge to place her own words, her own stories, right next to Susie's. She didn't think too much about why; she just followed the feeling to write. She had no idea if Hazel would ever see these words, these thoughts, but she knew she wanted to write them down for her. And with that, Jane took her journal and pen and wrote:

LETTER 1
MEETING YOUR FATHER
JANE

Dear Hazel,

The first thing I noticed about your father was his green, alchemic eyes. It reminded me of the very first bead I ever wanted to use to make a necklace out of. I noticed him at the market up in Grandor where I lived for a summer. It was closing and everyone had already started to take down their tents. There was always a sense of slowing down at this time of the day at the markets. Each artisan tucked their products away into bags and cases and boxes, occasionally slowing to a stop to inspect their own tapestry or necklace or candle or woven scarf. A trace of a smile would usually emerge before the thing was packed away until the next sunrise. Another chance to place their handmade things into the hands of a passerby.

Someone would tell me that whatever they were dangling in front of their eyes would look fabulous on me.

There would be trying the thing on, a mirror held up, and then usually a "thank you, but no thank you, I'll be back again later."

For me, the goal of coming up to Grandor was to escape with my things rather than to connect other people to them. I was determined to waste what was meant to be my premed education money on the experience of living on the great and moody lake of Grandor, Maine. There were many things a straight and well-paved path could lead you to. It could lead you to the love of your life seated next to you on the first day of medical school. (That was your great-grandparents, Hazel.) It could lead you to a nice home in Placer with a daughter you loved. (That was your grandparents.) It could lead that daughter to set out to pursue a medical degree of her own. (This was me.) And for the first five semesters this was true for me, if you can believe it. But that straight and well-paved path couldn't prevent a patch of black ice one early spring day from sending a car into a

tailspin. It couldn't prevent the front of the car from meeting a thick and strong tree. And it didn't prevent me from
becoming an orphan when I was twenty-one.

(I so wish you'd gotten to meet your grandparents. You
would have loved them. They would have loved you.)

The medical degree didn't seem as important to me anymore now that I was on my own. What called to me was
a great and moody lake that I stumbled on, in a small and
quiet town in northwestern Maine, where nobody's eyes
looked downward when they saw me walk by. I was so sick
of people saying, "How are you feeling, Jane?" with an em-
pathetic tilt of their head and pout of the lips.

The hefty sum of my parents' savings accounts appeared
in my bank account within days of the funeral. It was more
than enough to have all the things one needed in a lifetime,
I thought. But I was numb to what "having a life" could
mean without my parents, your grandparents. Their money
manager called me to confirm the transfer as I was walking
down the street in my hometown of Placer. I happened to
be next to a bead shop at the time, and I walked in, determined to spend as much money as one could at a bead shop.
The transactions of a normal life seemed meaningless now.

I was surprised to find that there was something cathar-
tic about rolling the tiny beads around between my fingers.
The way the colors swirled into one another in such a small
little orb. The way the light hit the glass. The differences
in texture, or patina, or shine, or color. It was subtle, and I
found the things that drew me to a given bead were arbi-
trary. I rested my favorites one by one in my left palm and
imagined myself arranging them into delicate glimmering

strings for necklaces. I imagined my hands occupied and productive while the rest of my body and mind and heart was a grieving mess. It seemed very appealing in that moment.

So I bought a large pile of beads and clasps and strings and wires and tweezers and pliers, found a place on a map with a stall where I could sell my yet-to-be-made jewelry. And then I packed up everything in my college apartment, sent in my notice of leave to the registrar at school, and went to that place on the map.

And soon after, I found myself on an uncomfortable wooden chair, behind a collapsible table full of jewelry that no one bought. I didn't mind, though.

While people walked past my tent, usually without a second look, I spent most of the day in the tent reading and decoding poetry. I had always been drawn to poetry in theory, but my life in pursuit of an MD wouldn't have allowed for such indulgences. But now, on my new path, in my new life resembling none of the old one, poetry could abound. I indulged in it as the cool spring turned into the summer heat next to my beads.

On a particularly hot Tuesday midmorning, I looked up from a collection of Emily Dickinson's greatest poems, peered over the spine and found myself intrigued by the green, alchemic eyes of the furniture designer across the way.

I shared that I liked his stuff and then pulled my fingertips along the edge of the wood. I had honestly just intended to start a conversation, but the wood felt smooth and strong. Like it was in the shape it was always meant to be in.

Your father descended from the black pickup truck into

which he was loading handcrafted chairs and tables and desks and bureaus.

He had a stunning mane of wild black curls that fell over his face. He was burly and handsome with strong hands and shoulders and pronounced cheekbones. He sat on the bed of his truck in a faded flannel shirt with specks of sawdust catching the light as he moved even slightly. The top two buttons were undone, revealing dark curls on his chest. He leaned back, crossed his legs and raised an eyebrow.

He responded to my comments with a certain look in his eyes that made me think he was flirting.

His long dark eyelashes were shining. He crossed one leg over the other and swung his foot back and forth. His boots were firm and rugged with holes and different-colored laces on each. His one foot came toward me and receded again. Like a metronome on an old piano.

I sat down on a lingering coffee table. "Sturdy," I said. It was the sexiest word I could think of at the time.

I don't know what had come over me, acting like that. As my fingers rounded the edge of the table, they dipped into a slight groove in the wood.

I quickly recovered by throwing something else out there. I told him I liked the finish. I continued to save myself the embarrassment of being so forward.

There was a geometric cube carved into the side. It was stained a darker wood.

I asked inquisitively about the engraving as confidently as I could.

To this day, I do not know what emboldened me in this moment. What force within my body pressed me up toward that man or brought my finger along his table so seductively. To ask such prying questions without hesitation. It was my first experience with bohemia. It felt meaningless, asinine even, but it enlivened all that was numb within me in those difficult days.

He told me it was his logo. A box. After his last name. And then he told me his whole name. Silas Box. It sounded as slick and cool as I expected.

Before Silas came down and greeted me properly, I pulled my finger along the wood once again and yelped out. I recoiled my finger from the table and brought it close to my chest and held on to it with my other hand.

Silas jumped from his position on the bed of the truck and took my fingers in his. His hands were calloused and scarred and manly. His eyes grew large and attentive as he inspected my finger.

He asked if I had caught a splinter, distress creeping up in his throat.

I playfully extended my finger right in front of Silas's and smiled generously. I was just faking and I let him know it.

Silas's shoulders fell and he tucked his chin, coarse with stubble, into his chest and shook his head at his own credulousness. His curly hair flopped back and forth effortlessly. He tucked a curl behind his ear as he lifted his head. Those green, alchemic eyes again. As my eyes met his, a grand and flitting feeling rushed into my heart. I hadn't felt anything in so long. It was glorious.

He asked if I was free for a beer and I told him okay, as casually as I could muster.

There was a time in my life that I considered what it

would have been like if I had never made my way across the market. If I had never seduced your father with my long dress and slightly sunburned chest. Or him me. If I hadn't said yes to that beer. If I had instead veered off this wild road, this directionless detour from my life, and returned to everything I was meant to see and do.

But it brought you to me, my dear Hazel. And I would never take that back. Not for anything in the world. Even if it started to make this mess.

We spent a lot of time together after that first beer. When I began falling in love, or in lust, with your father, I was young enough and aching over the loss of my parents enough to embrace the freedom that came with being in that place. Being with that man.

My relationship with your father was devoid of promises and apologies. Nobody bought flowers or left little love notes. Nobody folded laundry without being prompted or arranged weekend getaways. I never lit candles over a romantic home-cooked meal of Silas's favorite foods. Silas never came home from his day with something special he picked out just for me. If we wanted those things, we would do them together. Or not. There was nothing needed or compromised over. There was only want and lust and the simplicity of being just ourselves.

At the time, I believed in the expansive potential of my life. That Silas and I could grow into any kind of life together. Fill up the spaces of the world with our honest, naked, uncompromised selves. There was romance, true romance, in that. Togetherness in independence. (You can see how my mind has changed with Cam.)

There is a moment I often hearken back to when I think of that summer. The sun was high and the windows were open. There was no breeze to rattle windowpanes or billow curtains. There was just thick, drooping, hot air saturating the bedroom. White sheets were tangled at our ankles and pillows and bras and shorts and underwear peppered the room (I'm sorry to make you cringe!). My eyelids were heavy and I had my arm stretched across Silas's abdomen. I could feel his breathing. The rhythmic rise and fall of his belly. I lifted my arm to reach for a glass of water beside the bed and Silas's skin lifted with it. It was as if our bodies melted into one in that room. I let my arm linger for a moment, Silas's skin affixed to mine. Your father drew his heavy eyelids open and I instinctively thrust my hand toward the water glass. I knew Silas would not want to witness our bodies connected like that. It surprised me, though, how viscerally aware I was that this scene of skin stuck to skin would violate a sacred condition of our relationship.

It was in this moment that I realized it wasn't a free-spirited ideal that sustained us. It was the avoidance of all realities. That single flinch of my arm set into motion my scrupulous study of Silas's gestures. I became desperate for casualties. The conspiracies cloaked in every movement, every word. The way his jaw tensed when we made eye contact. The way his knees turned away from me when we spoke, even casually. The anxious twisting of his hair around his right pointer finger. The empty gaze that would sometimes befall him.

I asked once while we were sitting in his backyard where he went mentally. I put my hand on his hand tenderly.

Silas didn't blink once as he spoke of his own tragedies in his past.

He told me that he was only sixteen when he met his first love, Torrey, but he was sure that it would last a lifetime. I think I can recite almost verbatim what he told me about her. For many years I played that scene back over and over in my mind. He said that Torrey was an equal but opposite force. Calm and free-spirited. She never paid any mind to the rules but would break them only gently. Torrey got pregnant the year after they met and Silas's parents put them up in that lake house in Grandor (the one you're in right now). They redid the whole thing together. They were really making it work. Starting a life. Silas was just starting to earn some money from selling furniture, too. He told me with a sparkle in his eye about the rocking chair he had made for her. How excited she was to rock their little girl in it. I think they were going to name her Ruby. Cute, huh?

Then, one day, as Silas was preparing to meet Torrey for a picnic, the phone rang. It was the hospital. Torrey had gone in with some bleeding and cramps. Before long she was unconscious. They saved Torrey, but they couldn't save the baby.

He described, with such anguish, how Torrey reacted. I could tell the images of that horrible day were just ripping right through to the very moment that he was telling me this. They returned from the hospital to their home, but she was never the same. They as a couple were never the same.

I disclosed that unexpected death landed me in Grandor, too, and that he wasn't alone.

He took my hand and walked me into his workshop. He showed me a picture of her that he had tacked up onto the wall. Her eyes looked metallic and gray, reflecting the lake. Her lips were full and pink and burst out from her lush skin. Her shoulder was turned toward the camera and she was beautiful. Silas lifted up that photo to reveal two sonograms underneath. It was their baby. One sonogram at three months and one at five months of a baby that would never be.

My heart ached for him. And it was a deep, deep ache. I was never certain why he shared what he shared in that moment.

I felt a sadness both for him and with him. I sensed both an intimate attachment given our shared experience, but also a certainty that there would be an unnavigable distance between us.

From time to time, I would see him pick up the phone to try to call her. But, to my knowledge, he was never able to get himself to go through with it.

I don't know why I feel compelled to admit this now but I do. One day, I snuck into his phone and took down her number. I had a feeling I might need it at some point. I didn't want to acknowledge it yet, but I think it was my way of admitting to myself that we would have never lasted. I think if it wasn't going to be me in his life, I knew it would be her. I don't think there is a single woman on this earth that could replace Torrey for him. Or Ruby, for that matter.

But that doesn't mean he can't love you, and Eve, too. I really believe that.

I'm sorry if it made a mess of things,
Mom.

13

For Jane, the rest of the day almost felt normal. The twins woke up and still did all the twin things. Cam still did all the Cam things. And the door to Hazel's room was still slightly ajar with nothing but quiet behind it. The quiet behind the door wasn't new, but the feeling of emptiness was. Jane put her hand against the door and thought about pushing it wide open and lying down on Hazel's bed and calling her and closing her own eyes and listening to the sound of her daughter's voice. But she knew she shouldn't.

Hazel was beginning her own journey and she needed the space to do it. So Jane settled for a text message instead.

She typed, Thinking of you, hit Send and then held the phone against her chest. She would be lying to herself if she said she wasn't wishing that Hazel would call her immediately and want to come home. But the phone remained cold and dormant.

Jane continued down the hallway into her bedroom, where Cam was already in bed, reading by lamplight. She tucked herself in under the covers next to her husband.

"The twins went down easy tonight, huh?" Cam said

and then kissed her on the cheek. His lips lingered there for longer than usual.

Jane nodded and smiled. These were the kinds of moments she could look forward to without Hazel around.

"Which means I'll go down easy tonight, too!" Cam laid his book on the bedside table, turned the lamp off and pressed his ear into the pillow with his face turned away from Jane's. "Good night, love," he whispered and then didn't make another move or sound.

And neither did Jane, but her mind was swirling with thoughts of Hazel. Whether the girls had arrived safely. What Hazel was doing. How she was feeling. Whether she liked Silas. Whether she liked Eve. Whether she was homesick. What they ate for dinner. If they had dessert. What they would do tomorrow. It all swirled and swirled into a tornado picking up momentum and fear and anxiety.

Jane checked her phone for a response. Still nothing. She scrunched her eyes shut.

Her heart was pulsing. Sleep was not likely. Not likely at all.

Jane opened her eyes up wide, and as quietly as possible slipped out of the covers, out of the room and resumed reading Susie's notebook from right outside Hazel's door.

LETTER 2
LEARNING I WAS PREGNANT
SUSIE

Dear Eve,

Shortly after my trip up to Grandor, a pregnancy test I took alone in our bathroom revealed a second blue line. I clutched my belly. I pressed my open palm into my flesh tenderly. I remember that it surprised me that I was happy with how supple and bloated it was. I usually wanted my belly taut.

There were many other mixed feelings, too. I had wanted a baby so, so badly. I wanted you. But I was so, so ashamed to have betrayed my husband. It was very out of character. I felt a flash of wondering how I would ever live with myself. And then I thought of you, and it melted away.

It was pure elation, despite the memory of being in bed with a man that was not my husband. That was not your father. As I told you in my last letter, I was trying desperately to forget everything back home. It's no excuse, but Silas was the perfect man to violate the sanctity of everything I thought I once believed in. He was scruffy and dark and strong and his hands were calloused. He was a man so clear, so in control, of his own morality and attitude. It was as if there was an invisible boundary around him. One that I could not cross. Which was exactly what I wanted because I knew I was going back to my life at home with your father.

But still, this was something I had not yet encountered in another man. Something that intrigued me.

Especially after months of calendars and trackers and hollow lovemaking and waiting with your father for that second line on the pregnancy test to emerge. Of course, it never did. We learned soon after that that your father's sperm wasn't viable and that he would never be able to produce children. Imagine that, honey. It was heartbreaking. Everything felt so empty. My belly. My life. So I had run away to Grandor and done something so terrible. So unfair to your father. Something I want to say I would take back, but I never can because it led me to you.

And truth be told, when I woke up the next morning after

having been with Silas, he was gone. I vaguely remember him tiptoeing out and telling me he had to get home, but I was still hazy with sleep and the remnants of the prior evening's tequila. I was glad he wasn't there, though, because alone in that bed after doing something so unspeakable, my feelings for your father and our life at home intensified. They surged through me so fiercely. My heart beat with it. My blood was vicious with it. I'd believed I got everything I wanted from Silas. I committed to letting that memory live in a place so far away in my mind that no one would know about it. I vowed not to tell Parker. Not to tell my girlfriends. Anyone.

I clutched the pregnancy test in my hands. I had been wrong about what Silas would give me. I honestly felt relief more than anything. I had ached for this moment, this baby. I had yearned for it. And now here it was. Small and thirsty for life. A life that I could provide. If only it were your father's.

There was a time in my life that I wouldn't have lied about something so big, but there were things that were bigger than a single lie. Your father, and this baby growing inside of me, and our whole future together. Our family.

I closed my eyes and exhaled. I looked at myself in the mirror, straight into my own eyes, and then went to meet your father in the bedroom with the pregnancy test in hand.

I told him it was a miracle and thrust the plastic stick in front of the book he was reading. I told him we were pregnant. I tried to keep my voice from quivering. I paused and then swallowed to clear the lump that had formed in my throat.

Without hesitation, your father looked up from his book and flung his arms around me.

He agreed that it was a miracle in a soft and earnest voice.

He squeezed me even tighter and then pressed his lips into my neck.

It was everything I envisioned this moment to be.

With your father's arms around me and his voice in my ear, I was quick to let the tension of the lie dissolve. I relaxed into your father's arms and then hugged him back. I was surprised how simple it was for everything that happened with Silas to burrow its way even further from reality. For me to rewrite the story of my family. But I did.

I could tell by the weight of your father's body around me, the delicate way in which he kissed me, that he was so relieved, so ready, for this to be the truth, too.

And so, to me and your father and to everyone else, it was our truth.

After all these years of trying, we were having our baby. That was what we stuck to for so many years.

I'm sorry if it made a mess of things,

Mom.

And with that, Jane felt compelled to write her story.

LETTER 2
LEARNING I WAS PREGNANT
JANE

Dear Hazel,

When the pregnancy test revealed that there was a baby inside of me, I had a moment of clarity in my life. A moment of honesty with myself. I wanted more from Silas. And with this baby, I would want even more and more and more.

My wants would be exponential. After learning about you, I would keep finding my hands cradled around the bottom of my still-flat belly. I had been waiting for days to tell Silas what was inside, but I felt guilty. Guilty of wanting real, engulfing romance. Guilty of wanting to expand our love into more. Into parenthood. I thought of Torrey and Ruby. What they meant to Silas. I knew in my heart that I, that we—you and I—could never fill Silas up like they had.

I woke up one night just as Silas was making his way into our bedroom. It was four o'clock in the morning, much later than normal, and he curled his body around me. He reeked of beer and whiskey and cigarettes and someone else's perfume. I now know that someone else was Eve's mother.

He told me that he didn't think we should do this anymore. He told me he was in pieces and couldn't be put back together. He told me he wasn't a good man and then his words trailed off into mumbles and he fell asleep.

I reached down and held my belly. Despite the heat, I felt a chill up my spine. I realized that we had exposed each other's deepest vulnerabilities. Me wanting to be a mother. Him wanting to be alone. I knew that we had arrived at the painful but relieving place where all relationships end.

I rolled over in bed and faced Silas. He was lying on his back with his mouth open, snoring from the back of his throat. A lock of hair was plastered to his forehead, sticky from sweat and heat and probably sex.

It, of course, bothered me that he had been with another woman, but what really stung was the unequivocal knowledge that I would be raising you myself. I felt you inside me even though I had read that you were only the size of a lentil then.

I lurched over Silas and put my mouth close to his ear.

I told him I was leaving. It was the only thing I could do.

Without opening his eyes, Silas rolled onto his side and wrapped his tanned muscular arm around my hips and squeezed the flesh of my butt between his fingers.

It was hard to do it, but I peeled his fingers from my body.

And then I said that it was for good. I'm not sure he understood in his drunken, sleepy haze, but it didn't matter much. I was leaving for me.

He opened one green eye. The other one was pressed into the pillow.

I held his gaze for only a moment, but time stretched and stretched and stretched. There was an impermeable silence between us. I had thought we would be drenched with sadness or regret. Instead we seemed to be blooming with understanding and respect. With the acknowledgment of balance and rightness and possibility and relief.

I felt a tear emerge on the precipice of my bottom eyelid. I didn't want to cry, so I pressed my finger against it to prevent it from falling. I looked down at my finger and was happy to see that it was not as wet as I expected it to be. And then, I got up from the bed and walked out of the room without further ceremony or explanation.

If falling for Silas was the start of your life, this moment was the start of our life. From that moment on, it was you and me, baby.

I'm sorry if it made a mess of things,

Mom.

14

It was one of those days when Jane just wanted to melt into the couch and do nothing.

She wanted to get lost in a book or complete a movie uninterrupted or treat herself to a glass of wine and a bowl of ice cream in silence. But Cam was working late tonight, so after a full day with the twins, Jane was left to cook and feed them dinner.

Getting them to eat on this particular day was a challenge. Any bit of food placed on the tray was swiped off by Griffin, which made Trevor cry, which made Griffin cry, which made Trevor cry louder, which made Griffin cry louder, which made Jane want to scream. If one began to calm down, the other riled him right back up. It was one of those days when the reality of motherhood was grating.

To get a moment alone, Jane walked into the living room, sank into the couch and pressed her palms over her face. As soon as she did, Griffin and Trevor let out simultaneous and piercing screams from the next room over, where they were left to play.

By instinct, Jane called out for help from her daughter. "Hazel, honey, can you come grab the boys for a bath..." Her voice trailed off into the quiet. There was no Hazel to help. In fact, there was no sign of Hazel at all for days.

Jane picked up her phone to check for text messages. Nothing. Just a stream of unanswered Thinking of you messages.

Jane needed Hazel. And not just for help with the boys. She needed her for her soul. Her heart.

Her thoughts were interrupted by another set of shrieks. But she wasn't done with thinking about Hazel. She felt an intense pull back to Susie's notebook.

So she did a thing she vowed to do only in dire circumstances, which was to remove the twins from their high chairs and, without even cleaning off their faces, place them right in front of the television. It worked like a charm. The boys were probably not full, but they were quiet. So Jane retrieved Susie's book from the other room and returned to reading it.

LETTER 3
THE EARLY YEARS
SUSIE

Dear Eve,

I carried you in my belly a full nine months plus another eleven days. I told you to take your time if you wanted, as I rubbed my big swollen belly. I told you that you didn't have to come out until you were ready. And you took my words to heart. It took thirty hours of labor before you made it into the world and into the doctor's hands. You yelped under the bright lights of the delivery room. I burst into tears upon hearing the sound of your voice for the first time. I squeezed your father's hand; he was looking down at you with a quiet shock in his face. You were our "miracle."

The nurse placed you in your father's arms first. As he rocked you back and forth and smiled so warmly, so knowingly, down at you, I felt in my heart that you were his daughter. It may sound surprising to you, but it didn't even cross my mind that you were someone else's for another half a decade. You felt so fully, truly and wholly ours. I knew that together, your father and I would give you the very, very best life.

And, I felt we did. When you were hungry, we fed you. When you required a new diaper, we changed you. When you were sleepy, we rocked you. When you were fussy, we walked you. And even when you needed nothing at all, we lay with you and kissed you and hugged you and played with you and read with you. Just because we wanted to. Just because we loved you. Just because we were your parents.

The feeling that I could give another human, you, everything you needed was by far the greatest honor I had ever felt. For the first year of your life, I held you nearly all day long. I didn't want to let you go. I didn't want to miss a single moment of your life. There were so many intoxicating moments of unbridled joy just simply observing you. At the littlest cough or hiccup or giggle, I would just explode with joy.

In those early years, I felt I knew everything about you.

But still, the person you would become felt like a great mystery to me. It's going to sound odd to you, but I mourned the future version of you. I wanted to know everything about you forever, but I knew that it wouldn't be possible.

I studied your reactions to things—whether you preferred chocolate or vanilla ice cream, a dress or shorts, your hair up or hair down, the color marker you picked up first, your favorite toy, or movie, or bedtime book. I wondered whether any of these things indicated what you would choose when you were six, or twelve, or twenty, or fifty years old. I wondered how every little choice you made today would change you.

I felt desperate to know who you would be in addition to who you already were.

At the time, I didn't consider whether I felt this way because half of you, half of your genes and personality and preferences I suspected were alien to me. But upon writing this letter to you, I know this must have been a significant part of how I felt when I observed you, all those years ago. I suppose I also knew that the day you would meet your biological father would come eventually.

But I really, really didn't want it to. I wanted you to be all mine, all ours, forever.

I'm sorry if it made a mess of things,

Mom.

And with that, Jane took out her journal and pen and wrote.

This entry, she knew, was going to hurt.

LETTER 3
THE EARLY YEARS
JANE

Dear Hazel,

When I walked through the door of our house with you in my arms for the first time, I felt it would be reasonable to panic, but I didn't. I just exhaled slowly and tried to keep my thumping heart under control. It was just us now.

I placed the car seat gently onto the couch so as not to wake you and then lay back on the couch. My body was still aching and cramping from your birth. There was a mix of dull stinging and squeezing deep within my belly. Lying there with things quiet and slowed down made me acutely aware of all those throbbing feelings in my body. I pressed my eyes together even more tightly and exhaled slowly again. I felt a tear press up in my throat. I wished I could share these moments with someone that would re-member them. I wished my mother and father were there. I even for a moment wished Silas were there. I felt helpless and alone. Scorched by all the things that had happened in my life before motherhood was a part of it.

Sleep came in like a tide and tried to tug me into a slum-ber. I didn't know if I should let it happen. What if you were to wake up and need something? I thought about pulling my eyes open, but everything was so heavy and tired and sleep tugged some more. I wanted to give in to it. It seemed so sweet and luscious to be fueled back up by sleep. Even if it were just the littlest drop. I rolled over onto my side and brought more of the surface area of my body into contact with the couch cushions. And just as I prepared to give in fully, just as I was about to succumb to rest, my body jolted me awake. My baby! You couldn't just be left alone! My entire torso sprung up into a seated position, my eyes stretched out big and wide, my heart raced but in a new way. I frantically turned my attention to the car seat you were sleeping in.

You didn't appear to have moved or made a sound at all. You just lay there peacefully, angelically, in your car seat.

I shook out my body, dispelling any last traces of adrenaline. As my heartbeat slowed, and that dull ache in my belly returned, I was reminded that I was, in fact, supposed to sleep when you slept. I felt betrayed by my own body. This electric instinct to mother was more powerful than any of my own personal needs. I felt relieved and terrified all at once that I would be here at all hours of all days to take care of you. My body apparently wouldn't have it any other way. But who would be there to take care of me?

I inspected your face. You were small and fleshy and alien-like. Your skin's bluish hue at birth had turned to a splotchy pink. Your hair was dark and thick and two small pieces stuck up like a rogue patch of grass on the right side of your head. I felt an urge to pat it down and raised my hand to do it, but then something inside stopped me. *Let her sleep*, a voice spoke in my own head.

Looking down at you, I felt as if I had gone out and bought something too precious and too expensive. It was as if I had walked around a shop I knew I shouldn't have been in and walked out with something I couldn't afford. Something I didn't know how to integrate into my life. Now that

I owned it, I felt I had no idea how to interact with something so delicate.

Was I allowed to touch this baby? Would it wake you up if I did?

And even if I did touch you, and even if I did wake you up, who would know?

My once fierce desire for the thing had now shriveled up into a pathetic fear of it. I was weak in the presence of you, my love. But I also felt somewhat in control.

I thought about returning to sleep, but preferred instead to keep looking down at you, my sleeping little girl.

You had your mouth open the slightest bit. A small bubble of drool formed on your lips and then popped. You squirmed in your chair, your left leg and then right kicking out. You let out a little coo. It melted my heart a little bit.

I felt an urge to pick you up. I knew I should just let you rest but I felt I needed you in my arms. I felt I needed you close to my body and my heart. I needed the weight of your little body against mine.

So I did it. I tucked my hands underneath your tiny back and lifted you into my arms. Your little body was so warm. I wiggled your delicate head into the crease of my elbow and rocked you slowly back and forth. Your screaming and crying upon my picking you up was far more anguished and primitive than any scream or cry I had heard you scream or cry yet.

I was too tired to feel alarmed but too new to this to be calm. I just existed in the surreal and primal state of what I now understood as motherhood.

I wondered to myself how this baby could have all of these

things she needed in such close proximity and still feel so much agony? So much distress? How was I to care for you so constantly?

Still, I just rocked you back and forth, back and forth. Eventually, I felt you begin to relax. I could tell we were both relieved. Your gnarled fingers started to unwind. Your back started to sink into my arms. Your eyelids started drooping.

I remember it all so clearly, even though it was so long ago now. I felt a little buzz in my veins. Perhaps I could curl up on that couch and sleep, too, now.

Your eyelids drooped again.

Perhaps I could pick up that book I was in the middle of before you were born.

Your face was perfectly still and delicate now.

Perhaps I could go to the other room and call a friend. Make some contact with the outside world. Yes, that was what I would do. I smiled at the thought of how refreshing it might be to talk to someone.

I gingerly placed you down onto the couch and prepared to make that phone call. But just as I did, an alarming red color spread across your face. Your eyes pressed open, and your right green eye swirled violently. Your entire body began squirming and your mouth yawned open, promising even louder booming cries. The sound of all the grief and pain in the universe emerged from your little lungs. There was bellowing and roaring and agony.

It was as if you had discovered my infidelity—the mere idea of turning my attention to anybody but you.

I picked you up once more and rocked you. I was simultaneously excited and comforted by the fact that you needed me. Because I knew in that moment that I needed you, too. You whined a bit and I tried to offer a lullaby to get you back to sleep. And without thinking about what that lullaby should be, I began reciting the lines of a favorite poem to you. The same one I was reading when I met your father.

Sleep little baby, clean as a nut,
Your fingers uncurl and your eyes are shut…

I felt a clear understanding that my life had been divided into a before and after, and I was now, and would forever be, living in the after. I wondered how I would do this alone. And then I just I closed my eyes, recited the lines some more and let you sleep in my arms.

I knew I didn't know what I was doing, but I wanted so badly to do it right.

I'm sorry if it made a mess of things,

Mom.

15

It was Cam's turn to put the boys to bed and Jane's turn to pick the movie. She cued up *Lost in Translation*, one of their shared favorites, and sat beneath the covers with the remote control in hand until Cam joined her. As soon as Jane heard Cam's footsteps, a warm smile spread across her face. There were few things more pleasant to Jane these days than a quiet evening next to her husband with a favorite movie playing. Cam came in and was smiling, too. There was more pep in his step than usual, Jane thought. And his eyes looked particularly loving.

"I was thinking we could level up movie night!" he said and pulled a big bowl of popcorn from behind his back. He dug his hand right into the pile, pulled out a single kernel, tilted his head back and dropped one delicately in his mouth from a few inches above. He snapped his head back forward to look right at Jane, picked another kernel from the bowl and held it up next to his face in a position poised for throwing.

"Here, catch!" he said excitedly, and tossed the piece across to her. She opened her mouth and lurched to the side. The salty kernel landed right on her tongue and Jane crunched down on it with delight. Cam leaped up into the into the air to cheer—a few bits of popcorn toppled out of the bowl— and dove into Jane's arms as if she had just caught the winning touchdown in the Super Bowl. And then he kissed her sweetly on the ear.

"You know I'm more of a sweets girl," Jane said into the side of Cam's ear. "And now you got me jonesing for some ice cream."

"Oh yeah!" Cam replied, pulling back to look at Jane in the eyes. Jane smiled and slid out from beneath the covers with a sultry look in her eye. Ice cream felt nearly as alluring as sex these days.

"Get me some of that cookie dough," Cam yelled excitedly after her.

"You got it," Jane agreed and walked down the hallway into the kitchen.

She opened the freezer and reached for the cookie dough ice cream. Blocking its container was a second container of plain old vanilla. She contemplated which flavor she wanted for herself and just as she was about to push the carton of vanilla out of the way, she felt a pang of guilt. It was as if Hazel was right there, asking to share a bowl with her.

She wished she could. She wished she could right now.

Jane still hadn't heard from her daughter. And it was hurting more and more each day. She considered calling Silas, but she wanted to give Hazel the space she deserved. But Jane so wanted to connect again. In between moments of her normal life with Cam and the twins, it was painful to remember that Hazel wasn't there.

Forgetting Cam was in the other room waiting for his cookie dough ice cream, Jane went to go get Susie's journal that she had placed in her bedside drawer.

LETTER 4
SEEING SILAS IN YOU
SUSIE

Dear Eve,

I first saw Silas in you when you were about five years old. There was no great significance to the lead-up. It really just washed over me all at once.

You were fighting against heavy eyelids as I turned the final page of your favorite book at the time, *Rainbow Fish*. I wished you good-night and turned to kiss you.

Your eyes opened slowly as you prepared to receive your kiss and say good-night back. And when they opened, it was like Silas was greeting me with the full force of his deep green eyes. They swirled and held the light from your night-light in little black flecks just like Silas's, too.

I flinched back from the bed with a light gasp and brought my hands to my chest. My heartbeat was thick and powerful with the reminder that Silas was in there, too.

I thought about explaining everything to you right then and there. But instead I just said good-night again and turned out your light. I don't think I ever truly looked at you, or your father for that matter, the same again.

Over the years, I continued to catch the flicker of Silas in your eyes. I must admit that it caused me to observe you with a certain trepidation as you grew older. I wondered what other parts of Silas might emerge next without warning. What other reminders of a brief past might come crashing into our life. I watched you from afar sometimes, just waiting, as I scanned my fuzzy memory of him for things it could be.

His hair, his gait. The way his cheeks and ears lifted when he smiled. The way his temples flared as he listened. The slight bend at the end of his pinky.

Would you exhibit those things, too?

I watched carefully, constantly, but nothing would reveal the Silas in you. Nothing but those green eyes.

But then I began to consider that there were all the things I didn't know about Silas that could have made their way to you without me realizing. There could be things brewing inside your sweet little body after my flesh and genes collided with a man I knew almost nothing about. Did Silas have a temper? Was he smart or caring or generous? Was he wise or funny or spontaneous? Was he healthy? Were his parents healthy in their old age?

These thoughts and questions ricocheted around my mind. And ironically, it meant that I began to carry the memory of Silas with me all the time.

By the time you were six years old, I was heavy and achy with it. I wished I could expel it from my mind, my body, my bones. And yours, too. But I couldn't. It was a part of our family. It was part of our life. Part of the story of all of our lives. There was really no denying it no matter how much I willed it away.

I'm sorry if it made a mess of things,

Mom.

And with that, Jane wrote:

LETTER 4
SEEING SILAS IN YOU
JANE

Dear Hazel,

I first saw Silas in you the moment you were born. In the haze of bringing you into the world, I felt the past and the present begin to overlap. I saw the faint outline of my mother and father materialize across the room. They were holding hands delicately and smiling, looking calm and content. And Silas was there with them, too. His dark mane of hair and his swirling green eyes. His arms were folded across his chest but his eyes looked filled with pride.

I wanted to reach out to them, to walk toward them, but another wave of piercing pain surged through my body.

I was truly delirious through most of the labor, but I snapped right into full lucidity right before you emerged from between my legs. I was holding the nurse's hand. I didn't realize that I had envisioned anything else for myself, that I would have wanted a man's hand in mine when I gave birth, but it had become apparent when I shook my hand out of hers as soon as I came to.

Through gritted teeth I told the nurse that I could do it

myself and that I didn't need a hand. I didn't want to reach for the hand of a stranger at this life-changing moment of meeting my first daughter. The nurse slipped her fingers under my fingers anyway, and then I squeezed them with all my might. I thanked her with relief once you came out and a strand of hair, damp with sweat, fell across my forehead. And then there you were. In my arms.

The feeling of your small but heavy head in the crease of my arm filled me with the most warmth and pleasure and happiness I had ever felt. Your eyes were closed and your skin was dusted with a blue tint. You seemed so gentle. So pretty. I brought my hand to your cheek and you opened your eyes.

I had been expecting blue but they were already bold and full of color and life. Your left eye, at its center, was a deep and rich chocolaty brown. I could barely even detect where the iris ended and your pupil began. The outer edge was rimmed with a deep forest green and spots of an equally deep ocean blue that rippled in toward the middle to meet the brown. Where the two colors met, they swirled together like moss creeping over soil. The overall effect was a single hazel eye.

Your right eye, on the other hand, was a swirling mix of many shades of green. The color was fierce and powerful. The kind of green that sprang out from underneath the snow and enlivened brittle, wintry branches to remind you that spring was coming. The kind of stirring green that looked just like Silas's. The deep green of a forest after rain. The kind of green that was certainly straight from Silas. I was overwhelmed by the image of Silas's big green eye looking back into mine.

I looked from one eye to the other and back again. You were no doubt Silas's, not that there was any doubt.

I suddenly felt confronted by the realization that you would always carry the story of both your parents with you. It was already apparent in your eyes; one for your mother and one for your father. Your eyes had not mixed in their color, as your father and I had not mixed our lives.

I felt a pang of grief clench down tight onto my heart. You would never have the full family little girls deserved. I felt an emptiness for you that I knew I would never be able to fill on my own.

I had wanted so badly to do this all on my own. To forget your father was a part of it all. I imagined my life filled with just you and me. Free of everything that came before it. But looking down at you, and into that green eye, I knew this wouldn't be an option. You would always have Silas in you. Still, I felt a flurry of closeness and commitment and devotion and love swirling through my body.

The nurse interrupted and asked what I would name you.

I brought my lips gently down onto your forehead to kiss you. I looked into your surprisingly alert little eyes. One hazel one. One green one. You were a mix of your parents. A mix of our lives. I wanted to remember this moment. This feeling that Silas would always be with us, too, in some way.

I said I would name you Hazel. I wanted you to know where you came from. Know the things that made you, you. Hazel Box. I remember saying it with gusto.

I'm sorry if it made a mess of things,

Mom.

16

Jane was walking down the hallway one afternoon while the boys were napping just a few days after Hazel left, when she spotted Hazel's school backpack slouched in the corner of her bedroom through the crack in the doorway. It felt like a violation to go into Hazel's room when she wasn't there, but Jane couldn't help it. She ached for any connection to her daughter. Jane slipped furtively into the bedroom and pulled the backpack up from the floor. She held it up in front of her face as the zippers jingled at the sides. It smelled of pencil lead and spearmint gum and a sweet candy-like perfume. Precious smells of a teenage girl.

She pulled the backpack into her chest and hugged it as if it were Hazel. She pulled the straps over her shoulders and let the weight of contents of the bag tug down on her shoulders. As she embraced the backpack in her arms the notebooks and binders moved under the canvas like bones under skin. She thought of Hazel with that backpack on her own shoulders, spraying herself with that perfume, chewing that spearmint gum, scribbling notes in class. The rest of the room looked like it could belong to any girl, really. Clothes were piled in little stacks in corners, and on the carpet, and on the desk, and on the chair. Notebooks and textbooks and papers and pens and highlighters were strewn across the desk. A pile of different-flavored ChapSticks lay crisscross like pick-up sticks. There were a few posters on the wall featuring movies with actors Jane didn't recognize.

But then, there was the sign of the daughter she knew. On the bedside table, there was a picture of herself and Hazel at the park holding eaten watermelon slices in front of their mouths to form big green watermelon rind smiles. Hazel's two front teeth were missing but the rest were shining out from behind as she smiled. Jane remembered when this was taken, a few weeks before Hazel's seventh birthday. Hazel was wearing a white T-shirt with a big pink dinosaur on the front and Jane was wearing a blue tie-dyed T-shirt with vibrant, swirling circles. Her hair looked careless but free in a loose braid that slung in front of her shoulder. There was so much light in both their eyes. So much youth in their cheeks. And next to that photo was a picture of Hazel at fourteen years old, holding the twins right after they were born. Griffin and Trevor were each wrapped in a little blue blanket, barely discernible. Hazel was looking up at the camera from her seat and her mouth was closed and her lips curled up to form a calmer smile. Her hair was messy in front of her face, and her shirt was drooping off one shoulder. Hazel looked simultaneously so old and so young holding the boys like that. It was the first day of Hazel's new life.

It occurred to Jane that she might not know her daughter as well she thought she did. That perhaps Hazel was off in Grandor, Maine, truly starting her new life. Perhaps Eve and Silas were enough to fill her up. Enough to fill up all that space she knew she'd left empty here at home. Letting Hazel embark on this journey forced Jane to question if she was there enough as her daughter started to grow and change into a young woman. But still, this silent treatment from her very own daughter, her very own flesh and blood, felt like punishment.

Sure, Jane had been distracted by the twins and Cam. But how couldn't she have been? Sure, she should have noticed that Hazel was withdrawing and probably didn't do enough to intervene, but that could have been simple teenage stuff. It didn't have to mean that Hazel would leave her forever. And Jane was starting to feel increasingly anxious that that was the path they were going down.

When she decided to let Hazel go visit her real father, she assumed it would help quell some feelings of abandonment for Hazel. But when, when would that feeling of ease come? When would Hazel reach out? When would Hazel call? When would Hazel be back in her arms? How would she get her back? And what the hell was going on up there at the lake? Why had no one called her yet?

Jane's ears and cheeks started to get hot with a mix of sadness and anger. She dropped Hazel's backpack on the floor as if it were radioactive and sought comfort in immersing

herself in another one of Susie's letters. She found the journal and cozied into a spot on the couch and started reading.

LETTER 5
TELLING (OR NOT TELLING) SILAS ABOUT YOU
SUSIE

Dear Eve,

It wasn't until you were well into elementary school that
I felt compelled to tell Silas you existed. It started off as a
gentle idea and turned into a raging, pestering, daily need.
There was a steady drumbeat of it. I don't know why I felt
that compulsion but I did. Perhaps it was seeing you grow
up into your own person, finding your independence in
even the smallest of ways. And perhaps it was just because
the wind started blowing a new direction. But whatever it
was, I finally decided I would just head on up to Grandor,
Maine, where I first met Silas and do it. I needed an excuse
to tell your father so that I could make it up there for the
day. It wasn't challenging.

Your father was sitting peacefully with a book in his hand
and his reading glasses perched effortlessly on the bridge of
his nose. He was looking calm and natural and easy as ever.
One leg was crossed over the other and he was still in his
work clothes. I had never known another man that felt more
comfortable in slacks and a button-down. I had never even
seen him untuck his shirt when he came home for the day.
Your father licked the top of his finger and then turned a
page without breaking his attention.

I drew my palms firmly across my shirt and skirt, pressed my lips together and cleared my throat to get your father's attention. I stood as erect as I could in the corner of our living room, waiting for a response. Your father was engrossed in the book.

I cleared my throat again. This time a bit louder. I took a few steps toward him and my heels clicked against the floor.

I told him I was thinking about getting my business up and running again and he replied that he thought it would be a good idea. He said it without even looking up from his book.

I took a few more steps toward your father and crouched down in front of him and asked him if he was certain. He rested his book down on his lap and pulled his glasses off from his face.

He assured me that he was. Your father smiled with just his lips, returned his glasses to their position on his nose and brought his book back in front of his eyes.

It was so easy. He was so easy. About everything.

I pressed down on the top of the book with my palm and looked back at your father. I told him how much I loved him and kissed him on the forehead.

Later that weekend, I was off to Grandor again. When I arrived, the first thing that drew my attention was the great white tent filled with jars of honey sticks. I immediately flashed to that moment all those years ago in Grandor, when I'd allowed myself the indulgence of that one honey stick. I had all but given up sugar then in service of my figure. It was so unlike me to allow myself that kind of extravagance. To be so permissive of my petty desires. It was that single drip of sweet honey on my tongue that had spiraled into the meeting of eyes and tequila and then the brushing of hands and then more tequila and then the touching of lips and then more tequila and then spending the night with a man that made you, you.

I suddenly felt like I was making a mistake going up there. My jaw and neck and shoulders and ribs tensed up. I wanted to undo the memory of that evening so badly. I wanted to replace that tequila-drenched night in a musty room with a man I hardly knew with a sober, respectful evening with your father on our Duxiana bed with fifteen-hundred-thread-count sheets.

I felt another pang of not wanting to be up there.

I walked over to the tent with the honey sticks and again pulled a dark brown root beer–flavored one from the jar. I twirled it in between my fingers and thought of Silas and thought of you and your father. I truly wished that you were your father's daughter, biologically speaking, but I couldn't completely wish away that night because that night created you. My healthy, beautiful, sweet little girl.

I looked down at the honey stick between my fingers. The sweet little indulgence that started it all. I opened the change wallet from my beige leather purse, pulled out a small handful of coins and walked confidently over to the elderly woman in a wide-brimmed straw hat sitting behind the table. I asked how many honey sticks I could get for my change and placed the coins onto the table.

The woman organized the money with her wrinkled fingertips and looked back up at me.

She offered me ten and asked if they were going to go to someone special.

I told her that they would go to you, my daughter, and that you were seven years old.

She told me how lucky you were and that I was a good mother for getting you some treats. She placed her hand on top of mine. I winced a little bit at the feeling of another person's palms on mine and felt my eyes well up at this stranger's words. "A good mother." That's all I ever wanted to be. And you were happy and had a nice home and that was what mattered.

I didn't need Silas to know a thing about you. I had everything I needed, everything I wanted at home with you and your father.

I thanked her warmly, looking straight into her eyes. I blinked vigorously until my tears subsided and drew stick after stick from their jars until they formed a colorful bouquet of sticks.

She slid an extra honey stick my way with a wink. She told me little girls loved the cotton candy ones and that it'd be perfect for you. I thanked the woman again and then shoved the honey sticks into my purse. I decided I had gotten everything I had come for at the market and I marched back to my car and drove right back home to Connecticut and my real family.

Silas didn't need to know a thing about you.

I'm sorry if it made a mess of things,

Mom.

★ ★ ★

And with that, Jane wrote a counterpart letter to Hazel.

LETTER 5
TELLING (OR NOT TELLING) SILAS ABOUT YOU
JANE

Dear Hazel,

The first time I said "I'm pregnant" out loud, I was on the phone making a doctor's appointment. I felt dizzy when I did it. The woman on the other end of the phone congratulated me exuberantly. She was the first person to do so.

She instructed me to come right in because they had a cancellation.

The nurse was wearing bubblegum-pink scrubs and had a smile across her face when she greeted me and began preparing the sonogram machine.

She shared her name through an unwavering smile and explained that she would be prepping the room for my sonogram that day.

I hated everything about that room. The hard plastic on the machines. The frigid air wandering out of the vents. The smell of sterility. I had imagined soft light and tranquility. I had imagined warmth. What else was I supposed to expect from the moment of seeing you for the first time?

She asked if my husband would be joining us. I should have foreseen that question but I hadn't. It caught me off guard.

I explained that he wouldn't be, the words catching on

my throat. The nurse smiled and nodded and went about her preparations on the other side of the room.

I winced at my own mini deception. Why did I lie like that? What was I trying to prove about myself and my life? What was I afraid that the nurse would think? I put my hands over my belly and inhaled.

I felt ashamed of not telling the whole story. I didn't want to feel ashamed and the words kept busting out of me. I told her that I didn't have a husband. I must have said it too loudly and too frantically because she just smiled even wider and nodded and then fiddled with the contraptions in the corner of the room.

I wondered what that smile meant. I replayed the response in my mind over and over again, searching for signs of judgment, disapproval, reproach, condescension. I laughed nervously and just kept going. I explained that it would be just me. And how fun I thought it would be. I couldn't stop the spilling of words. I think I asked her who needed a man anyway. I'm a bit embarrassed the way I just let my insecurities pour out of me like that.

I pulled my lips together so I couldn't talk anymore and lay back in my chair. I could feel my own heartbeat. The rising and falling of my chest.

Finally the nurse put an end to the madness when she told me the technician would be in soon. She exited the room pretty swiftly after that.

Surely these were social interactions I was going to have to tolerate for the rest of my life. Surely these were conversations I would be forced to have as my belly grew for the world to see.

The quiet of the room set in. The machines hummed around me and I thought of my mother. I wished she was there. I was mad that she wasn't.

And then the door swung open again with a whoosh of air and another woman, this one taller and wearing glasses, took a seat right next to my chair.

The doctor eventually came in and introduced herself to me in an energetic and earnest tone. She explained the process of the ultrasound and how the gel would feel cold, but seeing the baby would be a thrill. The words flowed too easily from the doctor's mouth as she scanned the room and the ultrasound machine, making sure everything was in place. I could tell it was a well-rehearsed introduction, but I still welcomed the soothing voice. She sounded like my mother to me.

The technician hovered the tube of gel over my belly. Then she, too, asked me if my husband was going to join.

I was much more prepared this time. I told her it was just me. I liked the sound of saying that. It would be just me. Just me, your mother.

As the cold gel hit my belly, my fingers curled. The transducer glided across my tummy and I looked up at the screen. Suddenly, the darkness of the screen was replaced with what could not be mistaken for anything but a little head. The sleeping head of a little, little baby. Her eyes and nose and cheeks and mouth filled the screen. It looked pale and ethereal. Like a ghost suspended, waiting to be.

The doctor asked if I wanted to know the sex of the baby.

I was barely breathing, barely thinking, as I nodded.

She told me I was having a little girl. I felt stunned and in love already.

I walked out of the doctor's office with shaky legs and a printed sonogram in hand. I couldn't help but think of my mother again. I got in my car and closed the door behind me. I sat behind my steering wheel and breathed and rubbed my belly and breathed and rubbed my belly and breathed some more.

I felt hot and angry in my loneliness there in the parking lot. I slammed my hands on the steering wheel. I slammed my hands and stomped my feet and yelled and screamed and shook my long hair all around. I felt rage and passion and hopelessness and excitement and confusion and loss and heat, but mostly love. Mostly, I just felt love. Love for my parents. Love for the baby girl inside me. Even love for Silas.

Everything at once became calm again. My heartbeat slowed and my ears cooled down and my legs and arms stilled.

I knew I shouldn't be surprised at these violent contrasts stirring inside me. All of those things, all of those feelings, are just part of love. With this love, though, I felt in control. In charge of it all. The powerlessness of my old loves melted away in that moment. The loss of my parents. The loss of Silas. I vowed to love you completely and unambiguously. Mercilessly. Relentlessly.

I fixed the image of the sonogram below the rearview mirror and admired my little girl floating there. I pressed my lips into the shiny paper.

As I started the car, I looked down at the duplicate of the sonogram in my lap and thought about where this one belonged. And then I drove straight to the post office and mailed it to Silas. Before I slipped it in the envelope, I wrote on the back my favorite poem from memory. I think you'll recognize it.

Sleep little baby, clean as a nut,
Your fingers uncurl and your eyes are shut...

No questions, no requests. Just a grainy picture of his baby, our baby, and that poem.

I didn't have the courage to do it any other way.

I'm sorry if it made a mess of things,

Mom.

17

Cam had come home early, had gotten the boys up and had gone out with them when Jane finished reading and writing the letter, but she didn't feel done yet. She wasn't sated at all. She missed Hazel. She felt lost without her. She needed to feel like it would all end up okay. So she pulled Susie's book back toward her and turned the page, seeking the comfort of Susie's story. The familiarity of another mother's story.

LETTER 6
WHEN EVERYTHING CHANGED FOR OUR FAMILY
SUSIE

Dear Eve,

I think I would have gone on with the illusion of our family forever. And for a long time, I thought I could. It was your father who brought it out into the open. It was the thing that changed all of our lives forever.

I used to love to watch through the window as you descended the steps of the bus coming home from kindergarten. Your tiny hands clutched around the railing. Your tiny body twisting around as you brought one tiny wobbling leg and then the next tiny wobbling leg from one step to the next. The final dismount from the steps brought you so much joy, and me so much fear. It was a big step for a little girl, but you made it every time. Your tiny lips would press into a tiny smile and you would readjust your bright pink backpack, too large for your tiny body, and begin the run down the driveway toward the door. Your wispy brown hair in two pigtails pointing in different directions after a day of playing. Your backpack bouncing wildly up and down behind you.

Just before you would reach the door, I would swing it wide open and crouch down with open, loving arms, waiting for you to fall into them. And then you did. And I melted every time your little arms flung around me and squeezed tight around my chest. Every time your little head nuzzled into my chest.

I pressed kiss after kiss after kiss into your big round cheeks and you giggled and giggled. The kind of giggles that came straight from the belly.

I curled my fingers around your shoulders and held you out in front of me. I wanted to soak you in at the end of the day. Make sure you were the same girl that left the house in the morning. Make sure you were happy.

I looked straight into your eyes, your swirling emerald

eyes, and asked, "How was your day? What did you do? What did you learn?"

You smiled a big toothless smile and would recount the day. Who you played with at recess. What the other girls brought for lunch. What the teacher was wearing.

And I nodded along as you told me, letting the words flow all the way through me. But more important than any of the details was your face as you told the stories of your day. How your eyes lit up and your lips turned up and your cheeks stayed rosy.

You wiggled your backpack off your back and pulled the zipper open.

One day when you got home from school you told us that your homework was to make a family tree. I could tell you were excited.

You pulled out a piece of paper with a big tree drawn in crayon. The brown of the trunk and green of the leaves were so charmingly scribbled a bit outside the lines. You placed the paper delicately down on the floor. You sat down next to the paper and began to explain how this project would go.

You counted as you pointed to the empty spaces in the leaves of the tree that we were meant to fill in with pictures of your family. I remembered that you paused for an extra while on the spot where your picture was supposed to go. You looked up at me to make sure I was listening to the directions. I felt proud of how clear and confident you were. I knew I had a girl that would get what she wanted, what she needed, from her world. At a slight detection that I wasn't paying attention, you placed your palm on my cheek and directed the angle of my head down toward your drawing.

You pointed at the two blank spaces connected to yours and reminded me that this was where Mommy's and Daddy's photos were meant to go.

And then you continued describing where Grandma and Grandpa were meant to go at the four spaces at the top of the tree. You stood up and put your hands on my waist, apparently now finished with your explanation.

You asked if I understood the plans and I assured you that I did. I didn't want you to settle for anything less. And then I suggested that you find Dad to see if he had any good photos. Sometimes, I wonder if things would have been different if I hadn't told you to ask him.

Your eyes stretched big and wide and you yelled from your place in the foyer out for your father. Your voice was so much bigger than your body. You picked up the paper and ran toward the living room excitedly.

I picked up your backpack and followed slowly and measuredly behind you. When you reached the entranceway to the living room, I leaned my body against the doorway and observed the scene. Your father always made sure to get home early to see you after school, and you had already jumped up into his lap and perched up on his thighs with your family tree paper in hand.

I watched as you rested the paper onto the couch cushion next to your father and repeated the same explanation, pointing and all. Your father nodded along, just as I had, and then hoisted you up. He could hold you in one arm so effortlessly.

Your father set you down in front of the cabinet in the corner of the living room. I still remember where I came

across that piece: an antiques fair in northern Maine. I remembered falling in love with the smooth walnut wood
stain and the hallmark angled legs of a midcentury modern
piece. I imagined it sitting underneath a single shallow vase
of succulents in the second home of one of my clients or
lined with black-and-white pictures of family and friends
in another's single-story home with broad ceilings and open
rooms. I had made the mistake of bringing it home before
placing it elsewhere, and after putting it under my favorite
Matisse print, I couldn't manage to let go of it. So here it
was in our living room, living among us.

Your father pulled a shoebox full of photos out from the
dresser. I had always found it charming that your father still
printed photos. That he still enjoyed the ritual of picking
up a roll of prints from the shop, even though this was a
long-outdated pastime. He had to drive almost ten miles to
the only place in the area that still printed them, but he in-
sisted. And he always got great joy from lifting the flap of
the white envelope they came in, and flipping through the
photos. I did, too. There were stacks and stacks of shoeboxes
of photos in that cabinet. Stacks and stacks of memories and
catalogs of time spent together.

Your father lifted the lid from the shoebox labeled Christ-
mas and you both began sifting through them. I moved from
my spot in the doorway to meet you in the pile of our family memories. Memories of trips to the beach or the lake.
Memories of eating ice cream or spaghetti. Memories in the
cold of winter and the brightness of spring.

Your father sifted through the photos slowly and me-
thodically, looking at each one carefully, but you tried to

hurry him along, determined to find photos that would be the right size and shape to fit on the tree.

You were particular about which photos you wanted. They were either too big or too small or the subject wasn't turned quite in the right direction. You and your father went through the pile and tossed one after another photo to the side.

At once, your eyes got bright and you pulled a photo from the pile. You found the one you wanted and you held it out with pride.

It was a picture of me and your father, our faces big and smiling, pressed together and up close to the camera.

I remembered exactly when the photo was taken. The three of us were out for an early dinner. It was summer and it was still bright as midday along the coast. You must have been only three years old and we were teaching you how to use the camera. You were standing on your chair and leaning across the whole table and holding the camera up close to our faces.

You told us to smile and your father and I obliged and pressed our faces closer together for the photo.

You asked if we were ready to cut the figures out and your father told you where you could find the scissors, in the top drawer to the right on the kitchen cabinets. You stood up and skipped out of the room toward the kitchen, your pigtails flopping as you bounded.

I looked up at your father and smiled warmly, feeling nostalgic among all the wonderful family photos.

Your father looked straight into my eyes but didn't smile back. He touched the tip of his finger to the space labeled Dad on the tree.

And then he asked the question I thought would never come. He asked if his face belonged there on that family tree in the space where the father was supposed to go.

His tone wasn't challenging. It wasn't angry or fierce or argumentative. Just calm and measured. Matter-of-fact.

It was as if that question had long, stretching arms that reached inside me and squeezed my insides and rattled them around.

I felt the air drain from my lungs. My heart bulge. My vision blur.

I thought perhaps I misheard, so I asked him to ask again. And he did. He asked if his photo belonged in that spot for the father. He didn't ask more loudly or more firmly. No more challenging or angry or argumentative.

I stared back into your father's eyes. A pressure emerged in my throat and behind my eyes. I knew he knew the answer to his own question.

I opened my mouth to respond but there were no words to say. I lifted my arm to touch him, but there was so much space between us. Your father's gaze was still unwavering.

Before I could muster anything, you came skipping back into the room, still bouncing, your smile still stretched across your face. You rushed over to your father and handed him the scissors, which he accepted with a shockingly natural-looking smile.

Stunned, I kept my eyes locked on your father, who was now focused on moving the scissors along the contour of our faces in the photo. All at once, I interpreted my own life as hinging on this single fact that your father was not your biological father. A single fact that I had twisted into a single lie. A single lie that I had wrapped everything in our lives around.

I had surrounded the lie with a home built for three. With photos of a mom, a dad and their daughter outside on a summer evening tucked in a shoebox in their living room. With introductions to your new teachers with Parker as your father. With nodding along with my girlfriends as they said, "She has Parker's nose," or "That's such a Parker thing," while they watched you play. The more I wrapped and wound things around the lie, the further from the surface they were. But with that one question, that one look, your father had cut right to the center of it and unwound it all.

I felt afraid to move. I was afraid that any sudden motion would send the whole thing crashing down. Our whole life crashing down. I felt a tear form. Determined not to let it fall, I closed my eyes and inhaled. When I reopened them, you had his face at your cheek, kissing you. The image of my cut-out face next to your father's cut-out face looked so strange decoupled from their necks and bodies. They looked so out of place floating there like that on the wood floor. The images were overlapping slightly, but it was so clear that they were separate. So clear that they were disjointed, detached, parted. I couldn't bear to look at our faces like that and closed my eyes again.

Your father suggested that you go upstairs and wash up for dinner, like nothing had happened.

I opened my eyes again to your father organizing the pile of photos and replacing them into the shoebox. You were out of sight now.

All I could muster was an "I don't know."

Your father stayed silent without lifting his eyes from the pile of photos.

I asked how long he had known for. My voice was quivering.

Your father's hands stopped moving now. He sighed and looked up at me.

He told me he had always known. He reminded me how many times he had been tested and of the medical impossibility of his fathering a child.

He looked back down at the photos and started rustling them around, apparently now too frazzled to make sense or order out of them.

I asked why he hadn't said something sooner. I still needed to gasp to find the oxygen required to make words. He said there wouldn't have been any point. And he assured me that he loved our life and that he loved you. He paused and swallowed. I thought he might say that he was leaving me, leaving us, but he just kept saying that he loved us.

He was always so gentle. So understanding. At times I had found it annoying, but it felt so perfect now.

I felt the tear fall down my cheek. When I brought my fingertips to my face to wipe it away, I noticed that everything was already wet and salty.

I apologized as many times as I could. As many times as he had said *I love you*, plus some more. It was now a deluge of tears down my face. They rippled down my cheeks and chin and dripped onto the floor in front of me. My hands were shaking and my insides were vibrating.

He reassured me again that he loved us. That was the truest truth of all. And that he would never leave us.

I reached my hand out for your father's. He placed his hand on top of mine tenderly enough. His face remained stoic. Unemotional. I scooted up close next to your father and rested my head on his shoulder.

He told me that he had made peace with the circumstances on his own, but that he wanted you to know the real story someday. He wanted you to have a chance to make peace with it, too.

When he said that, everything paused. I don't know why I expected a different outcome for this conversation. I looked up at your father, preparing to protest. I didn't want your life to unravel. I didn't want to rob you of your reality. Your history. Your identity.

And then your adorable, piercing voice rang out from the upstairs.

Your father straightened his back and I lifted my head up. Your father looked confident. He looked sure of what he wanted. What he needed. And I wasn't in any position to set the terms.

I can't forget what he said to me then. He said that the lie was worse than the facts. And he didn't want lies in this house. He didn't want lies mixed up with love. And I believed him to be correct about this.

I had truly never envisioned this conversation with your father. I had resolved so long ago not to tell him. And so many years after that decision, I was still sure I would never have to have it. But if I had pictured this conversation, it wouldn't have gone like this. It wouldn't have been so short. It wouldn't have been so measured. So clarifying. It was rare that your father so firmly stood up for something he believed in.

And in this instance, I knew I had to give him what he wanted. And I knew deep down that it was the right thing to do.

I placed my head back on your father's shoulder and I told him we could and we would do it eventually.

And then your father returned the last picture to the box, tucked it into the cabinet and wiggled out from under the weight of my shoulder and left the room.

I'm sorry if it made a mess of things,
Mom.

And with that, Jane felt the need to write her own explanation for Hazel.

LETTER 6
WHEN EVERYTHING CHANGED FOR OUR FAMILY
JANE

Dear Hazel,

I think I would have gone on with a family comprised of just you and me forever. And for a long time, I thought I could. But deep down, I think I wanted something different. And one day Cam just walked into our lives. It was the thing that changed all of our lives forever.

You and I were enjoying our Saturday afternoon over a picnic in the small park near our house. There was a playground on the corner and a thin dirt running path that cut through the grass. The park was crowded with young families with strollers spilling with toys and young couples with overflowing picnic baskets. There was just enough grass and just enough trees for us to set down our blankets and remove the contents of our basket and sprawl our arms and legs and still not impose on anyone else's space. Still, it was hard for me not to notice that we were the only mother-daughter duo. I'm a little embarrassed to admit that I wondered if people might think we were sisters in our matching sun hats with big wide brims and matching sunglasses that stretched from cheekbone to forehead.

In an attempt to shake the thought, I gave you a big harsh smooch right on the side of your cheek and you giggled and blushed a little bit and pretended to try to squirm away and yelled out at me.

Hearing you say "Mom" in any capacity, in any tone, still made me gush with pride. It would never get old. I stopped thinking about the embarrassing sisters thing.

We munched on breads and cheese and jams and grapes and salamis. I liked the raspberry jam and you liked the fig preserves. I turned the shiny pages of *InStyle* while you did the same with your *Seventeen* magazine and we took turns pointing out particularly cute outfits and particularly cute men from our respective pages. The breeze would have been nice except that you kept losing your page to the gusts of winds. Exasperated, you turned over onto your back and watched as the clouds skated through the sky and I joined you immediately.

The clouds floated up there in perfect white puffs. They looked like the clouds you used to draw with your whole little hand gripping the crayon as you pulled it across the construction paper.

We both lay there calmly for a few moments until another gust of wind rushed through our hair. This one was bigger than the others, stirring up grass and leaves and sending the other people in the park running after rogue pieces of trash or toys set into a roll. I sat up and when I turned to my left, a tall, slight man in running sneakers was standing right next to our blanket. I flinched at the surprise of a person so close to our little bubble.

He apologized right away for startling us. I looked up from beneath the brim of my hat but didn't know how to respond. So I just smiled. And then he asked me if I could help him with something. I agreed, though I was a bit confused about what it could be. You had now sat up, too, with your hand pressed to the top of your hat to keep it from flying away.

He told us we looked like twins. What a ham!

I remained seated as I waited for more of an explanation of why he was standing there, my patience and the smile that came with it waning.

The man appeared to have been jolted back to reality and then asked if I wouldn't mind holding on to his shirt for a moment.

I was confused and turned to you to see if you had figured out what was going on, but you looked just as confused as I did, but perhaps more curious.

He explained that it was windy out and that he was worried about trying to take his sweatshirt off and the wind catching his shirt and making it fly up.

I had certainly seen this situation before—tummies or bras exposed after a man or woman intending to simply lift an overshirt above the head, mistakenly took the entire garment underneath with it.

I asked if he was serious, pulling my sunglasses down on the bridge of my nose so that I could get a better look at the man in front of me.

And he said that he was very serious with a real earnestness, but also a new charm. His eyes were clear and blue and his cheekbones and jawline were strong but still gentle. He could not be described as muscular or strapping like some of the other men I had been with, but he was fit. Athletic even. Like his flesh was tailored to his anatomy. I caught him scanning my left ring finger. I sensed a twinkle in his eye when he found it bare.

I could feel my cheeks get hot and I looked over at you. You gave me a smile back and a quick wink of your left eye helped me to realize what was going on here.

It had been so long since I had been with another man, even thought about another man. I was so busy, so happy, with you. Well, maybe I had thought about them, but none of them were men that were in front of me. None were men that I could feel or touch or flirt with.

I stood up slowly with as much composure as I could and stepped closer than I might otherwise step toward a stranger and pinched his T-shirt between my pointer finger and my thumb.

He expressed his relief, and might have even winked, before pulling his sweatshirt over his head.

As his sweatshirt came up, I caught a glimpse of his groin

lines disappearing below the waist of his shorts. Nervous that I shouldn't be looking there, I craned my neck and looked back up toward the man's face. I could see in my periphery that he now had his sweatshirt crumpled up in his right hand. When I realized my fingers still clasped his T-shirt, I pulled my hand away as quickly as I could.

The man smiled and thanked me. His teeth were big and white and straight. He seemed smart. And kind. And handsome. Definitely handsome.

My cheeks got hot again.

And then he introduced himself as Cam and stuck his hand out toward me for a shake.

I looked down at you and you were still sitting on the blanket on the grass, closely watching and listening. At the moment of eye contact with me, you put your hands over your mouth to hide your smile and lay down again on your back. I could detect you laughing by the shake of your belly and your shoulders.

I turned back to Cam and smiled.

I introduced myself, and then you, with pride. I felt you would be excited to have a father figure in your life after all these years.

And Cam smiled right back.

I was impressed he would come up to both of us like that.

A few days later, I found myself at a real, and quite up-scale, restaurant with white tablecloths, sitting across from a man I confirmed to be smart and kind and handsome. Definitely handsome. I giggled when Cam told me he was a tax attorney. It was the most adult job I had ever heard described over a beer on a date. He had kind light blue eyes and smiled easily as we talked easily.

I had sensed this when we first met in the park, but it was becoming increasingly clear that everything about Cam was right in place. Well arranged. Planned. He talked freely about his hopes and dreams for the future. About having a family. About moving to an old but well-constructed house in a beach town when he retired. He was near certain that he had his sights set on Kennebunkport, Maine, but was watching the housing markets up and down the eastern seaboard closely. He deliberated over the number of bedrooms and which direction the porch should face.

Before even spending an hour together, I felt safe with Cam. I found myself telling stories about you. A lot of stories about you. Opening my phone up to show him pictures of you in your Halloween costume or eating something sour or jumping off the diving board at the pool. At the sight of you, at the window into my life, our life, I could tell Cam's heart was at ease.

With a gentle smile and clear, sparkling eyes, he told me that I seemed like a really good mom.

I smiled back as I tried to keep my heart from exploding. I knew he could be a great father to not only you, but also to his own. I wanted that for him. For us.

Soon, as you'll almost certainly recall, I was spending many meals and nights with Cam while you stayed home with a babysitter. And I was becoming more and more enamored, and more and more in love every time.

You would help me get dressed for dates. I would ask you how I looked.

"Beautiful, Ma," you would say so sweetly. And I could tell you meant it. And then I would kiss you on the head and say, "Be good." And then you would say, "Always," with a smirk. And then I would slip out the door to Cam.

He was always, always, always steady and kind. He offered me big, honest love and he did it freely. More and more, I felt so deeply that he could give me what I wanted, what I needed, in a partner. And that he would do it forever.

And when he asked me to marry him nine months later, no frills, at city hall, I said yes and kissed him deeply. And when he said he wanted to have a baby of our own, I said yes and kissed him deeply again. I thought about you at each and every one of those moments, Hazel. I really did. I thought it would make us both so, so happy. He was so sweet with you. So considerate. So thoughtful about your role in our family. His role in our family.

I have to be honest. I was excited about my second chance at motherhood. This time, I would have Cam at my side.

Of all the decisions I had made quickly, from my heart, this one felt the most right.

I'm sorry if it made a mess of things,

Mom.

18

It was a slow Saturday morning with Cam and the boys. For all intents and purposes, it should have been a perfect morning. Cam was making pancakes and the smell of warm syrup and freshly brewed coffee filled the air. The twins were in their own world, playing charmingly with a set of blocks. Everything was peaceful but Jane.

Jane was a mess. She was in a fog of missing Hazel. There was nothing else she could think about but that.

"Honey! Pancakes are ready!" Cam bellowed from across the house. By the time she had shuffled one leg and the next into the kitchen, Cam had placed a stack of pancakes on the table and the twins in their high chairs. Cam whistled cheerily as he tore the pancakes into smaller pieces for the twins and then poured coffee for himself and for her.

Jane sat down on her chair and lifted her fork to eat, but she wasn't hungry. She could tell Cam was talking but she couldn't make out the words from the fog in her mind. All she could think about was Hazel. She felt the prickling of tears building up in her eyes.

She observed Cam's lips moving and felt an unusual pang in her belly from looking at him. It was hard to admit to herself until now, but she realized she had transferred all of her loving and tender feelings from Hazel straight to Cam and the twins. Drifting away from Hazel was less a conscious choice than a series of unconscious ones. She only blamed herself really, but it couldn't be denied that the moment Cam joined their family was the moment she'd started losing Hazel. Jane was having a hard time being the right kind of mother to the twins and Hazel and the right kind of wife to Cam.

But Jane wanted to change that now. She really, really did. She was still Hazel's mother. And she would be forever. She wanted to reclaim her place. She needed to reclaim it.

Jane excused herself from the table and went into the other room. She didn't do it consciously but she found herself picking up the phone and dialing Silas's number. Jane's heart was pulsing.

"Hello?" Silas's gravelly voice said from the other end of the line. She wanted to yell and scream and let everything out into the receiver, but she tried to stay calm.

"How are things going up there?" she asked, keeping her voice as steady as possible.

"Up where?" Silas asked. "Sorry, who is this?"

Jane felt a volcanic eruption begin. "Who is this?!" she asked indignantly, but then did her best to tone it down and in a softer voice, continued. "This is Jane. Hazel's mom."

"Ohhhh, hey!" Silas responded far too casually in Jane's opinion.

"I haven't heard a peep from anyone. So yes, how are things going up there?"

"They're...uh...going. They're going," Silas said with what sounded to Jane like some trepidation.

"Go on," Jane urged.

"You know, we've been doing the usual stuff. Hanging by the lake. Making s'mores. Cooking meals. Pretty breezy."

It was silent for a moment. And Jane was utterly unfulfilled. The volcanic eruption was brewing again.

"Anything else you would like to share with me about the human being that I carried within my body and underneath my heart for nine months and then for another fifteen years after that and haven't heard a single word from in over a week?"

"Oh, uh, yeah."

Jane thought perhaps Silas was getting what she was after now.

"The girls are, uh, getting along pretty well. I think they like it up here. Weather's been nice. I think I'll take 'em to the market this weekend. I'm just hanging on the dock right now solo while Hazel and Eve are hanging back up at the house. Uh..."

Nope, Jane thought. He wasn't getting it at all. Here was the eruption.

"Silas, can you please cut the crap? I want to know how my little girl is doing up there in your custody. So, please, can you find something to say that will make me feel like a human and a mother again. PLEASE!" Jane felt herself out of breath. It felt good to say it out loud.

There was a thick silence, and then a loud exhale from Silas.

"I'm sorry, Jane. Last summer when it was just me and Eve, it was different. We each kind of just did our own thing, you know. But it's different with Hazel here, too. There's more connection. There's more meaning infused in every little thing. It's hard to explain. But let me tell you, she's really special. I don't think I was expecting all this. You've raised such a great girl. You really have. She's just the kind of daughter I feel like I'd want to have. Well, I guess I do have."

Jane's eyes were filling up with tears.

"Ugh, I'm sorry. This is hard for me."

Jane's throat was in a knot but she wanted to hear more.

"What's hard?" she asked, gentler and meaning it.

"It's just so weird when I look into these girls' eyes, Jane. It's like they're my eyes. And I know in some ways they kind of are. Eve's eyes are like the forest after rain. Lush and rich. Teeming with life and energy. Hazel's eyes are softer, calmer. Her left eye is a mosaic of greens and blues and browns, all subtly integrated into a single appearance of hazel. And that green eye is emerald green. Definitely mine. Both definitely, definitely mine. And the different sides of me, too. It's amazing to look at your own flesh and blood. It really is. It makes me want to love them like daughters, like my very own, but really it…" He paused and took a deep breath. "It just makes me think of Ruby. And that makes me think of Torrey. And it's getting unbearable."

Jane could taste the salty tears that fell from her eyes onto her lips.

"Ugh, Jane. I feel like a terrible person for saying it," Silas said. "I don't know why I'm even saying it but I feel like I just have to get it off my chest. I don't even know if you want to hear it. You probably, almost certainly don't. But you're the only one I know that knows anything about Torrey and Ruby. Well, aside from Torrey herself. But I haven't talked to her in years. Years."

Jane was just quiet. The call had started off being for her, but she knew she had to hand that over to Silas. It was for him now. He needed this.

"I keep zoning out of my life and then snapping back into things, pining after Ruby and Torrey. The other day I took a rose down to the garden in the woods Torrey and I made. And the day after that, I found myself in my workshop unable to work, just holding up a picture of Torrey and the sonograms of Ruby. Those grainy ghostlike images of my little girl, our little girl. Our little girl that never was. And the night after that I couldn't sleep, and I found myself sitting in Ruby's would-be rocking chair in her bedroom, which I usually just keep locked."

Jane found herself nodding along as Silas spoke. The words, the emotions, were flowing out of him like a waterfall.

"Part of me expected that that room would have fallen into disrepair, just like my life had. That everything in there would be crumbled and broken. But it was just there, like a fossil. A perfectly preserved snapshot of a moment in time. This is weird to say, but I think having Hazel and Eve here makes me want that life back. Makes me feel like I could have that life with a wife and daughters. Like I could actually be happy someday."

Silas seemed exasperated now. "Does that make any sense at all? Like any at all?"

"It does," Jane replied, through tears and a tight throat. "Children are the most special thing in this world. They make you see everything, *everything*, differently. And you're never the same again once you meet them."

"Yeah. I get that now. I really do," Silas said, trailing off.

"Well, then, it seems like their trip up to you is worthwhile for everyone, not just the girls, huh?"

"Seems like it."

"Well, see if you can get Hazel to call her mother, all right?" Jane urged, but without much belief that he would.

"All right," Silas said.

"Bye now," Jane said, almost desperate to hang up the phone. It was all too much.

"Bye, Jane. Thanks for listening."

Another moment of quiet.

"Oh, and one more thing," Silas added. "I don't know if I ever told you this, but I really did care for you that summer. It was different with you than the other women. Even Susie. I really did care for you. If I wasn't so broken, maybe things would have worked out. But I really did care for you."

Jane's heart stopped for a moment. What could she say?

"Goodbye, Silas" was all she could muster.

As soon as Jane put the receiver down, she burst into tears. Being a good mother, a good parent, was the most important thing she, and all the other parents out there, could do in this world. She felt a strange comfort that this was all part of Hazel's journey. And hers and Eve's and Jane's and Silas's and Susie's, and even Torrey's, too. That thought calmed her, but not enough to go back to the breakfast table.

She pulled out Susie's book and read another letter and prepared to write her own.

LETTER 7
WHEN YOU LEARNED ABOUT SILAS
SUSIE

Dear Eve,

Telling you about Silas being your biological father was one of the hardest things I've ever done. I wish the truth wasn't so painful. I know it was painful for you, too, and I know you were there to experience it, but I want to share my side of things. I remember every detail of this day. I've replayed it so often in my mind since.

When it was time to tell you, your father and I sat on the couch in the living room. I took a deep breath, smoothed my skirt, and crossed and recrossed my legs, searching for a position that would alleviate my discomfort. It didn't work at all. My heart felt like a hundred moths fluttering around in my chest. Your father nodded reassuringly and brought his hand onto my thigh for comfort, but his lips remained tight and solemn.

He called out for you.

We could never be sure about your whereabouts in the house. You were always lost in some cranny, alone, where no one could disturb you.

He asked you to join us on the couch for a chat. I was glad he was the one calling for you because I don't think I could have done it myself. My throat was so tight and nervous.

Soon, we could hear the pattering of feet on the floor above us and then winding down the staircase. When you appeared in the room, you looked as you always looked then: indifferent.

"What?" you asked sharply.

He said it was nice to see you, too, with more than a hint of sarcasm. I loved him so much in that moment, trying to bring an ease to things. And then he asked you to have a seat. I loved him even more for his warmth.

You rolled your eyes, threw your head back and shuffled over to the couch, where you dramatically fell onto the cushions and looked up at us. I wondered what you were expecting to talk about.

I turned to your father and nodded slightly, encouraging him to talk. We had agreed in our preparation for this moment that the news would be best coming from him. The quiet in the room became thicker. Leave it to you to call it out.

I could tell you were getting nervous and you hurriedly kept asking what we wanted to talk about.

You sat up a little straighter now and opened your eyes wide. I couldn't help but catch another glimpse of Silas in your green eyes. I squeezed your father's hand and he puffed out his chest and began.

He said that there was something we wanted to share with you. His voice was steady and his words were slow and methodical. I wonder if you thought the same.

And first, he reminded you that we loved you very much.

You had reached maximum impatience by now and folded your arms in front of your chest. I understood, and in some ways shared, your sense of urgency to get it out in the open already.

He reminded you that he was your real father.

I braced myself for the deluge and could tell you were doing the same.

And then he explained that he was not your *biological* father.

The room all of a sudden felt colder and more cavernous. I locked my fingers into a neat pile on my lap to keep them from flitting around nervously. I didn't want to force you into any kind of reaction. The look in your eyes started to change immediately.

He matter-of-factly stated that he could not have biological children of his own. Which was the truth. But it was the part that I knew would make my insides squirm.

You asked who your biological father was.

I felt it was my turn to chime in and bear some of the burden of the conversation. We decided that we were not going to lie to you about any of it. I explained that it was someone I had met on a trip to purchase furniture a long time ago.

You caught on quickly and asked if it happened more than the one time. I was surprised that your view of relationships was already that sophisticated.

I could feel that your words were picking up momentum and heat. I squeezed my eyes together and tried not to cry. Or scream. Or run out of the room. Or throw my arms around you and your father or both and then grovel and cry.

Your father tried to interfere and his voice boomed when he did. It was rare he sounded so big and strong. But he did right then. I knew how badly he wanted things to go smoothly. But how could they?

Something raw and fragile had taken over you, but there was also vicious grief apparent in your eyes. A hint of a tear danced on your eyelid. Your cheeks got hot and red and your green eyes began swirling with something even more fierce. You looked like you were capable of doing anything.

It scared me.

And then, without another word, you got up from your seat.

And then there was a full teenage explosion, in a fashion that only you could summon.

Your fingers balled up into tight little fists and your knees popped up and your heels slammed down on the floor as you walked to the other side of the living room. You picked up the picture frame from the sleek midcentury modern console pressed up against the wall. It was a vintage Tiffany's silver frame I'd got a decade ago in a town in Virginia, and I'd placed a photo in it of the three of us at a baseball game. We were smiling in our seats, wearing matching Yankees baseball uniforms with our arms slung around each other. You were in the middle, with a big pile of peanuts in your lap, smiling up at the camera through missing teeth. You tilted the frame to one side and then the other, staring into the image at the center.

I tried to figure out what you were thinking. Was it sadness? Longing? Fury? Hope? Love? I wanted to know so I could soothe you. For a brief instant I thought the rage may be subsiding but then, in an instant, you brought the frame above your head and slammed it down onto the floor. The silver clanked against the wood floor and the glass of the frame shattered immediately; shards flew in every direction.

Your father and I both gasped. I reached for your father's hand, but he had already brought one to his heart and the other right on top of it. I expected this would be the main event of the tantrum—that you would march right on up-stairs to your room and slam the door, having made your statement. But you just stared down at the pile of glass, your green eyes swirling with what I was now sure was rage.

You bent down and pulled the picture from the pile of glass and pinched it between the tips of your fingers. The photo itself appeared unscathed despite the mess underneath it. But I was sure it wouldn't remain this way for long. And still without saying a word, you opened the drawer of the console and pulled out a sleek black pen.

You picked your head up slowly and looked straight into my eyes. There was heat and fire and aching in them. And then you assertively twisted the back of the pen and forced the inky point from its tip straight through my eyeballs in the photo. And then you did the same to your father's eye-balls. And then you dropped the photo at your feet care-lessly.

I instinctively lunged toward you. "Honey, plea—" I started.

But before I could finish my plea, you stamped your foot into the ground and, through gritted teeth, flinched back into place and remained motionless next to me, stunned.

You took a slow step forward. Your foot rocked over the broken glass, crackling slowly as you transferred your weight from your heel to your toes and walked toward the small table next to the couch, where three more family photos were propped up with pride. Smiling faces with white teeth and joyful eyes. Ice cream and beaches and gorgeous scenery. Bodies huddled together with love.

You picked each one up and smashed them onto the ground. And again, through the craggy piles of glass, you picked up each photo and stabbed through the eyes with that same sharp black pen.

I felt my cheeks tense and I began weeping. Tears spilled from my eyes as I watched you destroy the memories of our happy life. But it seemed only fair. I had certainly just shattered your image of a happy life.

When I snapped back to the scene, I noticed you were heading for the dresser that your father kept all our family photos in. My throat constricted and my feet felt stuck in their place. Without even realizing, my hands had come up for cover over my mouth. I couldn't fathom what you were about to do, but then you did it. You pulled open the drawer and vigorously tore out photo after photo, stabbing each quickly and haphazardly with the pen.

Your father launched over and wrapped his arms around you. Why hadn't I been able to do that?

He pulled you tight and close and your body went limp. I watched your arms slink over your father's shoulder and then your fingers uncurled from the pen. Finally, you dropped the photos that were in your hands and as you sank down to the floor, your father sank down with you, his arms still tight around your body.

He reminded you how much he loved you. He let it sink in.

He said again and again that he loved you, with his eyes closed, rocking you back and forth a little.

My fingers were now clutching my sweater over my heart as I watched the reality I had created and then sat here so pathetically observing from afar. I felt, at once, the inevitable consequence of my actions all those years ago. I felt my own tears coming down my cheeks.

As you lay your head on your father's shoulder and sank into his arms even further, I thought I heard you whisper that you hated him.

I thought the incident was over after you stormed into your room but you came flying back out within a few minutes. You just yelled and yelled, asking for his name.

And no lies. So I told you. And I told you with shame in my voice that it was Silas Box.

I couldn't say I regretted everything because it brought you to me. But I'm so sorry I caused you any pain, my love. So, so sorry.

I later learned that immediately after you slammed your bedroom door, you opened your computer and you found your biological father. I guess it wasn't too hard to find him. You said that his website just popped right up.

It started off a whole new journey of you meeting him up in Grandor, where the whole thing happened.

I'm sorry if it made a mess of things,

Mom.

★ ★ ★

And with that, Jane wrote:

LETTER 7
JANE

Dear Hazel,

There wasn't ever a time in your life that you didn't know about your father. About Silas.

I made sure of that when I saw that green eye of yours for the first time and gave you his last name. I wanted you to know about him because I wanted you to know yourself and your story. It was never any secret.

But now I realize that knowing about him isn't the same as knowing him.

I suppose I expected you to ask more questions as you got older. Things about what your father looked like, or sounded like, or acted like. The things he loved and the things he hated. I expected you to wonder if the things you were seeing or feeling or thinking came from him. But you never did.

I guess I assumed that you never got curious. That you never would get curious.

In hindsight, I think part of feeling this way was knowing your father. I knew he would not be a good husband at that time. I knew he would not be a good father at that time. On the surface he was too independent, too selfish. But it was the thing that was deeper down that would have really stopped him from being good to us. It was the fact that he was still reeling from losing the other loves of his life.

That was the woman and that was the daughter he would have been perfect for. Those were the people he needed to be perfect for.

And I inadvertently assumed that if I wanted to have you without him, live my life without him, that you would, too. I should have known that questions about him rested latent within you. I shouldn't have been surprised when that message from Eve activated everything. In hindsight, it was silly to think this but I really thought I might be enough for you.

Still, when I saw your eyes light up in front of that computer screen, I was in shock at how quickly, how effortlessly, how simply you gave yourself away to your father. And Eve.

It was in that moment that I realized just how slow I had been to believe that you would need to explore, really explore, this side of you.

Until this moment, I thought of you as an extension of me. When I felt warm and loving and happy with you, I felt warm and loving and happy with myself. When I felt anxious and angry and annoyed with you, I felt anxious and angry and annoyed with myself. When I talked to you, I felt I was talking to myself.

It's different with the twins. With them, I think about the parts of them that come from Cam. And I love those parts of them. Without your father in our lives, I supposed I felt like you were all mine. But of course you are not. And Silas's coming into your life forced me to remember that.

If I am being honest, I didn't know whether to mourn or embrace that truth. To stop you in your tracks or to push you toward it.

I was scared. I'm still scared.

I didn't know whether to allow you to go on this journey and learn more about yourself, and in doing so, certainly learn that you were more like him and less like me.
Or scarier yet, that you are simply your own person. Not
just a mix of me and your father.

As we sat in front of that computer, I felt an overwhelming
urge to keep you close. To ask you to stay. To demand that
you do. I know it was within my ability as a mother to make
that so.

But I knew deep down that I had to let you go. I knew I
had to let you explore that part of yourself.

I barely thought of Silas or Eve or Cam or your brothers
and to some extent even myself. I was mostly just thinking of you. Your story. Your journey to womanhood. Your
journey to knowing who you are and where you came from.

I'm sorry if I made a mess of things,

Mom.

19

Jane sat on the couch with Susie's book of letters next to her and her phone between her fingers as she waited for it to light up with a text from Hazel. She was running out of Susie's letters to read, and there was an emptiness around her she hadn't felt before. She stared at the blank, dark surface of the phone. She willed it to move. To buzz. To connect her with Hazel.

Nothing.

Jane looked up to the ceiling to distract herself. She had sent Cam and the boys out for a walk so she could get some space with her own thoughts.

Still no buzz.

Jane considered whether she may have had the settings mixed up and opened the phone herself to check on her texts.

Even though she had been the one sending texts, it surprised Jane just how long, embarrassing, desperate the string of messages to Hazel was. It was a string with no responses—everything from Call your mother...now to Miss you, love you honey to How was today, send pics! They covered the full spectrum of her emotions, felt and feigned. Anything to get a response, but still nothing.

Jane sat with the phone in her lap for a while longer. The silence of the room and the blankness of the phone weighed heavy on her.

She settled on another Hi, honey. Thinking of you and hit the send button and decided to distract herself while she waited for, hoped for, the answer to come in.

She lifted herself from the couch and began pacing across the carpet, her cell phone still tight in her grip in case Hazel was going to reply.

She turned back to Susie's book for what she knew was the final letter as she waited for the reply.

LETTER 8
DECIDING TO LET YOU GO
SUSIE

Dear Eve,

I'm sure you felt it, too. Our house was quiet in the days after you told your father and me that you wanted to meet Silas.

I think we all felt a longing for simpler times. But then I remembered that even if those times felt simple, they were also shrouded in a lie. A lie that your father and I had allowed to persist. But it was all out in the open now and we could never go back.

At first I felt a sadness, but then I felt a freedom. A freedom from the lies. A freedom to live in truth. A freedom to love each other with everything laid bare on the table.

I had managed to hang on to your father by what sometimes felt like only a thread. I wondered if I would be so lucky with you. There's a fire, a fierceness, in you that your father (your real father, not the one whose genes you have) doesn't possess. It scared me. But I knew that holding you close, holding you back, would only make it worse. That you would never forgive me if you never got to know this side of you.

I dialed the number on the crumpled piece of paper you gave to me with Silas's phone number on it.

He answered the phone, not suspecting anything at all.

I was matter-of-fact and clear.

I told him who I was and began to explain that you were my daughter.

He told me he had a feeling that I'd be calling and he was right.

I told him that I understood he and you had been chatting for quite some time and had arranged for a summer meetup. I challenged him with my tone. I wanted to see what he was made of. See if he could handle you. And also make clear who was the boss around here.

He was on his heels a bit. Silas was bumbling on every word. He might have been able to charm me the first time we met, but I was in control this time.

I reminded him that you were only fifteen years old and that fifteen-year-olds didn't do much without their mothers. I didn't leave much wiggle room.

Silas exhaled. Slowly.

And then he said something that warmed me.

He said that he never knew you existed but that he was excited you did. My heart simultaneously sank and lifted.

There was a moment of silence.

He shared that he always wanted a daughter, this time with more warmth.

I wasn't ready to turn to go. But then he took me there.

He confessed that he messed up with this fatherhood stuff, and that he had been messing up for a long time and that he wanted the chance to redeem himself. He wanted a chance to get to know you.

I could feel, deep down in my bones, that he meant it. I really could, Eve. And not being in the picture wasn't his fault. It was my fault. You deserved to be part of each other's stories.

He said he wanted to know what a little Silas would look like.

I set the record straight and reminded him that if you were a little anything, you were a little me. I was smiling now. More comfortable now. I unfolded another piece of paper with some prepared notes.

I continued with some set questions. I asked if he carried sunscreen or kept liquor accessible and whether he had a nice bed for you to sleep in. And as he confirmed, I added little checks next to the items on my checklist.

And then finally I asked him what I really cared about. I asked whether he was a good man. He said he was trying to be. And then I asked him who your real father was. And he said my husband was. And that was the right answer.

I told him right then and there that he would see you next month and that was that.

I put down the receiver and then I cried big wobbling tears. I knew what I had to do. I knew what you had to do.

I'm sorry if it made a mess of things,

Mom.

And with that, Jane wrote:

LETTER 8
DECIDING TO LET YOU GO
JANE

Dear Hazel,

After you asked me to meet your father, I retreated to my room to not only collect my thoughts, but also to prevent myself from reaching my arms around you and never letting you go. When I decided to let you go and envisioned you headed up there by yourself, forging your own path, I never felt more proud of who you have been, and who I knew you would become...

20

Jane put her pen down. Even as she just started to write this letter, she felt exasperated. She wanted to tell Hazel these things to her face. Not in a letter Hazel would probably never read. She wanted to tell Hazel she was sorry. So, so sorry. And she wanted to make it better as soon as she could. The silence between them now while she was at Silas's was bigger and thicker than ever. Jane wanted, she needed, to reach across the gap and bring Hazel back close. Explain to her what she now knew. She wanted, she needed, to make it better. For herself and Hazel, and the rest of the family, all the same.

Just then, her phone rang.

"Hello?" Jane responded, nearly out of breath with relief.

"Mom," Hazel said but didn't say it warmly.

"Hello?" Jane asked again, with more urgency this time. She wanted to hear from her daughter so, so badly.

"I'm staying here," her daughter said into the phone and then hung up.

Before Jane could say anything else, there was an empty dial tone on the other side of the phone.

She felt an impulse to call Hazel right back; at the same time she felt a compulsion to write in her book. She thought of the words Susie had written about how she felt like she was losing Eve. And Jane had felt the same. The very same. She felt she could record and revisit the ways in which she was making a mess of things. To write it all down in a place where Hazel could one day read it when they one day might reconcile. But she needed something now. Not someday. Now. She needed Hazel to have her perfect love story. And she desperately wanted to be a part of it.

She couldn't leave this in anyone else's hands anymore. Not Cam's, not Silas's, not Hazel's, not Susie's. No one's. She had to reclaim her daughter, her life, their life, for herself. No more letters. No more thinking. No more contemplating.

It was time for her to start doing.

And it was time to bring a perfect love story to everyone else. To bring everyone peace. She picked up the phone and called one of the other women in this mess of a love story. She was sorry if she made a mess of things. But she was ready to turn it around now.

She couldn't wait a minute longer.

She stood up and decided to take action into her own hands.

PART III

Hazel in Maine

21

With the crackle of tires against asphalt, the bus rolled out of the parking lot. Hazel looked out the tinted windows at her mother, who was becoming a smaller and smaller form in the distance, until at once she disappeared. Hazel felt a great ball of heat gathering behind her ribs and press up into her throat.

This was a feeling she did not recognize. Was it satisfaction or sadness? The vitriol of going or the guilt of leaving? The sense that she was transforming while everyone she knew remained the same?

With each rotation of the wheels of the bus, Hazel felt the increasing separation from everything she used to be and everywhere she used to go and everything she used to think. Hazel was, in the slightest increments, becoming distanced from the person she had been, while by those same slight increments becoming someone new.

She looked over at Eve, who had already covered her ears

with her bright pink headphones and closed her eyes. The vibration of the seats and the hum of the engine had already put her to sleep. As Hazel looked at Eve, that ball of heat beneath her ribs began to cool. It was almost unbelievable that her life could have led her to this moment—to this seat on this bus next to Eve Warrington. Her sister.

Hazel thought back to all those days and nights at home in New York. All those times observing Cam and her mother steal away. All those moments changing, and bathing, and dressing the twins and playing with them. All those evenings alone in her bedroom, with a phone that never lit up with a friend calling. She longed for friends but never made any that would stick around. She longed for attention from teachers but didn't get the grades to earn it. She longed for a pat on the back from sports coaches but didn't have the athleticism to deserve it. Looking back on it, she thought everything seemed so small, so insignificant, compared to what was about to happen now.

Hazel considered how each of those tiny, meaningless, insignificant moments stacked on top of one another and created a tower. A tower high enough to free-fall off and land right where everything started. Where she could construct from nothing a brand-new tower of experiences. A brand-new life.

This was a chance at a new life that was all her own. This was freedom.

The roads became narrower, choppier and more serpentine as the ride continued. First there were four lanes, and then two, and then just one. The buildings on the side of the road became shorter and the parking lots became emptier. The neon signs dulled into painted ones. And soon there were no buildings at all. Just long stretches of grass and trees. The roads unfurling with a monotony, only revealing the sliver that lay immediately ahead. Skies echoed blue for miles, and then turned to gold as the sun slipped behind the horizon. A sense of calm had Hazel entranced, until she heard the familiar pop of gravel under the tires as the bus slowed to a stop.

Eve shook herself awake and barely took a moment to rub her eyes before pressing her face into the window.

"That's our dad!" Eve announced. "Isn't he kind of hot?"

Hazel giggled and blushed a little and slapped Eve playfully on the arm. "Ew, that's seriously gross."

Ignoring the retort, Eve climbed over Hazel's legs, scooped up her bags and rushed down the aisle. Hazel followed, breathing deeply to slow her heart down.

Eve, and then Hazel, stepped off the bus.

The world suddenly felt so muted and still. It was as if time had stopped entirely.

And then a playful, gravelly voice broke the silence. "Hey," Silas said and lifted his sunglasses from his eyes to look down at Hazel and Eve in front of him. He reached out with both hands and rubbed his palms brashly, paternally, on top of their heads, as if they were little boys that had just hit their first home runs.

Eve winced and Hazel soaked it up, keeping her eyes open the entire time as her black hair swished back and forth in front of her eyes. Silas held his hands there for a moment longer than expected, eyes shifting from one face to the other.

Hazel locked in on Silas's eyes. They were like smooth

rocks in the bottom of a sparkling lake. The centers were dark and green. Heavy and austere.

Hazel blinked and shook her head to pull herself out of her transfixion. Her cheeks and arms and belly were all tingly. This was her father. This man, right here in front of her, was her father. This was the man who made her, her. The man who could save her from her life. She felt an overwhelming urge to wrap her arms around him and squeeze him with all her might. Before she could talk herself out of it, her body lurched forward and her arms swung around his waist with the force of fifteen years of missing someone she never knew she should miss. She tilted her head to press it onto the side of his body and closed her eyes tight. This was home.

Silas patted Eve on the head, somewhat robotically, and then curled his arm, somewhat rigidly, around Hazel's back. Hazel wiggled her body to fit more naturally under his arm, but there was still an awkwardness to the orientation.

"Bah, ha!" Eve guffawed, tearing Hazel right back into reality. Her eyes sprung open and she looked over at Eve.

"I wouldn't say Silas is much of a hugger, really," she said through a slightly devilish smirk.

Hazel unraveled her arms from Silas as quickly as she could and took a few steps back. The tingling in her cheeks and arms and belly were replaced with a fiery heat of embarrassment. She looked right into Silas's eyes, which were brighter and warmer than his hug had felt.

"Oh, would you cut it out, Eve," Silas said with a smile and a slight shake of his head.

Hazel was taken by the fact that her father looked like a man that could do things. Silas's chest was big and wide, and

he had a wild mane of black curls and a face thick with stubble. He looked tanned, relaxed and strong in a way that was
unplanned. He wore a loose gray-and-green plaid shirt that
was tattered and chalky with age and repeated launderings.
Her mother seemed like such a helpless person to her now.
So weak, so tired, so needy. Hazel was glad that somewhere
in her genes was the capacity for independence, ability.

"It's good to see you again, kiddo," Silas said and bumped
Eve lightly with his hip. They smiled warmly at each other.

"And I guess this makes you Hazel," he said, smiling
down at her.

"Yup!" Eve chimed in, even though Hazel thought Silas was
talking to her, and smiled a big smile that showed all her teeth.

"All right, then. Let me grab these," Silas said as he lifted
up all four of their bags at once. Hazel watched his fingers curl around the straps. They were broad and calloused
with thin scars like tally marks scattered across them. Silas
remained sturdy and unencumbered as he swung the bags
up onto his back and walked them over toward his pickup
truck. His forearms and shoulders bulged as he swung them
over the ledge of the truck bed without undoing the latch.

He walked toward the driver's-side door, dragging the
heels of work boots through the dirt of the road. The air
was tense, and thick and exciting. The possibility occurred
to Hazel that Silas could just drive away in that car and
leave her standing there. But as if he had forgotten something, Silas turned around and opened the back seat door.
"Get on in, girls."

Silas leaned back in his seat, turned on the car and put all
the windows down. He drove casually behind his mirrored

sunglasses with his left leg bent up, foot on the seat and a single finger resting on the steering wheel. Despite the indifference of his slouch, each turn from one dirt road to the next seemed deliberate and careful. Occasionally he would rake his fingers through his hair and inhale the sylvan scent of the trees. There were no words exchanged, no music playing. Just the sound of the increasingly thick woods. And the silent anticipation of it all.

"There's our lake," Silas stated matter-of-factly with a hint of pride.

"Yeah, there's our lake!" Eve repeated with more panache. Hazel could tell Eve felt an ownership over that body of water. Eve stuck her head out the window and shouted loudly and wildly—almost diabolically. She shook her head side to side and stretched the tip of her tongue all the way to the bottom of her chin. Her hair whipped viciously, but still elegantly, through the wind. Her voice carried in wobbling waves through the air. Silas pressed his foot into the pedal and the car began to accelerate. Hazel observed Silas's shoulders bouncing up and down above the seat, chuckling. She instinctively stuck her head out the window to join in Eve's entertainment. Hazel was at first taken aback at the force of the wind against her face but soon found a voice of her own.

"We're going to our lake!" she screamed, with all the intensity and joy and frenzy and ecstasy she had been waiting for.

Eve pulled her body back into the car, slapped Hazel squarely on her bottom with a maniacal laugh, and then stuck her head out the window once more.

"We're going to the lake!" she joined in.

Silas pressed his hand into the horn for three short beeps and then held it there for a fourth long, reverberating honk. Without slowing down, Silas ripped the wheel to the left into a narrow clearing between trees. A tremendous cabin, wrapped with porches and ivy and chirping animals, emerged in front of the car.

"We're here," Silas said, bringing the car to a slow stop. "Welcome to your getaway, girls."

There was a pathway of once carefully laid stones, now bulging in places, leading toward the door. Eve rushed out of the car and leaped through the front door, feet not even touching the ground on her way. She made it inside before Silas could even open the car door. As Hazel began approaching the cabin, Eve poked her head back out the front.

"Oh my god, this place is cool!" Hazel yelled, to Silas or Eve, or to no one at all.

Hazel looked at Silas. He raised his eyebrows, which grew unexpectedly coarsely. "Uh, is that a word that's fine to say?"

Eve popped her hip out to the side and leaned against the doorframe. "Yeah, totally." She winked toward Hazel. "Give Hazel the tour!" she demanded.

"Yes, yes, of course," Silas said as he walked toward the front door, bags already assembled effortlessly on his back. He pressed through the door and Hazel followed closely behind him. The door wobbled loose in its bracket. Hazel could tell the doorframe had been recently painted, but she could still spot the vestiges of bumps and dings.

Silas ushered them from room to room, the first a dining room that appeared to have not been used in a decade. Three gold-toned branching chandeliers hung from the ceiling, their reflections duplicated in an enormous spiderweb-lined mirror spanning one of the walls above an ornate fireplace mantel. A long, dark wooden table, covered in a membrane of dust, sprawled from one end of the room to the other. Heavy velvet drapes caressed the window frame in a swirling pattern of jewel tones. The walls were covered in a thick but worn wallpaper with a blistering rash-like texture that appeared to be caused by an unattended leak. Each room they walked through thereafter was a variation of the one before, full of things in various phases of disrepair. There was lopsided furniture, dented pots and pans, peeling wallpaper, discolored rugs, dusty armoires, tarnished doorknobs and chipped doorframes. But there was something about the way the light came so respectfully through the windows or the way Eve rushed to inspect every cranny, that obscured the line between treasure and junk. Especially because Silas narrated a story for every last thing in every last room. His words and his voice felt wise and paternal.

When they reached the living room, Hazel bent down and grazed the edge of a beautifully crafted coffee table, a stack of books in place of one of its legs. Her fingers slowed at the broken corner, feeling for flaws.

Silas crouched down next to her. "It's just that if you spend all day working on other people's furniture, sometimes you just don't have that much energy left for fixing your own."

His face was so close to Hazel's. His green eyes looked straight into hers. Hazel smiled. And Silas did, too.

"Let's head on over to your room, huh?" he suggested, nudging her with his shoulder lightly.

Silas, Hazel and Eve walked together down a long hallway with creaking, undulating floors. Eve dragged her arm along the wall and hummed a song Hazel didn't recognize. There were several closed doors along the hallway and Eve twisted the knob of each one as she passed by. Each door opened with a poof of an ephemeral cloud of dust. It didn't seem to surprise Silas that Eve wanted to generate a little chaos. He just chuckled, and Hazel followed behind him. But then the whooshing rhythm of doors flying open was interrupted by a tense clicking sound. Eve couldn't turn the doorknob. Silas's jaw tensed and he rushed toward the door. Eve tried turning the knob again, but there was no movement. She whipped her body around toward Silas, who was already right behind her, chest puffed up and shoulders pressing toward his ear. "Ugh, this annoying one that doesn't open!" she said familiarly.

"That's right," he said firmly, but with a faint indication of melancholy. Eve didn't seem to notice the melancholy.

"Well, I'd like to remind you that I don't think you should call it a door if it doesn't open. Doors open. And if it doesn't, you should just call it a wall."

Eve popped her hip out to the side and raised her eyebrows, as if to challenge Silas. The exchange amused Hazel, but Eve surprisingly seemed more interested in the semantics than what lay behind the door. Hazel felt differently.

"Keep it moving." Silas pressed his hand into Eve's back gently and smirked, ushering her away from the door.

Eve kept walking without ceremony or protest. She was quick to shift her attention, her green eyes darting around. Silas stood with his feet firmly pressed into the floor in front of the door, his left hand pressed into the doorframe.

His body took on the shape of an X. It seemed instinctual. "You'll both stay in that room this summer," Silas said and pointed down the hallway to the last door on the end.

Silas followed Eve down the hallway and Hazel trailed behind. As she did, she slowly and quietly twisted the knob of the locked door. She wanted to see for herself. Still locked. She pressed her ear into the door and closed her eyes. No sound. She wanted to know what was behind that door, but it wasn't only out of curiosity. It was something about the way Silas had stood in front of that door when Eve tried to open it. As if he were protecting it. Or himself.

Before Silas could turn around, Hazel rushed back to meet him and Eve toward the end of the hallway. Silas had already started pressing open the paint-chipped and creaky-hinged door to their room.

"Voilà."

As soon as the door opened, Eve leaped inside. Hazel took deep breaths and stepped as calmly and as slowly as she could behind Eve.

There was a majesty in the sum of the parts of the rooms in Silas's house, but no room was as majestic, as personal, as this one. The room was bright and fresh and smelled like paint and wood and wax and something special like sweat or love. The floors were old but must have been recently refinished. Light poured in through the grand window at the other end of the room and reflected a sheen on the floor.

Against the wall to the left were two queen-size beds, each with its own four towering bedposts and sheer canopies draped open. The bedding and the pillows were all varying shades of pastel pink and paisley. The light colors and delicate patterns were in sharp contrast to the rest of the house. It was as if the entire room stood for the concept of daughters rather than Eve and Hazel themselves, but it felt sweet and honest between those four walls.

Eve ran toward the bed closest to the window and jumped right on top of it onto her back. As she fell into the mattress, the down bedding swelled up like a gentle wave around her body.

She giggled quietly and then exhaled audibly. Hazel almost felt a moment of calm coming, but then Eve abruptly sprang up onto her knees and ran her hand slowly along one of the bedposts.

"Holy shit, these are cool!" she exclaimed.

Hazel walked over to the other bed to inspect the bedposts for herself. There were deep and intricate carvings of flowers and ivy running all the way up the posts. Hazel gently placed her finger into the center groove of a carved rose and traced her finger in concentric circles out toward the edge of the blooming flower.

"Why, thank you, Eve. I made them," Silas said confidently but much more modestly than Hazel expected, given how magnificent they were. Hazel turned to look at Silas. His big shoulder was leaning against the doorway and he had one big clunky work boot crossed over the other.

"You made them?" Hazel asked, her throat constricting a bit at the idea of Silas, her father, preparing such a grand gesture for their arrival. She was touched, and happy and warmed. Relieved, even.

Hazel felt an urge in her body to get up and wrap her arms around Silas and squeeze him tight and never let go. But she found herself paralyzed. It had been a long time since she felt that free with her love and her body. It had been a long time since she felt love and attention like that.

Before Hazel could get herself to move, or eke out an underwhelming "Thanks," Silas had moved from the doorway and was walking to the window.

Hazel followed him there and looked out the window. She could make out a view of the great and moody lake outside and a slightly dilapidated but sizable and prominent barnlike structure.

"What's that?" she asked.

"Ah, that's where the magic happens," Silas responded. "The workshop."

"Will you finally let me inside?" Eve asked and opened her eyes wildly. Something about the way she asked things always made them feel illicit.

"Oh, it's all just sawdust and old tools in there," Silas responded. "Nothing interesting at all."

"Whatever," Eve replied, as if she had never been impassioned about it in the first place. She threw her body back onto her bed, sprawling her arms out and letting her back bounce flat against the bed. She bounced up and down slightly, her breasts bouncing for slightly longer than the rest of her body.

"You guys take it easy for a bit. I'll make us some dinner and call you down. Sound good?"

"Sure does!" Eve yelled from her supine position on the bed.

Hazel lay back in her bed on top of the comforters and pillows.

Silas left the room and closed the door behind him.

"This is going to be great," Eve murmured.

Hazel nodded.

22

Hazel didn't even realize she had fallen asleep when she woke up to the alluring aroma of cooking. It didn't resemble the smells of her home at all. The scents were rich and fatty. Spicy and full. Hazel looked over at Eve's bed, which had the imprint of a body but no Eve.

Hazel followed the smell down the stairs and arrived at an already-set dinner table, with Eve sitting casually in one of the chairs watching Silas prepare the meal. At the precise moment Hazel stepped into the room, Silas was pulling a great big perfectly charred chicken out of the oven. Another waft of smell came over Hazel and her tummy let out a loud and gurgling grumble.

She heard Eve cackling in reaction and then Silas turned around. He was wearing an apron that was stained with all kinds of colors and textures.

"Perfect timing!" he said as he placed the steaming chicken down at the center of the table.

"Come sit down."

Eve was still chuckling as Hazel sat down next to Eve.

"I guess you're hungry," Eve teased.

Hazel nudged her shoulder into Eve's. "Oh, shut up," she retorted, slightly surprised by her own boldness.

Typical sibling rivalry, Hazel thought warmly and took a seat at the table. She felt a smile spread across her lips.

Hazel scanned the spread. It was full of colorful roasted vegetables, a fresh salad of lettuce topped with creamy, crumbled cheese, and golden, toasty bread with a pat of butter that was just starting to melt.

Silas unraveled his apron, tossed it onto the counter next to the remaining mess of bowls and littered cutting boards, and joined the girls at the table.

"Oh, one more thing!" he yelled, bounced back up and made his way toward the refrigerator. He emerged with three cold beers, the necks of the bottles crossed between his fingers.

Hazel found it curious that he didn't want to leave some of the bottles in the refrigerator while he drank his first. Silas tucked his big knees under the table and placed the group of beers next to his plate. Then, he picked one up, meticulously leaned the bottle cap on the edge of the tabletop and then slammed his big hand down on the bottle. She heard the air release from the bottle with a gentle swish and then the light clink of the bottle cap hitting the floor.

Hazel expected him to take a gulping sip, but instead he reached for a second, and then the third bottle, and repeated the same dramatic performance. Silas took up one open bottle in each hand and then proudly stretched them out in front of Hazel and Eve, respectively.

"Uh, what are you doing, Pops?" Eve asked, one eyebrow arching up.

There was a brief moment of confusion in Silas's eyes, followed by a deep sense of understanding and almost terror. He was asked if he kept liquor accessible. But beer was different from liquor.

Hazel's body was still tense and rigid at the scene. She had never had a drink before, let alone in front of an adult.

"Oh, uh, yeah. What am I doing?" Silas asked rhetorically, now averting his eyes.

Eve let out a sinister giggle.

"You know we're only fifteen, right? As in like not even close to drinking age?"

"Um, yeah. Sorry. Uh, I must..." Silas stumbled awkwardly over his words.

But then Eve's eyes lit up and her spine straightened.

"Can we have them anyway?" Eve asked, in that same illicit, excited tone.

The question itself relaxed Silas. His jaw loosened and his shoulders relaxed and then a slight smile moved slowly across his lips.

"Really? Have you ever had one before?"

Eve snatched the bottle from his hand and took it confidently into possession between her index finger and thumb. "Of course I've had one before. What do you think I am? Some kind of prude loser?"

Eve brought the bottle to her lips and tilted her head back.

Hazel could see the outline of her throat, swelling and then relaxing, effortlessly allowing the cascade of beer down it.

"Ah," she said as she tilted her neck back up and slammed the beer onto the table. Hazel could make out the fill line from behind the label. Eve had swallowed nearly half the bottle in one sip.

"Well, okay, then," Silas said, seeming impressed at the feat. "And how about you, Hazel?"

Hazel felt her tummy do a flip again as she made eye contact with Silas. She could feel a tingle in her cheeks and her palms start to sweat. She hadn't even held a bottle before. She felt scared, but even more, she felt excited.

"Uh, yeah. Of course," she mumbled. She looked over at Eve, who had her eyes locked on Hazel, urging her to drink it, too.

"You sure now? You know you don't have to…" Silas started to say, but then Hazel tore the bottle from his hand with a furious rush of something inside her she had never felt before.

She exhaled fully and then poured the liquid into her mouth. The bubbles were angry and sharp going down. The beer was bitter and nasty on her tongue. Hazel felt her face begin to contort—her lips pursing, her nose scrunching up, her eyebrows pressing together. But she stopped herself from wincing and continued to gulp it all down. She gulped and gulped until the entire bottle was finished and then she slammed it down on the table next to Eve's.

Eve looked impressed. And Hazel felt cool and sexy and interesting and mature and alive. She had discovered what it felt like to do something dangerous at the same time as she had rediscovered what it felt like to be part of something. The combination of feelings strengthened the validity of both. It made her want to do more, feel more. To sink deeper. To be part of this new family.

For so long she had been thirsting for someone that understood her, and in this moment she had felt fulfilled at a mere admiring gaze from Eve and Silas. This place, these people in it, would be more than enough. Her mother would have never let an adventure like this happen anymore. Not since the twins were born. Hazel was ready for newness in her life. Ready for connection.

"Looks like you two have got some Box genes in ya, after all!" Silas said, swelling with pride.

He slapped Hazel on the back firmly, which caused her to belch.

All three of them laughed and laughed and laughed, and then belched some more.

"Well, I'll get us some more, then. It's going to be a fun night, you guys." Silas got up to get another set of beers from the refrigerator and Hazel was already spinning.

"Dig in," Silas instructed as he set the new cold beers down onto the table. Hazel reached for the bread and butter. Her hands felt foreign and wobbly as she placed a slice on her plate and took a buttered knife across the surface. She took another sip of her beer. This one felt smoother, less shocking. And then she piled more food onto her plate.

All three of them ate and drank and told stories and laughed and ate and drank and told stories and laughed some more. They all inhaled the conversation as much as they inhaled their dinners. And as much as Hazel inhaled her beer.

None of them even bothered to pause in moments between words leaving their lips and their meal entering it. Soon, the outlines of Eve's and Silas's bodies began to get fuzzy and then the food at the table began to blur. But Hazel ate and drank and drank and ate even more. And then everything blurred some more.

When Hazel came to, her bare bottom felt cold against the tile beneath her and her head and body felt as if they were filled with lead. The room was dark and quiet and water poured down on her from the showerhead above in a constant stream, splattering around her. Hazel's knees were tucked into her chest and her arms wrapped around them. Everything was still blurry and she could taste the acidity of vomit lingering inside her cheeks. Her eyes were closed but all she could see was green. That same putrid, nauseating green of her bedroom wall. The image enlarged and contracted with the throbbing of her head as if it were a breathing lung.

Hazel stood up slowly, continuing to let the water pour over her. Her legs wobbled as she did it but it felt good to stand. She opened her mouth to the stream and let the water overflow in her open mouth and roll down her chin. She motioned to turn the water off, but her stomach contracted violently. She pressed her palm into the wall of the shower and tilted her head down. Chunks of food and slimy chyme from her stomach spewed from her mouth and fell into a warm and viscous mound on her feet. She moved her head away to let the water wash her toes. Through watery eyes,

Hazel observed muculent globs of food stuck to the drain, resisting the force of the water trying to wash it down.

Her throat felt sore from the stomach acid, the stench of which filled her nostrils. She turned her mouth up toward the water to cleanse it again. Her stomach contracted again, but this time Hazel only dry-heaved. She dropped back down to the floor of the shower and pulled her knees into her chest, trying to stay clear of the lingering vomit. As she returned to this position with the water running over her, Hazel wondered how many times she had already repeated this pattern—stand up, vomit, sink down, let the water cleanse her, stand up, vomit, sink down, let the water cleanse her.

Hazel could feel her pulse in her temples. The world around her was glitchy and dark. Her mouth tasted sticky and stale. Her insides felt empty and aching. Hazel pressed her forehead into her knees and squeezed her shins. Her wet hair stuck to the outsides of her calves and she let out a groan, perhaps as a way to transfer all the horrible, disgusting, vile things from her insides out into the world, hoping something else would absorb them. Take away her agony, her embarrassment.

She pressed her forehead further into her knees, resigning herself to sit under that showerhead next to her own vomit for eternity when the door to the bathroom creaked open. Hazel rolled her head over, leaving one ear on her knee, and looked toward the door. Eve appeared in the doorway, rubbing her eye with the heel of her palm.

"What are you doing in here?" she mumbled through sleepy lips.

Hazel turned her forehead back into the tops of her knees and groaned again.

Eve opened the door to the shower and reached to turn the water off and then crouched down next to Hazel. Eve shimmied her legs around Hazel's curled body and then tucked Hazel's wet hair behind her ear.

"Ew!" she shrieked, presumably having just identified the vomit at the center of the drain. She chuckled a bit as she tickled Hazel's back up and down with her fingertips.

"Oh yeah, been here before." She tickled Hazel's back again. It felt good to have another body next to hers. It felt good to have help. It felt good to know that Eve had gone through this before. That Hazel had a partner.

"Hold on, gotta piss," Eve interrupted and then popped up.

Hazel moaned again and followed Eve with her gaze.

Eve pulled her pants down and sat down onto the toilet.

Hazel thought to close her eyes, or turn her head away at the sound of the rushing urine, but her reaction time was slow and her movements were viscous.

"Yup, that's what three beers will get you!" Eve said from the toilet seat as the gush of water turned into a gentle tinkling sound and her pee came to an end.

"You're a pretty fun drunk, though, I have to say."

Hazel couldn't help smiling.

Eve pulled a big wad of toilet paper from the roll, wiped her crotch, stood up and then pulled her pajamas back up.

"Let's get you back to bed."

Eve joined Hazel again in the shower, this time with a towel. She shook it, rubbed it vigorously across Hazel's wet hair and then wrapped it around her. Eve cupped one hand beneath Hazel's elbow and then grabbed onto her opposite arm with her other hand.

"All right, up we go, drunky."

Hazel stood up on wobbly legs again. Her heavy throbbing head fell onto Eve's shoulder.

"Thank you," Hazel mustered and stumbled along with Eve.

When they reached the bed, Hazel tumbled over onto it and felt her towel slip off. Too weak to react, Hazel splayed her bare body out across her sheets.

"Hey! I knew you had good tits!" Eve said and gave her underbreast a pinch.

Hazel smiled limply and motioned to swat Eve's hand away playfully, but Eve had already left the side of the bed and come back with a clean T-shirt and a glass of water. Eve pulled Hazel into a seated position by her arms and then pulled the shirt over her head, and then her arms through the armholes.

"All right, you, drink this whole glass of water and then sleep it off."

Hazel curled her fingers around the glass and brought it to her lips. Eve left her hands on top of Hazel's as she did it. Eve slid one, and then the other of Hazel's legs under the sheets, and then pulled the comforter over her.

Eve returned to her own bed, and said good-night through the darkness and from across the room. Hazel began to drift into sleep with the lingering feeling of Eve's fingers on her fingers. With the lingering feeling of friendship and sisterhood and happiness. Despite the feeling of her head throbbing and water sloshing around in her empty belly.

23

Hazel woke up still in a fog, got dressed and made her way downstairs to the kitchen and gulped down a cold cup of water. Just as she finished the final drop, Silas burst in the room.

"Hellooo—" he began but stopped abruptly upon seeing Hazel. "You look really terrible."

Hazel paused for a moment, trying to put words together in a retort.

Silas opened a cabinet, pulled out a bottle, shook out two maroon ibuprofen pills and placed them on the countertop in front of her. "Two pills and two more glasses of water will do the trick." He smiled at Hazel knowingly, perhaps even paternally, as he watched her swallow the ibuprofen and water down.

"Plus, we'll head out on the lake today, take the boat out for a drive. Some fresh air will be nice."

Eve emerged on the staircase, her hair still wet from the

shower. "Yes! The boat's the best! Do I have to wear one of those disgusting life—" Eve also stopped abruptly upon seeing Hazel.

"You look terrible," she said similarly matter-of-factly, but with a glimmer of enjoyment in her eye.

Hazel felt the cool water running through her empty stomach.

She picked her head up to look over at Eve. "That's what he tells me, too."

"Bad morning is a sign of a good night. That's what I always say!" Silas chimed in, overly chipper.

"That's what you *always* say?" Eve asked smugly.

Silas smiled and tucked a piece of dark hair behind his ear.

Before a moment of silence could even briefly hang in the air, Eve reclaimed it. "Okay, but seriously, do I have to wear the life jacket?"

"Yes, you do. You both do! Follow me down toward the shed. Fresh air is going to be really nice for you especially, Hazel!"

Hazel pulled her feet under her again and followed Silas and Eve out the back door. They traversed the backyard and made their way to a path between two trees sloping down toward the lake. As soon as they passed by the two large trees, the full view of the sparkling lake emerged.

Hazel inhaled. She could feel her lingering nausea escaping her body, replaced by the crisp air. She felt a little tickle in her belly as she thought of getting out onto the water. Silas, Eve and Hazel all enjoying the great big lake and the great big sun together.

The ground leveled out into a small sandy beach. Timid

waves from the lake washed up gently and rhythmically onto the sand. A long wooden dock stretched out over the lake, a big white boat bouncing on the side.

Eve's face lit up and she leaped toward the dock swiftly, her long legs beginning a stride.

"Wait a minute, you!" Silas shouted.

Eve stopped in her tracks without even turning around.

Silas made his way to a rickety old shed set into the hill and emerged with two life jackets. They were faded from too many hours in the sun but did not seem like they had been used much. As Silas pulled the two life jackets apart, wisps of cobwebs clung delicately between them. Silas began slapping each jacket on the ground, his tanned and powerful arm in sharp juxtaposition to the dull and lifeless jackets. Flecks of dust formed a transitory opaque cloud around them.

"These look way worse than last time! I'm serious! I'm not putting that on," Eve shrieked.

Without even lifting his head, Silas tossed one jacket each girl's way. "Sure you are!" he said breezily, sarcasm dripping from every word.

Eve pinched the edge of the jacket between two fingers and held it away from her body. "It stinks!"

Hazel laughed and slipped hers on each shoulder, zipped it shut and clicked the buckle in place.

"As soon you're ready, princess," Silas urged, tapping his sandal into the ground.

Eve, in a dramatic and drawn-out performance, slipped one arm through the armhole and then the other, wincing a bit as each part of the jacket touched her bare skin. She pulled the zipper up, having to tug it with a bit of added force to get it over her breasts. Eve then snapped her legs to-gether, stretched her arms out to the sides and took a bow.

"The princess is now ready," she declared as she tipped her chin and nose into the sky.

Silas took her into a playful headlock and messed her hair with his palm.

He then released her from his hold. "You're a pain in my butt. You really are. You know that, right? I know you know that."

Eve just smirked and raked her fingers through her hair. "Ugh! You messed my hair up!"

Silas, Eve and Hazel continued down the overgrown path toward the dock. It was already hot even though it was early in the morning. There was an acerbic but still captivating odor of earth and grass drying in the sun. Eve's glossy hair swayed back and forth as she walked, glimmering sporadi-cally as it caught the sun.

When they reached the dock, Silas hopped straight into the boat. With one leg in the boat and the other stepped up onto the dock to stabilize the swaying, he reached his hands out to help the girls in. Hazel joined first, paying careful at-tention to her feet but self-conscious about displaying even a trace of uneasiness. Eve followed next, with another dramatic display of precisely placed feet and hands and squeals. There was something admirable about how free and accessible Eve made her discontent. She was so bold and open with it. She wanted her thoughts and feelings out there for the world to see. For Hazel, those reactions were far too precious, far too private, to expose to anyone, let alone everyone. She used to feel she could show her mom, but her mom had other priorities now. And even if Hazel did share how she felt, she wouldn't get anything in return. So she kept all of her feelings close and clung to them with such resolve that no one would even think she had them.

Hazel followed Eve into position on the back seats of the boat. Eve stretched her leg out casually across the bench and draped her arm along the edge of the boat—a swift, Eve-like transition from the theatrics to such graceful comfort. Silas assiduously fiddled around with ropes and strings and levers, and then sat behind the wheel of the boat and slipped his sunglasses on. He turned the key and the boat began to rumble. The boat drifted slowly away from the dock and the smell of fuel displaced the fresh aroma of summer lake. They were in near open water now, and without even turning around, Silas moved the boat into a different gear.

The boat suddenly leaped forward. It jerked with such force that Hazel nearly fell over the back. She giggled and grabbed the rail on the edge of the boat to brace herself and looked over at Eve, who was still lying comfortably on the cushions with her eyes shut, enjoying the sun. The thunderous clang of the engine drowned out the sounds of the lake. As they rode across the lake, the nose of the boat rose into the air and then thumped back down onto the water. This repeated over and over with a slightly syncopated rhythm. The rumble of the engine reached its crescendo just as the tip of the boat reached its zenith. Hazel's grip around the rail relaxed as she became more expectant of the seesawing patterns of the boat beneath her body. She looked over at Eve, who was now kneeling on the bench, her torso angled out over the edge of the boat into the considerable spray fanning out from all sides. Her silken hair thrashed around in the wind and then fell over her cheeks for just a moment before being lifted and thrashed again by another whoosh of air. It didn't surprise Hazel that Eve looked so effortless. She always did. Hazel's face, on the other hand, began to feel stiff and ungraceful against the pressure of the wind, and she tucked her knees into her chest and pressed her face into her legs for protection. The vibration of the seat beneath her body provided some reprieve.

After only a few minutes, the sound of the engine faded, and the boat puttered to a stop not far from a small, rocky island. Silas twisted the key to the engine, and the faint chirps, crackles and splashes of the lake became audible once more. Hazel lifted her head up to find Silas rooting around in a compartment in the center of the boat. He eventually hauled a small anchor from the pit and tossed it by its chain over the side. Hazel tilted her body over the ledge to watch the anchor fall deeper and deeper through the clear water, its shape losing its form and wiggling at the edges until it was completely out of sight. Silas declared it a good place to swim, and took his shirt and sandals off. He stepped up onto the bow and dived into the lake. As Silas's body dipped beneath the water, Hazel noticed a feeling of being left behind creep up through her. It surprised her.

By the time Hazel had turned to Eve, Eve had already pulled her phone from the pocket of her shorts to inspect. Eve shook her phone again, as if she were shaking an ensnared snack from a vending machine.

"Ugh," she groaned. "This place has *literally* no service."

Hazel had learned by now that she need not respond to

all of Eve's grievances. Hazel just let Eve's words evaporate into the clear air.

Eve lay back onto the cushion harshly, unzipped her life jacket to expose her slim belly and chest to the sun, and slid her long legs out in front of her. They looked more tanned, and perhaps even a bit more toned, here at the lake. Her breasts were so full and round, even in her supine position. Her hair draped perfectly over the side, still glimmering in the sun. Hazel lay back and observed her own breasts. Gravity had already pulled them flat into her chest. She looked down at her own legs, a little chubby with a stubble of hairs poking out from her skin. She tried to pull one out but failed. She pulled her hair out of her ponytail and shaped it in front of her shoulders. She could see in her shadow that her hair's awkward waves and thin layer of frizz persisted.

Across the lake on a distant shore, Hazel spotted a fuzzy image of tiny shapes and figures sitting out on their beach. She could hear people talking and laughing, though she was unable to make out any of the words. Two small boys played in the shallow water in neon-colored bathing suits. They were shrieking as they splashed each other and jumped up and down, their little bodies glittering in the water. They transferred water in various-sized buckets, back and forth from the lake, into what appeared to be a moat crafted around a messy sandcastle. Hazel thought of her little brothers. How much they would like it here. Hazel's heart clenched at the thought of it. Did she miss them? Her heart clenched again. She needed to distract herself from the thought as quickly as possible, so she jumped into the water. It was cold and refreshing. After swimming a few small circles, Hazel felt tired. She was out of practice and so she pulled herself back into the boat. Eve propped herself up on her elbows and peeked out from behind her sunglasses to watch Hazel. Silas, too, had returned to the boat in that time and was sitting on the nose with his feet dipping in and out of the water as the boat rose and fell.

"Look who's back!" Eve remarked with a smile.

"Nice out here, isn't it?" Silas half declared, half asked proudly and spread a towel out between his hands for Hazel.

"Oh yeah!" Hazel said and walked into the towel. Silas wrapped her in it tightly and gave her a firm pat on the back. If Hazel had any chill before, it was entirely gone now. Everything felt warm inside. This was exactly what she had hoped this new life would be like.

24

After dinner that next night, Silas held the screen door open and suggested Hazel and Eve join him outside for another treat.

"Ugh, it's always full of bugs out there," Eve complained and then slunk down in her chair.

Silas smirked and removed his hand from the door and let it slam shut. The door creaked, bouncing in the doorframe as Silas stood there, eyes locked on Eve, willing her to move. When she didn't, Silas shifted his weight and then walked over to her. Eve had already begun smiling in anticipation of the creative ways Silas could convince her to move from her position in the chair.

"Come on, look at them swarming out there! They're obsessed with that light." Eve pointed out the window at a dozen moths fluttering around a light. "Ew, they're so gross!"

Silas, mildly amused, rolled his eyes, ensuring Eve could see them, and then placed his hands underneath Eve's armpits and lifted her from the chair. Eve tried to leave her body heavy and limp, but her narrow delicate body was no match for Silas's strong, burly arms and shoulders and hands.

Eve yelped and laughed and then steadied her intentionally wobbling legs beneath her torso until she was standing.

"Okay, okay, we'll go!"

Hazel giggled and then made her way toward the screen door herself. It was so thrilling to see Silas so casually outdo Eve like that. Hazel wondered if that was how it went with fathers and daughters. If she would have what Silas and Eve had. She hoped she would.

"That's what I thought," Silas responded confidently and smiled too widely, with all his big white teeth showing for Eve. Eve tucked her hair behind her ears and recomposed herself and then dragged her feet across the floor toward the outside.

Just when Silas's shoulders relaxed, Eve allowed her legs to become wobbly below her again. She yelped and laughed again as she pretended to droop down to the floor. But before her buttocks could reach the floor, Silas's hands were underneath Eve's back again, sparing her from the hardwood.

He playfully lifted his boot to Eve's bottom and ushered her out the door. "One of these days you being a pain in my butt is going to cause a pain in your butt!" Silas joked as he lifted Eve back up to her feet.

Hazel giggled again, this time with a little extra warmth in her heart. She was sure this was how it went with fathers and daughters.

Down a short walkway out in the grass of the backyard was a small but sturdy firepit surrounded by three red camping chairs. Like most items inside the house, the firepit, too, had a handmade quality. Three layers of gray, slightly crumbly cinderblocks formed a two-foot pit on top of a gravelly bed.

Despite the rustic, handmade feel, there was a certain newness to the thing. The three chairs were not tattered, or worn, or stained. The pit had no ash or burnt remnants inside of it. A stack of freshly chopped wood lay beside it.

Three long sticks leaned against the blocks next to a pack of unopened marshmallows, a box of graham crackers and a stack of chocolate.

"You girls ever make a s'more before?" Silas asked earnestly.

"S'mores?" Eve asked.

"Yes!" Hazel interjected excitedly and moved the stack of logs into the pit, flush against the gravel on the bottom.

Silas watched skeptically and then raised one eyebrow at Hazel's lackluster wood placement.

"I suppose I should have asked the more important question first. Have you ever made a fire before?"

Hazel felt her cheeks get hot and she pulled her body away from the pit.

"No," Hazel mumbled. She felt the enchantment of the firepit and Silas and the sparkly twilight start to spill out of her.

"Well, this is a new activity," Eve chimed in with a slight roll of her eyes. "And I don't think it's one that I'm too interested in."

"That's fine," Silas responded calmly. "Hazel and I will do it."

Hazel felt her tummy turn. Silas looked up and his clear, earnest eyes met Hazel's. And then a big smile spread across his lips.

"Any girl of mine better know how to make a fire! Go on and get me some sticks."

Hazel bounced into motion before he could finish getting the words out. She skipped over to the edge of the wooded area and started collecting sticks without even turning back.

"Mostly skinny ones," Silas shouted from behind her. "And gotta be dry!"

She hurried back with a pile and dropped them at Silas's feet.

"That, my girl, is some good-looking kindling!"

Silas knelt down in front of the firepit and told her about stick placement and airflow. He told her about his first fire on a camping trip long, long ago. He told her where to light the wood so that the flame would catch the fastest. He told her how to blow gently on the flames to keep the fire going.

And Silas looked right at Hazel while he said it all. He looked at her and directed her hands when she was making a mistake and smiled and cheered when she was doing it right.

And then there it was. A roaring, dancing, deep orange fire. Hazel felt her heart swell until it felt like it was going to pop.

She stood still and smiled softly, observing her creation. And she felt Silas watching her. Perhaps observing his creation.

Hazel was so happy to have been taught by Silas. She didn't know whether it was the flames of fire or the sense of pride that was warming her belly.

Silas slapped Hazel on the back firmly with a big open palm. The force of it caused Hazel to stumble forward a bit. The place where Silas's hand had been tingled, even stung, but she enjoyed the feeling.

Hazel never considered that she might be one for that kind of firm-pat-on-the-back or teach-the-kiddo-how-to-do-things kind of love. At home, with her mother, it had always been soft kisses and long hugs. Lick-the-spoon-after-baking and sing-our-favorite-songs-in-harmony kind of love.

Thinking on it now, Hazel couldn't remember anything but a love that just grew and grew into bigger and bigger love. It was always like a snowball accumulating layer after layer of fresh powdery snow. Until Cam came along, there were no discrete moments or milestones that built their love up or yanked it down. No shared stepwise changes in togetherness or closeness or happiness or sadness. Nothing to point to and say, "That's when Mom and I became this." Or "That's when I turned into a person that could do this."

Hazel knew she would remember this moment forever. The moment she turned into a girl that could make a fire from a few coarsely chopped logs and some newspaper. The moment that she and Silas became a team. It meant everything.

Hazel looked over at Silas, who was standing with his feet wider than his shoulders and his hands on his hips, watching the fire. The light caught his cheekbones and danced across his black hair as the fire jerked around in the pit. He looked so firm and steady standing there. So calm and focused.

Hazel turned around to Eve, who was reclined in her camping chair, one leg dangling over the armrest, mesmerized by the fire. Hazel smiled even more thoroughly.

Hazel hoped they were both proud of what they had created. In that firepit and in this cabin. It was just the three of them out there in the backyard. Enjoying a warm fire and a quiet sense of peace.

Silas interrupted the quiet by handing each of the girls a stick.

"This fire is ready for some s'mores!"

He tossed the bag of marshmallows into Eve's lap.

"Come on. Slide those puffy little 'mallows onto the stick."

Eve wiggled herself upright in the chair, flipped the bag of marshmallows over and began scanning the back of the bag.

"These are basically like all sugar. Do you want me to get fat?"

Eve slumped back into the chair and dipped her head back.

She tossed the bag back at Silas, with a bit more force than appropriate for a short toss.

"Party pooper!" Silas said while shrugging his shoulders. He turned and held the bag out in front of Hazel.

"How about you?"

Hazel looked over at Eve. Her long legs stretched over the side, her hip bone popping out from the bottom of her shirt. Her back arched over the armrest, which pressed her breasts into the sky. Hazel was surprised Eve had to make any sacrifices at all for that body. Her beauty, her allure, always looked so natural on her.

Hazel looked back at Silas, who was now shaking the bag seductively in front of her. This firepit. These carefully chosen sticks. This warm, humid evening. His black hair. His full eyebrows. The charming look in his stirring green eyes.

Hazel snatched the bag from Silas's hand, tore the plastic open and popped a marshmallow into her mouth.

"That's my girl!" Silas rubbed the back of Hazel's hair. And Hazel felt cool. And carefree. Like she belonged at the lake.

Silas grabbed a marshmallow, and then another one, and then another one, and slid them onto a stick. Hazel did the same, feeling rebellious by adding a third marshmallow, and then both Silas and Hazel held their sticks over the now calmer flames.

Hazel looked at Eve out of the side of her eye, hoping she was being watched, but Eve still had her head tilted back and her eyes closed and face toward the sky.

"The glowing logs are where it's at. It's where the heat is. It's where you get that sweet golden brown."

The wind picked up for a moment, creating a whirl of fire in the pit.

"See that. Don't trust those flames. Too unpredictable. Too susceptible to the elements. They'll burn you every time."

Silas kept his focus on the flickering flames, until he pulled the stick back from out of the fire, three perfectly browned marshmallows stacked on the stick.

"Quick, we gotta get them on the grahams while they're still gooey. Load up the rest of the s'mores!"

Hazel leaned her stick with her half-roasted marshmallows against the edge of the firepit and tore open the box of graham crackers and then the chocolate wrapper. She snapped a piece of chocolate from the edge.

"Ah, I just love that sound," Silas said. Hazel knew he meant it. He said it right from his gut.

Hazel presented a graham cracker with the piece of chocolate on it to Silas.

"That, Hazel Box, is the perfect ratio of chocolate to graham. It's a beautiful thing."

Silas sandwiched his marshmallows between two graham crackers and slid the stick out. Hazel watched the chocolate begin to melt underneath the hot, drooping marshmallows.

He shuffled slowly toward Eve and then sat down next to her on the dirt. Eve peeked one eye open, skeptically.

"Yes?" she asked, drawing out the question.

"Oh, nothing. Just thought this was a good seat," Silas responded with an overt lightness in his voice.

And then he aggressively bit into the s'more. The graham cracker broke awkwardly, leaving a big chunk of s'more with gooey marshmallow and melted chocolate hanging outside his mouth. Crumbs fell down into his lap as he struggled to get his mouth around the bite.

"Mmm!" Silas mumbled dramatically, leaning in toward Eve's ear.

Eve squeezed her eyes tighter together as Hazel watched in amusement. She sat down on the edge of the firepit and tilted the marshmallows back over a glowing log.

"Mmm…mmm!" Silas mumbled even louder now. More crumbs rolled down the front of his shirt.

"Ugh, fine. Give me a bite of that already!"

Eve sat back up in the chair and Silas slowly raised the broken s'more to her lips. Just as she was about to take a bite, Silas shoved the whole piece of it into her mouth. Eve shrieked and instinctively slapped Silas on the shoulder. He laughed and laughed, his shoulders bouncing up and down, and it made Eve laugh, too. And then Hazel.

Eve chomped down on her s'more as Silas licked the sticky marshmallow and traces of chocolate from his fingers.

Silas and Hazel watched Eve until she swallowed the whole thing, ready for the histrionics to unleash.

Without saying a word, Eve walked over to Hazel and sat down next to her on the edge of the firepit. Eve laid her head onto Hazel's shoulder and looked up at her with earnest, begging green eyes. She blinked twice, batting her eyelashes.

"What do you think about giving me one of those marshmallows?"

Hazel paused for a moment, smiled down at Eve and then nudged her hip into Eve's, nearly pushing her off the side. She had been emboldened by the evening. The fire and Silas and the s'more and the evening and this whole week at the lake.

"What I think is that you should make your own marshmallow!"

Hazel almost didn't recognize herself but those almost taunting but still lighthearted words felt so right coming off her lips. It occurred to Hazel that it must be a thing sisters can do with each other. It occurred to her that this could be her life. And she could be a confident, cool, competent, fire-making girl, sister, in that life.

Silas chuckled again and tossed Eve a stick. Eve held her eye contact with Silas, urging him to back her up.

"Don't look at me, kiddo. The gals I know never give up their 'mallows."

Eve rolled her eyes, sat harshly onto the edge of the firepit and tilted her marshmallow-lined stick over the fire.

Hazel finished making her s'more and took a big bite as she watched Eve roast hers.

She was happy. They were all happy.

At some point, Hazel, Silas and Eve found themselves draped in the darkness. But until then, there had been no sense of progression to mark the time. It didn't get cooler or quieter. The crackle of the fire didn't get louder and the flames didn't get hotter. The moment was eternal and still.

Hazel looked over at the house. The lighted rooms had become a great illuminated stage with each window aglow. It surprised Hazel just how much she could make out from each window. Furniture and books and beds and night-stands. All except for one dark, evasive window. Just as the question of what was in that room began to bubble up inside of Hazel again, her thought was interrupted by a wet droplet on her arm.

The drop was thick and full, and remained in its orbed form for a moment before sliding off the side. And then there was another thick raindrop. And another. And another. With increased frequency.

Hazel looked over at Eve, who had popped up from her chair but was surprisingly not yet covering her hair. Silas had his face up toward the clouds.

A booming rumble of thunder filled the air.

"You girls ready for this?"

"Ready for wha—" A great crack of lightning lit up the sky and the great moody lake beneath it. Eve yelped but then pulled back into silence.

"Ready for a real Grandor rainstorm?" Silas said calmly.

Within seconds, the rain unleashed itself with a sudden burst of intensity. The ragged sheets of rain covered the chairs, and the trees, and the fire, and their bodies.

Eve yelped again, but this time with more excitement

than anxiety. And then she spread her arms out and let the rain fall all over her. Drenching her clothes and her hair. And then she lay down in the grass and let the rain fall all over her some more.

Hazel looked over at Silas. Perhaps for permission to join. But perhaps just because it was becoming an instinct to look up at him when she felt uncertain of anything. Anything at all.

Silas shrugged and then joined Eve on the ground with his head near Eve's and his feet out in the opposite direction. And then Hazel did the same. It was dark but the moon was bright and Hazel could turn her head to either side to find Eve and Silas enjoying the rain. Her sister and her father enjoying the rain.

Hazel closed her eyes and listened to the clicking sound of big wobbling raindrops hitting the roof.

And then out of the peace, Hazel felt Eve's hand on hers, squeezing it tight. Hazel opened one eye to look over at Eve, but Eve's eyes were still closed. Hazel gave it a squeeze right back and then she felt Silas take her other hand. It had caused their arms and shoulders to touch and it sent a chill all the way down Hazel's spine.

She could feel his imminence. The fullness of his attention. His love. And Eve's, too.

Hazel considered that this unexpected access to unadulterated happiness, this surprising feeling of boundless tenderness for someone else seemingly out of nowhere, must be what it was like to have a real family.

Even though it was raining, she wanted to stay out there forever.

25

Eventually, Hazel, Silas and Eve returned to the shelter of the house. The sound of the screen door slamming could barely be made out against the backdrop of the still-pounding rain. Hazel realized she was short of breath from the rush of it all. The darkness. The rain. The togetherness. She could feel the quick pulse of her heart and her lungs filling and then deflating. She noticed Silas's and Eve's chests rising and falling, as well. They, too, were feeling the rush of it all.

Three distinct puddles had already formed on the wood floor beneath each of their feet, a result of their dripping clothes.

"Let me get us some towels," Silas said as he pulled his soaking wet T-shirt over his head.

Silas's chest and shoulders were slippery from the rain. Small beads of water had collected on the tips of Silas's curled chest hair. A few droplets were streaming down his chest onto his abdomen. Hazel could just make out Silas's musculature beneath the thick skin of his belly. His slightly protruding belly only made him appear more manly, more capable. He then stepped out of his shorts, leaving him in just his tight black boxers for a moment. He dropped his saturated clothing onto the floor with a heavy thud and then turned toward the hallway. His thighs were trunk-like and solid and bulged as he walked away to get the towels.

"Ah, that was fun," Hazel said to Eve as she ran her fingers through her hair.

Eve had her head tilted to the side and her long wet hair was dripping next to her. Eve's wet white T-shirt had become see-through, hugging the contour of her breasts and her black bra. Hazel turned away bashfully as she felt her cheeks begin to get hot.

"Ugh, is my mascara running?" Eve had reinserted herself into Hazel's view, now with her belly exposed as she wrung out the front of her T-shirt. Eve never had any shame about her body. She was always so carefree about exposing her belly button, or hip or breasts or collarbones, but she was always paranoid about her makeup.

Hazel wondered what Eve thought a face revealed that a body did not.

"Hello! Earth to Hazel!" Eve snapped her fingers in front of her Hazel's face. "Well, is it?"

"Who cares?" Hazel replied and giggled a bit.

Eve smiled and giggled a bit, too. And then nudged Hazel with her hip.

It was so easy to crack Eve's demanding exterior. And

Hazel was delighted about how quickly she could do it. How confident she had become.

Silas returned with a towel around his waist and one more for each of his daughters.

"All right, you two, I'm hitting the hay." He tossed the towels firmly their way. "I'll see you in the morning."

Hazel and Eve wrapped the big towels around their dripping clothes and walked toward their room, leaving watery footprints on their way.

"I call first shower!" Eve shouted and picked up her pace. Her legs were constricted by the towel, turning her attempted run into a straight-legged shuffle.

"Of course you do," Hazel muttered with feigned annoyance and allowed Eve to disappear down the hallway into their room.

Hazel maintained her lackadaisical stride, turning her head side to side and observing the old and creaking walls of the hallway. They were starting to feel like her walls. Walls she liked living between.

Hazel stepped into an already steamy bathroom to take her turn for a shower. She undressed, left her clothes in a sopping pile on the tiled floor and stepped into the spray. As the warm water washed over her body, she became aware of how cold the rain had been against her skin and hair. Cold water flowed from her hair, replaced by the warm stream of water from the showerhead. She closed her eyes and let the water wash over her. Hazel was warmed inside and out. She felt satisfied and safe. Comfortable and happy.

It had been so long since she had felt those things back at home. So long since she had participated in family life.

Hazel had a sense that many girls her age had chosen to recoil from family life. She had a sense that one day they came home from school and decided to reject their life and home and look to something bigger. She had a sense they looked to friends, or boyfriends, or places far away. That one day they yearned to leave their home and their parents and their younger selves behind. That it happened without consequence.

But this feeling was forced onto Hazel as soon as Cam walked into her home. It was the day that she started to feel as if she were watching her life rather than being a part of it. That her home shifted from hers to Cam's. That Jane shifted from being hers to Cam's. That everything she built and loved had been lost. She would sit at the dinner table with them and watch as they talked and ate. There was a time that felt like long ago now in which she wanted so badly to get back inside those dinners, to get back inside her life. But she learned over time that she couldn't. Something impenetrable had been built. And, whether it was on purpose or not, Cam and the twins had built it. It wasn't this way in the beginning with Cam, but it was the reality now.

But she didn't have any of those feelings up here in Grandor with Eve and Silas.

Her sense of being wanted, being loved, being part of something had finally returned to her. It was everything she needed. Everything she wanted.

The next morning, Hazel woke up to Eve inspecting herself in front of the mirror. It had become a familiar scene and Hazel was surprised at the constant upkeep required of a girl. The diligence required for a look like Eve's. Eve could occupy hours putting her hair up into a wild bun on the top of her head and pulling it back down again, picking at blackheads with the tip of a pin, or looking at her own body in the mirror.

As Eve stood in front of the mirror so slightly tilting her hips forward, arching her back, and craning her neck to observe her own butt, it occurred to Hazel that it was something more than vanity. It was almost as if Eve was conducting an intellectual study of her own anatomy. Her skin and her bones, and how it all moved. Measuring the slope of every curve, capturing the memory of a body at a discrete moment in time.

Hazel was no match for Eve. Eve always looked so cool and smart. She was a simultaneous participant and critic of all things in her world. She was angular and athletic but soft and provocative all at once. Even if Hazel could manicure her eyebrows and wear ripped jeans and expensive sunglasses, she would always be just fine. She would never hold up more than medium well under scrutiny. There were so many things Hazel didn't have. Would never have. She was no match at all for Eve.

Eve caught Hazel's eye in the reflection of the mirror. It moved Hazel.

"What are you doing when you look in the mirror like that?"

Hazel knew she had so much to learn from Eve. From her sister.

Eve pursed her lips together and kissed the mirror, right

on her own lips. Green eyes open and locked on her own eyes the entire time.

Her attention on the mirror was sharp and focused. And then it wasn't.

Eve reached for her phone, which had been glowing and buzzing without Eve paying it any mind, but she looked at it now as if she were under a spell. Her eyes were wide and absorbent as she lay on her belly poring over her phone. Her knees bent and her feet were swinging behind her as she jammed her fingers into the face of the phone with an impressive speed and rhythm. The phone buzzed and glowed some more in response. There seemed to be a symbiosis between Eve and the phone. She fed the phone and it fed her. They were both wild and abuzz with it. Even watching Eve mesmerized by the phone was mesmerizing in itself. Despite the trance, every now and then Hazel could make out the slightest hint at what the messages on her phone evoked in Eve. Her lips might perk up at the edges. Her eyebrows might press the slightest bit up. Her green eyes might soften sensually.

And then, as suddenly as Eve had been sucked into her phone, she released herself. Eve popped back up from her position on the bed and posed back in front of the mirror. Back to her sharp and focused attention. And from there, Eve continued as if she had never stopped in the first place.

"I just don't believe anyone who says that they didn't get cool until after college," she said matter-of-factly. "After these years, Hazel, it's all downhill. We get uglier and uglier, less and less cool, and then we die." Eve snapped her fingers and popped her hip out.

"And since I am a teenager, I am at peak cool." She finally turned around to Hazel.

"Which means that I know everything." She pulled her mouth into a subdued smirk and popped her shoulders up toward her chin.

It was hard to argue with her as she stood there with her long legs stretching out from her worn denim shorts and her golden brown hair draping across her narrow back.

Eve reached her arms out to pull Hazel in front of the mirror, presumably to pore over Hazel's anatomy instead. Hazel tried to wiggle out of her Eve's fingers and divert her attention to another activity, but it was no use.

Eve held Hazel in front of the mirror, her palms firmly pressing down on Hazel's shoulders, and scanned her from top to bottom several times. She squinted her eyes. The black mascara on her eyelids enhanced the drama in her gaze. And then her eyes suddenly appeared more bright and shining emerald than the mossy green they usually were and a smile spread across her lips.

"I think we should try some red lips on you. Pucker 'em up like this," Eve demanded and then pursed her own plump lips and made kissing noises.

Hazel obliged like girls do—like sisters do—and stuck her lips out and closed her eyes. She felt the cold lip gloss streaking across her mouth. She felt Eve's face close to hers. She could feel her hot breath on her cheeks.

"Okay, now smack them together so it doesn't get clumpy."

Hazel obliged.

"Now smile!"

Hazel obliged again.

"Getting there. Now eyes. Shut them."

And Hazel obliged once more. She felt Eve's fingers roll-ing back and forth on her eyelid. Hazel couldn't help smiling as she succumbed to Eve's gentle touch, but she made sure not to move her eyes. She inhaled the scent of the makeup powder and what she had come to recognize as the smell of Eve's hair.

Hazel felt Eve take a step away from her. Hazel opened her eyes. Eve was still laser focused on Hazel's face. But not in the overall sense. Hazel could see her pick out specific details. Probably the awkward slope of her nose. The size of her pores. The curve of her cheekbones.

Eve squinted briefly and then smiled with pride.

"Almost there," Eve declared, standing back and looking at Hazel in the mirror.

"Now take this off," she said, tugging gently at the bot-tom of Hazel's T-shirt. "I think you should wear some-thing sexier."

"What's the point?" Hazel asked. "There's literally no one here but us…and Silas."

"Ugh, why did you have to remind me?" Eve responded dramatically and picked her phone up off the side table and started texting. Resuming her indifference.

But Hazel wasn't ready for their time together to come to an end.

"It looks so nice out and who knows where Silas is. Let's go for a walk or explore or something."

"Fi…ne," Eve responded, her face gnarled with feigned

acrimony, and then threw down her phone and bent down to pull her sneakers over her feet.

Hazel tugged at Eve's elbow to hurry her along and as Hazel and Eve walked out of their bedroom, Hazel snuck a glance at herself in the mirror once more. She tried catching her reflection with only a subtle movement of the eyes. She wanted to see herself as she looked to others now. For the first time she could remember, she liked what she saw. Wearing Eve's makeup and walking beside her, Hazel felt prettier, wittier. Cooler. She felt the possibility of reinvention pulsing through her blood. Her new life was upon her.

26

H azel led Eve out the door at the side of the house. They had taken the path down to the lake many times already, and Hazel felt a pull toward the woods on the other side of the yard. The crowd of thick trees with their serpentine roots protruding from the earth seemed simultaneously impenetrable and enticing. Hazel took a small step in the direction of the edge of the trees.

"Let's go that way!" Eve shrieked in excitement. "I've never gone that way before!" Eve was always craving newness.

As they reached the threshold of the trees and the cabin got lost in the distance behind them, Hazel thought about the twins. How they always appeared to be in a world all their own. She considered the belief that there was something, some place, in this world that only the two of them could see was definition of siblinghood. Or love. Hazel felt a submerged, prickling sense of happiness as she navigated the indistinct path in the woods with Eve. With her sister.

Stacks of white stones were oriented as if they were the entrance to a pathway. There was evidence of a prior clearing, but it was overgrown with sticks and weeds.

"Ooh. Let's follow this!" Eve's energy was building.

Back at home in Verona, Hazel had felt a frantic presence of something trapped inside her. Something big and important that wanted to come out. Something that was all her own. Not her mother's, or Cam's or the twins'. Something that was meant to be wild. Unencumbered. She wanted to experience newness. Traverse boundaries. And here she was doing it. With Eve. Surviving more and more on adrenaline. Living in the moment. Preparing for her new life.

The outline of the path was becoming increasingly difficult to decipher as they marched over budding plants and fallen leaves. The woods were quiet, not a word spoken, but both Hazel and Eve were radiating energy. The silence intensified the reality of being out there by themselves. They climbed over sprawling bushes and fallen sticks. They swiveled their heads to take in the crackle of the branches and buzzing of insects, and the patter of little animal paws.

Hazel had her eyes on the back of Eve's heels moving rhythmically, when her feet stopped abruptly in the dirt. Her head tilted back, her long, flowing locks now reaching down to her butt. Hazel followed the line of her gaze.

A pergola, at least ten feet tall, emerged in front of them. It was strange to see wood so neatly ordered in a geometric grid amongst the gnarled and sprawling trunks and branches of the wild trees. The legs of the entranceway, firmly planted in the soil, appeared to grow straight and strong directly from the earth. The structure itself was erect and rigid, but the vines hanging down from it were twisted and winding. They poured over the roof and meandered around the wooden posts. The leaves of the vines were ornate and ambrosial, bursting freely outward in every direction. Some of the leaves appeared brown and untended at their tips, but it didn't detract from the lifelike quality of the thick, verdant cloak wrapped maternally around the frame. It almost appeared as if the whole thing were breathing.

It was enchanting.

First Eve and then Hazel inched toward it, so as not to disrupt it.

Hazel pulled the tips of her fingers down along the wooden post on the right side of the entranceway. As she crouched down and reached the base, her pointer dipped into a slight groove in the wood, stained in a slightly darker color.

Silas's signature cube.

Eve was now standing before the opening in the front, the tips of her toes a centimeter from the shadow line of the overhanging vines. Eve turned her head toward Hazel. Her eyes were glowing and thirsty for more adventure.

Hazel stood up and walked the few steps over toward Eve until their hips were touching. The entrance was darker than Hazel expected. The pergola appeared to stretch several yards back but the distance was distorted and obscured with only a luminous, and oddly two-dimensional, circle at the exit, so they couldn't gauge the distance. Light shone through the tunnel in random beams between the spaces in the leaf cover.

The girls held each other by the hand and apprehensively entered. The air was cooler and more fresh underneath the cover of the leaves. The earth felt moist and soft beneath their feet, occasionally making a faint gushing noise as they pressed their feet in.

Then Eve let out a guttural, exploding shout. It was short and piercing. And then her shout turned into a vivid, fervent laugh. Hazel yelped, too. The loud freakish sound amplified and then diminished the quiet and tension that had previously engulfed them.

Hazel smiled and then yelped again, and laughed and took off into a run. Eve dashed off behind her and with just a few long strides they reached the opposite end of the pergola, the clamor of their voices rippling off into the woods.

The ground sloped down in a slight gradient and small gray stones of varying geometries and sizes lined another short path into a clearing. There were the remnants of a beautifully constructed garden that appeared to have once been tended with great care and contemplation, despite evidence of current neglect.

There were neatly tilled dirt rectangles, some with fences around them and narrow stone-lined walkways between them. Smashed flowerpots exploding with soil and chipped ceramic orbs were interspersed around the site. A rusty wheelbarrow was turned over on its side and a pair of gloves and sneakers that had been stiffened and distorted from rain and the sun lay in one of the fenced-in areas. There was a bench off to the right that had been scratched and defecated on by woodland critters but still maintained the elegance of its form. The armrests curled down gracefully into the seat, which was gently curved to accommodate the roundness of a body. A stack of stones formed a short set of steps up to a grassy area that was matted with rotting leaves. A tire swing hung over the area from a substantial but old tree branch above. A thick sinewy spiderweb stretched across the entire center of the tire. On the adjacent branch hung a bird feeder with scraps of pecked-at seeds and pellets. In the corner of the area was an assortment of bold, colorful flowers resting in a large basket that caught Hazel's eye.

The richness of the amber marigolds and silky tulips with long stems, the vitality of their nourished petals, the stability of their long green stems lay there in sharp contrast to the drab, crumbling, neglected objects that surrounded them.

Drawn to the flowers, Hazel stepped forward gingerly, so as not to disturb the sanctuary. When she crouched down to take the flowers up in her hands, she noticed some worn painted red lettering on the end of the basket.

Torrey's Picks. The letters were delicate and feminine, and slanted gently and elegantly backward.

Hazel twisted the basket toward her to look for more. Behind that basket, originally hidden from sight, was another, smaller basket with similarly graceful lettering, but pinker and more youthful, carrying a teeny pair of gardening gloves.

Ruby's Picks. The letters curled at the ends and concluded in playful dots.

"Who are Torrey and Ruby?" Eve yelled from behind Hazel too loudly, given the quiet of the place.

Hazel flinched, startled by Eve's voice. Hazel hadn't realized Eve had been towering behind her in her transfixion with the baskets. And, in earnest, the whole garden. The whole shrine.

Hazel twirled her body and started to say, "I don't know,"

but paused when she observed a figure emerging from the end of the pergola. As it moved closer, the fuzzy outline of its silhouette hardened into the unambiguous contour of Silas's broad, strong body.

There was suddenly a feeling that they were in a place they were not meant to be. Seeing things they were not meant to see. Hazel's body tensed, and she could sense that the same was true for Eve.

"You girls really leave no rock unturned, huh?" His tenor was buoyant and breezy as he marched toward them with his typically clunky strides.

"Torrey and Ruby are just two gals I know. Well, more like used to know." He winked, casually. But Hazel could detect restraint in his voice.

There was something fabricated about his vagueness. It gave the impression that he was deeply and intimately connected with these facets he pretended not to know. That Torrey and Ruby, whoever they were, once meant something to him. Probably still meant something to him. Something big and painful even.

Hazel and Eve remained still and quiet.

Silas sat down on the old bench and tapped on the seat, urging Hazel and Eve to join him. Both girls slowly broke free from their fixed positions to join Silas.

"What *is* this place?" Eve asked brashly, ignoring the thick tension that had enveloped the garden since Silas came, before her bottom even met the bench.

He pulled three cold cans of Coke from a small bag he was holding. They had little beads of cold around the outside.

There was a crisp crack when he opened one and handed it over to Eve.

"Well, this place *was* a garden." Silas opened a second can and pretended to take a sip before handing it to Hazel. He leaned back, crossed his legs and extended his arms along the back of the bench, one arm resting casually behind each girl's back.

"But it appears it has been turned over to the woods now." He smiled and took a big long gulp from his can. Hazel watched his throat ripple.

"Cool," Eve said and returned to her drink. "I like that thing," she continued, pointing at the pergola.

Hazel had her eyes on Silas, though. There was a quality of discomfort in his position. She detected a tension in his chest and shoulders. A disquiet in his legs that he crossed and recrossed as if to displace or dispel it. His long dark lashes were shining. The green in his eyes was dustier than usual.

After another brief moment of silence, Silas abruptly lunged forward.

"Well, that's enough of this," he said impatiently, interrupting nothing but quiet. "Let's head on up to the house, yeah?"

Eve popped right up off the bench, sipping from her frosty Coke, and walked briskly back into the pergola.

Hazel lingered on the bench for a moment, as Silas turned around to follow. There were two big roses, one a vivid pink and one a deep ruby, sticking out of his back pocket. The flowers were crushed from Silas neglecting them as he'd sat there on the bench with Hazel and Eve, drinking soda.

27

The next day was hot and sunny again in Grandor, and Hazel found herself in the kitchen quietly swirling the last bits of her cereal in its milky lake and trying not to make eye contact with Silas and Eve as they did the same. She did not want to appear too desperate for attention. Eve poured herself a glass of water, making the sound of the ice clanking against the glass the only sound in the room.

Silas eventually looked up from his newspaper to greet the girls. He did it with a curious weight in his smile.

"Listen, gals, I'm sorry to do this but I just got word of a big job with a deadline pretty soon. I really hate to leave you to your own devices when there's so much fun we could be having together today, but I've gotta take a day to get this stuff done."

Hazel and Eve both looked up but didn't respond.

Hazel had the impression that although she was absorbing the scene, there was an energy in the air, scattering around her, that she couldn't identify. A shifting momentum. A cause for unease that she couldn't quite grasp.

"You know how it goes. Get the materials. Get into the shop. Cut, saw, sand, hammer, you name it."

She had never heard Silas talk like this. Hint at even the smallest particle of sentimentality. Or remorse. He always carried himself so confidently. As if at every moment he was doing precisely the thing he wanted to be doing. And that nothing could sway him otherwise. This wavering was unconvincing, sliding across his lips.

Neither Hazel nor Eve uttered a word, but Hazel found herself nodding.

"I knew you girls would understand," Silas said.

But he grabbed his car keys and rubbed his palm against Eve's head.

"You know I hate when you do that!" she said, not fully in good spirits, as she tried to duck out of the way.

"I know, but it's our thing now," he responded, unfazed by her annoyance. And then he winked and slipped out the door.

Hazel and Eve returned to the quiet. Eve scrolled through her phone and Hazel scanned the kitchen looking for things she could busy her hands with by cleaning. She was starting to really hate the quiet.

The sounds of home back in Verona always vexed her, too—the twins babbling nonsense, the murmurs of her mother and Cam scheming their next parenting move, the drone of the TV as she took care of the boys at her mother's request. But this silence, it was worse.

With nothing else noticeably dirty in sight, Hazel rinsed

a set of large bowls from last night's dinner that were possibly already clean.

And then Eve's luring voice broke the silence.

"Let's go see if there are any hot dudes with boats."

Hazel rolled her eyes. "I think we both know that's not an option here."

"Can't you let a girl dream?" Eve responded, and flipped her hair over to one side of her head. "Plus, I need something new to post that doesn't look like it's part of this rickety old cabin."

Hazel wasn't convinced.

"Come on. I'll get one of you laughing or looking cool by the lake. People have been asking me for sister pics."

Hazel couldn't help it but she swelled with excitement at the idea of appearing on Eve's feed. It wasn't even about how many followers she had. It was more about memorializing their connection. Documenting their togetherness. Showing the world that they were a part of each other. It was curious, even to Hazel, that she could spend all these days with Eve and still feel a gaping hole in their relationship without being pictured in her digital world. Hazel thought back to the moments she'd first come across Eve, clicking through her Wassup? profile. She had learned so much about her that way. And surely others were looking for a glimpse into the life and thoughts of Eve Warrington. Hazel felt another rush course through her veins at the idea that she could be a part of that story.

She sat up from her position and said, "Fine," as casually as she could muster.

Hazel followed Eve, who had her phone clutched between

her fingers, down toward the lake's edge. Hazel took note of the workshop as they passed it and pressed her ear in that direction to see if she could get even a hint of what Silas was up to in there, but she didn't hear anything.

As they traipsed down the path and toward the water, Hazel made out the silhouette of a figure lying on the dock. It was almost certainly a man's body, legs splayed out and hands resting behind the head. With just a few more steps closer toward it, the outline of the sweeping curls of hair, the broad hairy chest and shoulders, and the shape of the aviator sunglasses revealed themselves. By now, Eve had caught on, too.

"Oh my god, is that Silas, literally doing nothing when he told us he was working all day?"

It couldn't be anyone other than Silas. As they got closer, they could identify a cooler filled with icy beers and an upright fishing rod lodged into the dock keeping him company as he lay there. It was almost comical how bad a liar he was. He could have gone anywhere that wasn't that dock.

"He really wanted an excuse to get away from us, huh?" Eve threw her hands up, apparently stricken but not showing any signs of distress. "Ugh, he's so moody sometimes! He did this last year, too, but whatever."

Hazel, on the other hand, felt as if she had been punched in the gut. She thought of her mother. The great void in Hazel's life Jane had created by inviting Cam and the twins into their home. The gaping hole that Hazel felt Silas and Eve to be filling. All of a sudden, she was empty again. Stuck in a sad limbo of home and alone.

The feeling was compact and familiar. She felt it right in her heart.

"Whatever." Eve shrugged and pushed Hazel into a beam of sunlight caressing the trunk of a tree. "Stand there and look out onto the lake. I'll snap a few and we can decide which one to post."

Hazel debated whether this was what she'd come all the way to the lake for. And in the absence of answers, she stood next to the tree and looked out toward the lake like Eve told her. She couldn't help but stare at Silas's body sprawled on that dock as she did it, though.

"Why do you think he lied to us?" Hazel blurted out. She couldn't keep it inside. She was so scared it would all come crumbling down.

"Who knows! Parents are weird. Sometimes they love you, sometimes they really, really act like dicks."

"Tell me about it," Hazel responded, feeling increasingly comforted.

"So, sometimes I'm a dick right back," Eve said smugly and then whipped her long hair around to her other shoulder.

"What do you mean?" Hazel responded, the anxiety creeping back up in her now.

"I mean, that's pretty much why I'm here anyway."

There was a pause that was long enough to indicate that it may be the end of the conversation, but then Eve continued.

"My parents only told me that my dad wasn't really my dad like two years ago. I was so pissed. They lied to me my entire life and expected me to just sit around and take it? No! I had to punish them. So I found Silas online. To punish them. It was seriously so easy. They *freaked* out when I told them I had arranged with Silas to come here. I think they thought I was going to like Silas and Grandor better than I like my life at home. What a joke. Silas is a total mess and this place is a shithole."

Hazel's heart was pounding and her breathing became audible. Eve continued on without a trace of pain behind her words.

"But the more I say I want to come back, the more and more upset my parents get, so it seems like a good idea to keep doing it. At least until I graduate high school. And, oh my god, when you responded to my Wassup? message, I was like 'This is perfect!' Seriously, you should have seen my mom's face. It's not like they're going to give me a sibling, so they're totally panicked that this is the final straw and I'll never come back home. Ha!"

Hazel could barely breathe. She felt an intense pressure behind her eyes and down in her throat. She placed her hand on a tree next to her to make sure she wouldn't fall over if her knees gave out. The cracks were starting to form and her whole life, her whole new life, could sink through. She hoped it wouldn't. She hoped so badly it wouldn't. Eve swung her hair back to the other side and flashed another smile. She may have detected something in Hazel's face because she dropped her smile.

"No offense or anything."

There was a big, thick pause.

"Oka-yyyyy, well," Eve said with wide eyes. "Guess we should get back to the house."

Hazel thought she heard Eve mutter "awkward," as she skipped away as quickly as she could back up the hill. Hazel sat right down in the grass and alternated between looking down at Silas on the dock and up at Eve walking away.

★ ★ ★

Later that evening, Hazel and Eve slipped right into what had become their routine of sitting in their own beds on opposite sides of the room. Eve, as usual, alternated between jamming her fingers into the screen, giggling or scowling at whatever was on the screen, taking pictures of herself and scrolling through pictures of and messages from others. Hazel, as usual, sat either observing Eve on her phone or trying to pretend like she was equally enraptured by her own. Occasionally, Eve blurted out a comment, not necessarily directed at Hazel, but she felt entitled to respond.

"Christie Channer has the best hair but I heard she gets a $400 highlight job every month even though she won't admit it."

"Tommy Dens is fucking hot but I heard he got a blow job from Rainey Popper, which makes him *a lot* less hot."

"Don't you think it's funny when people have two first names? Elizabeth Aaron has that and also yellow teeth. Once, John Spencer left an electric toothbrush in her locker for her birthday and when she opened it she cried."

"Pam Jackson went from barely an A-cup to a D in like a month. Tyler Hanner used to think she stuffed but I checked her out in the locker room before gym class and she *definitely* doesn't."

Hazel wondered if it would be better to be scrutinized by Eve, or ignored, but always netted out on scrutinized. Hazel had certainly been held under Eve's microscope and latched on to her editorial review of her body. Hazel always felt Eve appreciated her physiognomy in a way that was not as disconnected or brutal as she scrutinized others. Eve understood Hazel's body in a way she didn't have to contemplate. They had been created from the same genes, after all.

Suddenly, Eve interrupted her own trance and stared right at Hazel. Her green eyes were swirling and sparkling.

"You're not going to believe this. Connor Samuelson wants to FaceTime! He said he's going to call me in an hour."

"Who is Connor Samuelson?" Hazel asked.

And Eve just laughed, pulled her hair out of its messy bun on the top of her head and then dragged Hazel from her bed to her feet.

"Come downstairs with me," Eve urged and disappeared into the hallway with the lure of her energy trailing behind her.

Hazel instinctively followed Eve, who was racing down the stairway so quickly she appeared to be floating over several stairs at once. The energy was contagious and Hazel found herself running down the stairs, too. She finally caught up to Eve, who was standing in the cold white glow of the open refrigerator. Eve popped her head out from behind the refrigerator door when she heard Hazel's footsteps. Her green eyes had now acquired a menacing stir.

"We're getting drunk!" Eve announced without hesitation.

Hazel felt a wrenching in her gut but before she could say anything, the refrigerator door closed with a whoosh and Eve took off past Hazel and back up the stairway.

Hazel's heart and whole body immediately became heavier, and she pulled one leg and then the other up the stairs, following Eve back to their room. As Hazel reached the top of the steps, she could just make out Eve's socks sliding across the wood floor of the hallway and back into their bedroom. When Hazel entered the room, Eve was already sitting on the floor with two open beer bottles and wild eyes.

"Cheers!" Eve declared as she tilted the neck of the bottle up toward Hazel.

Hazel sank into a cross-legged seat across from Eve and clanked the neck of the bottle against Eve's.

Eve immediately tilted her head back and gulped sips of beer down. She removed the tip of the bottle from her mouth and let out a deep and grumbling belch. She cackled briefly before throwing her head back and dumping the carbonated amber liquid into her mouth again.

Hazel brought the rim of the bottle to her lips. Her tummy seized immediately at the fermented smell but she inhaled through her nose and tilted the bottle up. As soon as a drop of beer hit her tongue, her throat constricted and tummy seized again.

Hazel placed the bottle delicately on the floor.

"I'm actually okay without the beer," Hazel said, with a quiver in her voice, afraid of how Eve might react.

"Are you serious?" Eve responded. Her eyes were focused and piercing. Hazel saw black flecks in Eve's eyes she hadn't noticed before. They held the light in exotic ways that made them swirl into a deeper, darker spiral.

Hazel felt stunned. A tingling began in her cheeks and then made its way all the way down to her fingertips. She looked right back into Eve's eyes, unsure of what to do next.

"Whatever," Eve said and scooped Hazel's beer into her fingertips and repositioned herself in front of the mirror.

In seemingly opposite forces, Eve ran her fingers through

her hair to pull it straight and smooth and then rubbed her palm into the side of her head to tousle and muss it. She puckered her lips and pressed her chest out and pulled her shirt down and moved her head from side to side, keeping her eyes fixed on her own eyes as she did it.

It was hard for Hazel to tell whether Eve was harboring any disappointment with Hazel's declining to participate or whether she had swiftly moved on to more important things.

Hazel observed quietly as Eve guzzled down beer after beer between painting her eyes and cheeks and lips with makeup. Neither Hazel nor Eve lost focus for a moment.

And then, Eve's phone vibrated against the floor. Eve's spine straightened even further and she gave herself one last look in the mirror before snatching the phone and hopping up into her bed.

"Don't make a peep!" Eve said, looking back at Hazel for an instant before returning her attention to the phone.

As the phone vibrated in her hand, Eve lay back against her pillows and then pulled a few strands of hair in front of her face. She found a moment of stillness, exhaled, and then pressed the green answer button on the phone.

"Hey," she said casually.

Hazel waited to hear the sound of this famous Connor Samuelson. She expected something raspy and upbeat. Youthful but mature. But she just heard nothing.

"Hey," Eve said again, with the same tone, staring into the face of the phone.

"Ughhhh!" Eve grumbled, ditching the casual glamour look and throwing her phone down into the bedding. "No service!"

The phone rang again and Eve held it up in front of her face.

"Hey," she tried again. But this time with a little more panic in her voice.

This time a sound did emerge from the other end of the phone but it was chopped and crackling and garbled.

Eve brought the phone close up to her lips. "Helloooo!" she said, now without any trace of collectedness. Another spotty jumble of words escaped the phone and then got cut.

Eve collapsed over her phone and pressed her entire face and chest into the comforter of her bed.

"I fucking hate this place!" Eve yelled again. Her words were muffled by the sheets but Hazel could tell that they were hot with ire.

Hazel got up from her spot on the floor and scurried into the bathroom, trying to get out of the path of Eve's rage. As she slipped behind the door, she saw Eve's phone fly across the room, denting the wall and falling to the floor with a thud.

"I seriously fucking hate it!" Eve shouted. This time her words were clear and open to the air for all to hear.

"Who lives like this without cell service or Wi-Fi?" she continued. "Seriously! It's like you don't want to have a life."

There was a moment of silence and Hazel contemplated whether it would be a good time to head back into the room.

But then she heard Eve's words ring out again.

"Everyone here is a huge fucking loser," she shouted manically.

Hazel pressed her back to the door and tried to ignore everything happening on the other side of it.

"A hu-u-u-ge fucking loser."

Hazel brought her hands to her ears and pressed them tightly against her head, hoping to prevent hearing another sound.

"Get me the fuck out of here!"

There was a moment of silence that filled Hazel with relief. But then Eve filled it again with more sharp, piercing words that ripped right through her.

"These summer visits are a fucking scam to my parents, anyway. What the hell am I still here for?"

No matter how hard she pushed her hands into her ears, Hazel could not keep out the ferocity of Eve's words.

28

When Hazel woke up the next morning, she felt a new force in her bedroom. A new force everywhere. The house felt more vulnerable. Unshielded and permeable. Everything still felt tired. Her bones, her shoulders, her neck, her back, her heart were still tense and knotted. Hazel had stirred through the night, thoughts of this new family in this cabin by the lake disintegrating ricocheting and clanking around in her mind.

Hazel rubbed her eyes, sat upright and looked toward Eve's bed. It was empty. An intentional signal that Eve was no longer interested, Hazel thought.

Hazel moved into the bathroom and splashed water over her face. She heard the hum of chatter down the stairs and followed the sounds to the kitchen.

Eve and Silas were sitting at the table and Hazel stood quietly at the bottom of the staircase, observing. Was she welcome there?

Silas brought a mug to his lips in between his conversation with Eve and made eye contact with Hazel over the edge of the cup. He brought his mug down to the table gently, revealing a full smile.

"Whatcha doin' over there, Hazel?"

Hazel's belly warmed at the levity in his question. She took a step closer toward the kitchen. She could feel that force shifting. She could feel a comfort, a warmth, return to her.

"Come have a seat—we're making some plans for the day." Silas patted the seat at the table beside him, slamming his big palm into the chair.

Hazel took another step forward. Still gingerly.

"What is with you today, kiddo?" Silas got up from his seat and walked to meet Hazel in the corner of the kitchen. He looked into Hazel's eyes. His own softened at the corners as he did. And it melted Hazel's core. He did care. Her lips pressed into a smile. Silas's green eyes lit back up as he rubbed his palm on the top of Hazel's hair and then brought his arm around her shoulders. He walked with her to the kitchen table and they both sat down.

"Someone was snoring last night!" Eve said, looking at Hazel out of the corner of her eye.

"Oh, shut up," Hazel retorted, emboldened from Silas's pat on the head, and then snatched a piece of toast from Eve's plate and bit down on it tauntingly.

"I made that for you, you dork!" Eve said with a big proud smile.

"Well, it is delicious," Hazel replied, trying to be casual.

THAT SUMMER IN MAINE

It felt good to be the subject of Eve's anything. Toast, taunts, smiles. Anything but quiet.

"I thought we could go to the craft fair today?" Silas interrupted. The girls turned their attention toward him. Eve lit up.

"Really?! I heard that place is cool!"

Silas nodded confidently.

"I also heard that's where you met my mom," Eve added. "Is it true?"

Silas shifted in his chair and rubbed the scruff on his chin as if he needed to pull a response from his own lips. He cleared his throat, still squirming in his place.

"Well, is it?" Eve rushed.

"It is," Silas answered earnestly, but through a tension in his throat. "It is actually where I met both of your mothers."

Hazel felt her tummy do a flip. This was the first moment it occurred to Hazel that her mother was anyone else's before she was hers. That her mother had a life, and possibly a love, before there was Hazel. Sure, she understood the biology of it, but she had never considered the story. She had never considered that this man before her, her father, and her mother had ever shared anything. A first glance, a romance, an anything. It made her feel more connected to her mother to think that there were so many parts of her story before Cam and the twins came into the picture.

"We-i-rd," Eve said, interrupting the tense silence with eyes wider than ever.

It brought Hazel back to reality.

Silas pressed his lips together and rubbed the scruff on his chin some more. He wasn't squirming anymore, but there was a self-reflective glint in his eye. An embarrassment, perhaps. A sadness, perhaps.

"You're going to *have* to tell us that story sometime," Eve declared.

Silas chuckled and shook his head back and forth in Eve's direction. "You can ask your mothers about this one," he said, raising one eyebrow.

"I will!" Eve challenged back, surely telling the truth. She whipped out her phone and looked up at Silas.

"First of all, I know your phone doesn't work here. Second of all, you watch too much reality television, princess."

Eve's shoulders slunk and Silas stood up and rubbed the top of Eve's hair.

"I hate when you do that, you know," Eve said as she tried to duck away, still smiling. "It's such a dad thing."

"Well, I like it," Silas said. He paused, apparently catching his own earnestness. "Go ahead and get dressed. We're leaving in fifteen."

Eve hopped up to stand on the seat of her chair, raised her arms and began swaying her hips around. "We're going to the market. Woo!"

Silas rolled his eyes but was charmed as always by the theatrics.

"Get down, ya weirdo," he muttered as he left the kitchen. "I'll wait for you in the truck."

The market was full of everything. People and food and things and energy. Flimsy white tents lined the street in rows and rows. People poured out of tents and walkways in every direction. Piles of leafy greens were stacked on tables.

Fruits in purples and reds and oranges overflowed in their baskets. The sun was bright and the warble of chatter filled the air. Hazel barely managed a single deep inhale before Eve grabbed her hand and gave it a squeeze. Her hand and arm and eyes pulsed with energy.

"Oh my god, those honey sticks! I haven't had those since I was a kid!"

Eve pointed straight at a modest white tent a few yards away. The centerpiece was a single rickety foldout table lined with bell jars, each jar with its own brightly colored collection of plastic honey-filled straws. Each jar was labeled with its flavor in hastily written cursive with a thick and apparently unforgiving black marker. Shades of purples and reds for watermelon, or grape, or cinnamon. Shades of yellow and green for green apple, or lemon lime, or banana. Even blues for blueberry and blue raspberry.

Eve looked up at Silas with longing and earnest eyes.

"Can we get some?"

Eve looked and sounded so small, so young, so daughterly standing there next to Silas, neck craned back, asking for sweets.

Silas smiled, dug his hand into his pocket and pulled out a big handful of change. He extended his palm and Eve, and then Hazel, picked the quarters and dimes out from the pile and dashed over to the tent.

Eve delicately pulled a stick from the jar labeled Root Beer. She held it up in front of her eyes and tilted it back and forth, the light passing right through the deep brown honey until it was translucent at the edges. It looked holy. Meaningful.

Eve whipped her hair around and thrust the stick in front of Hazel. She held it triumphantly between Hazel's two eyes, centimeters from the bridge of her nose. Hazel found her eyes inadvertently crossed as she stared at the thin stick.

"You gotta try this," Eve urged, almost short of breath in her excitement. "I don't care what anyone says, root beer is by far the best flavor. You want one?"

Before Hazel could nod, Eve had drawn another root beer stick from its jar and turned to the woman behind the table, who glanced up from underneath the wide brim of her straw hat once she felt Eve's energy turn her way.

"How much for these two?" Eve asked eagerly.

"Twenty-five cents a pop. So that's fifty in total."

"Twenty-five cents?" Eve uncurled her hand to count the coins in her palm. "We can get like ten more!"

Eve immediately turned her attention back to the row of jars, manically pulling sticks from their jars and clutching them in her grip. Hazel just stood and watched. As Eve moved down the table, she would pull out some more and return others to their places, until she presented a pile of assorted honey sticks—no single color repeating except for the root beer—in front of the woman at the table.

"We'll take these!" Eve declared, stomping one foot down into the asphalt and completing one decisive nod.

"Okay, then," the woman said with an upbeat relief in her voice. "That'll be $2.50. I'll throw in those root beer ones for free."

The woman winked and Eve's eyes lit up again. Eve shuffled coin after coin from her palm onto the table until she made up the change and then squeezed Hazel's hand again and took off down the row of tents.

"Thanks, lady!" she yelled as she darted away, before pulling Hazel through the crowd. Eve's excitement was contagious, infectious. Hazel felt alive and spirited with her hand in Eve's hand, even as her feet clomped awkwardly beneath her.

They landed at an emptier spot behind the tents and Eve pulled out the two brown root beer straws. She pinched her index finger and thumb around one edge. A gentle click ensued. Eve smiled and then placed the end of the stick in her mouth and then slid her fingers up the straw, pushing the honey onto her tongue. She closed her eyes and her shoulders sank down.

"They are. So. Freakin'. Good."

Eve squeezed another bit into her mouth.

"My mom used to bring these back for me from her trips." Eve's voice had lowered and calmed. The corners of her eyes and mouth softened. "She would come home after a few days away and I would run into her arms for a big hug and she would crouch down and let me bowl her over. I wouldn't even let her put her bags down. And after a few seconds of her arms around me, squeezing my little body so tight, she would reach back over my shoulder with two root beer honey sticks. One for me and one for her. And we would pop them open and eat one."

And then, as if distracted from her own story, Eve's shoulders perked back up and her hip popped back out to the side.

"Ew, I was such a loser running at her for a hug like a little baby." She turned her attention to Hazel. "Want one?"

"Sure," Hazel replied, pulling the stick from Eve's outstretched hand.

Hazel popped the edge of the straw open and squeezed the smallest drop of honey onto her tongue. It was so sweet and full of flavor.

"These *are* good," Hazel exclaimed and pulled her fingers up the tube to enjoy some more. The viscous honey swirled around her tongue. She quickly reached the end of the stick.

Eve extended her hands out with the full pile of purchased straws. More greens and yellows and reds and blues but no dark brown root beer.

"I don't want to even try another flavor!" Hazel joked in a moment. "The root beer is just so good."

"Well, that can be arranged," Eve replied and reached into her back pocket for two more straws, curiously separate from the rest of the pile.

"Whoa, where'd those come from?" Hazel asked, her voice a bit shaky and nervous as her stomach did a turn.

"Stole 'em," Eve said casually, but her eyes were aglow again.

"Very funny," Hazel responded, now relaxing a little bit.

"I'm serious." Eve looked firmer this time. More insistent. Something started bubbling within Hazel. First in her belly and then it made its way up to her chest. Her heart was beating faster and her ears were hot.

"What the hell, Eve. Give those back!"

Eve remained nonchalant, with her hip still popped out to one side.

"What's the point? They're basically free, anyway."

Eve flipped her long hair from one side to the other and then rolled her eyes.

"Don't be such a prude, Hazel. It's just fun. Trust me. You get a little rush when you do it!" Eve's eyes widened and bulged when she said *rush*. The greens in Eve's irises swirled and raved.

"I don't trust you!" The words leaped off Hazel's tongue before she could catch then. Hazel was surprised they were even within her at all. But the way they burst out of her, the way they were flung like a dagger right at Eve, she knew she must have meant it somewhere.

Hazel and Eve locked eyes for a moment. Just long enough for the weight of the words to thicken the air between them. Just long enough for the words to begin sinking into their chests.

Hazel interrupted the stillness and abruptly grabbed the sticks from Eve's hand. She marched confidently back in the direction of the tent they had just come from. Her legs and arms were tingling. Her mind was racing and her heart was beating. She expected to feel Eve's hand on her shoulder any moment. Yanking her back. Trying to convince her to play along with her antics. To bewitch her with her hair and her fun and her everything else. To step further into her world and ignore her own.

But there was nothing. And Hazel found herself back in the tent, looking at the rim of the straw hat of the woman behind the table. Hazel slammed the two honey sticks onto the table.

"We ended up with too many," Hazel said, waiting for the woman's head to turn up. But she continued to stare down.

"It was an accident."

Still nothing.

"We didn't count right, I think."

The woman brought her hand to the honey sticks and slowly pulled them toward her. She looked up from beneath her hat. She had kind brown eyes. They were big and full. Earnest. Wise.

"Your friend seems like trouble," she said plainly, and then turned her head back down.

"She's my sister, actually," Hazel said with more pride than she expected. More pride than she wanted to embody.

29

Hazel turned from her position and looked Eve's way, but there was just an empty space where she had been standing. Hazel turned her head further around toward the place where she'd left Silas. The space was filled with people walking back and forth. It was just her in this whole big place. This whole new world.

Still buzzing from the confrontation with Eve and the things that oozed out of her, Hazel inhaled and try to take it all in. All the people and things and energy.

She observed all these people at the market in the morning. Saying "good morning" as they passed each other in their rows. Sifting through the basket of apples until they found the perfect one. Trying on earrings and bracelets and scarves. Showing them off to their partner with a tilt of their head and a smile. Exchanging dollars and vegetables and handshakes and hugs. She thought of where she usually was while all those things were happening: tucked away in a creaky old house with Eve and Silas. Hidden away at the end of a long dusty road amid towering, draping trees.

She felt energized to be a part of it all here at the market. She took a step into the moving crowd and began walking through the rows in a swiftly moving mass of people. Inertia kept her going and going through the market. Passing tent after tent. Table after table brimming with foods and colors and things.

Hazel felt present. Alive and independent and back in her body. There was a surprising lightness, a surprising sense of relief, without Eve or Silas. She hadn't realized how heavy and viscous the air was in Silas's house until this moment. How much it must have been pressing down on her. The air felt thinner here. Easier to breathe.

From the corner of her eye, Hazel spotted a two-seated stroller nestled in the corner of one of the tents. There was one precious light-haired little boy in each seat. They were both dressed in the same blue shorts and hunter green T-shirts, both speckled with crumbs and drool. Their thin blond hair both falling to the side in the same way. Their cheeks similarly pink and smooth. Their big eyes in the same position on their little heads. The corners of their little lips turned up in the same curvature.

Two little twins right in front of her. Little Griffin and little Trevor right in front of her.

Hazel felt her center soften and then a magnetic pull toward the little boys. Without directing them herself, Hazel's legs began to move beneath her.

She crouched down in front of the stroller inches from the boys' faces. They both began kicking their legs out and cooing in excitement. Those sounds softened her center even more. She felt a warmth around her heart.

Still crouched, Hazel looked straight into the eyes of the one on the left. Big and blue and glistening with a blank and gentle ease. Like Griffin. Like Trevor. The baby looked back at her. Straight in her eye. She saw the innocent ease in his existence. A calm optimism. A sweet and simple happiness.

She thought of the times at home lying on her bed, Griffin and Trevor curled up in front of her by her belly. Giggling and reaching their small hands out. The feeling of their soft palms on her lips. The gentle scratch of their little nails along her nose. Their little whimpers and outstretched arms when they wanted their pacifiers. The gentle suction on her fingertips when she placed the pacifiers into their mouths.

Hazel noticed a pacifier in the lap of one of the boys in front of her. And then she felt a tingle of longing in her fingertips. Hazel picked up the pacifier and placed it in the boy's mouth. There was light tug on her fingers and he began sucking. It gave Hazel a warm chill, and then the longing in her fingertips moved to her arms and chest and heart. It moved into a longing for Griffin's and Trevor's bodies against her body. A baby's body against her body again.

As automatically as her legs had started moving toward the stroller, her fingers started moving to the seat belt of the stroller. She unfastened the buckle and slid her hands behind the little boy's back. His back was soft and warm.

Hazel stood up from her crouched position, lifted the boy and pressed his belly into her face. The smell was a little flowery with the faint acidity of old milk. She inhaled it deeply. She closed her eyes and thought of the boys. Of home. She ached for it.

And then she felt a hand on her shoulder, accompanied by a frantic shriek. "My baby!"

Hazel shook her head and relinquished the child as if her hands had been on a hot stove.

A sharp pain seared through Hazel's head, and she closed her eyes to cope.

"What are you doing with my baby?" the woman yelled, her voice now shakier.

"I... I... I don't know," Hazel stuttered and took two wobbling steps backward.

"I... I..." Hazel stuttered some more, still backing away.

The woman had now picked the boy back up into her arms and pressed him against her chest. Tears were wobbling in her eyes now.

"They remind me of my brothers," Hazel explained, her voice assured and earnest now. "How I miss them."

She could see that the woman had tightened her arms around her child more thoroughly.

"I'm sorry," Hazel said in the same earnest tone, tears now welling up in her own eyes, her feet still backing her away from the scene. "I'm sorry. I don't know what I was thinking."

The woman closed her eyes and kissed the top of the boy's head.

Hazel turned away and lost herself in the rush of the crowd again, eager to get completely out of sight. He chest was rising and falling, her heartbeat quick and anxious. All of these things she didn't know she felt were oozing out of her. She didn't know what was happening inside her. What had caused her to pick that baby up. To frighten that mother like that. To shout at Eve and run from her.

Hazel's chest rose and fell some more. And her heart skipped and skipped.

And then she caught a glimpse of the back of Silas's head, his loose black curls swaying above his strong shoulders.

"Silas," Hazel tried to yell, but it came out in a whisper.

The back of his flannel shirt billowed slightly behind him as his legs paced forward. They were picking up speed.

"Silas," she said again, this time louder, but he still didn't hear her. Hazel widened her stride and increased her pace, trying to at least maintain the guise of a walk. Her arms were swinging at her sides like a pendulum, thrusting her forward.

"Silas," Hazel yelled again, this time certain her shout was in earshot.

She rocked onto her toes and started a light jog after him. As she rounded the side of his body and observed the profile of his face, Hazel could tell his attention was locked on a woman just a few feet ahead of him. She had deeply tanned skin and was wearing a flowing dress held up by two slim straps around her shoulders. Her arms were long and casual at her side, and the crisp white of the dress contrasted sharply with her skin. Her long honey-colored hair hung down her back and swayed and flecked with sunshine as she walked.

Silas was now within inches of the woman and reached out to touch her shoulder. Hazel stopped in her tracks so as not to disturb the moment.

"Torrey," he said hopefully as the woman flinched and then whipped around in the direction of Silas's hand. Her eyebrows were pressed up like two exclamation marks and her jaw and shoulders were tense.

And then Silas tensed up himself. His knees locked back and his shoulders crept up toward his ears. He pulled at the scruff on his chin and then nervously pulled at his curly hair.

"I'm, uh, sorry, miss."

The woman stood there for another moment.

"I just thought you were someone else." His voice had sunk into a garble.

"No worries," the woman responded, a restored pep in her voice. And then she took off again.

Hazel walked toward Silas, who was raking his fingers through his hair.

"Who's Torrey?" she asked.

Silas popped his head back up, a bit startled.

"Ah, just an old friend," he said, attempting a cheery tone.

"Wait, isn't that the same name I saw on the buckets in the garden?"

Silas looked stunned for a moment and then appeared to pretend he hadn't heard her. He placed his palm into Hazel's back and rubbed it around.

"How are you doing, kiddo?" He had stretched a smile across his face now and looked down at Hazel. She could sense a solemnity in his eyes. A longing.

They held eye contact for a brief instant, until Silas's attention was diverted over Hazel's shoulder.

"Ah, look. There's Eve. Eve! Eve!" he shouted and waved his hands around.

Hazel turned around and saw Eve in the crowd. Her sunglasses were perched on top of her head in front of the wild mess of hair collected behind it. She walked over slowly and confidently, her hips rocking to one side and then the other.

Hazel's tummy flipped as her mind raced back to what had just transpired with Eve. Her heart beat and clanked around behind her ribs.

Would Eve talk to her? Look at her? Acknowledge her?

Eve planted her feet right next to Hazel. Without a millisecond of delay, she flipped another brown honey stick in front of Hazel's nose.

"Bought ya another one!" she said, the words buoyant and upbeat.

Hazel looked at Eve skeptically but couldn't hold back a smile.

"Seriously. Bought it with my own money. Well, his own money." She stuck her thumb out in Silas's direction.

Hazel snatched the honey stick from her hand, popped the top and brought the honey to her lips.

Eve winked and then brought her sunglasses in front of her eyes.

Eve turned her attention toward Silas.

"Can we get out of here or what, old man?" she said harshly.

"Oh, I'm an old man now, huh?" Silas retorted.

"Every dad is an old man!" she replied, not missing a beat.

Silas pressed his lips together and nodded slowly. "Well, I guess I am a dad. So I guess that makes me old."

He looked at Eve and then at Hazel. Really looked at them. With a weight in his eyes. He pressed his lips together and nodded some more. As if he was assuring himself of a truth. A truth of his fatherhood. A truth of his daughters. These daughters. These two girls in front of him.

And then his eyes went vacant for an instant. And then he blinked.

"I'll grab the truck. You guys wait here for a minute."

Eve crossed her legs under her and dropped to the ground to sit.

"Can you believe our moms met Silas at this popsicle stand?" Eve rested her elbow on the inside of her knee, and her head in her palm.

Hazel looked back out at the market. She thought of her mother in this place, all those years ago. The sound of Silas's horn blared and interrupted her from the thoughts.

30

Night fell and Silas prepared another dinner for the three of them using the meats and produce and cheese he'd got at the market.

Hazel pulled her chair underneath the table. The legs of the chair screeching against the floor created an unfamiliar echo in the room that made Hazel aware of the hollowness in the space. There was usually a cacophony in the background, pans slamming together and chatter between the girls to fill the air. But this evening, it was quieter.

"Dig in," Silas said with feigned cheeriness. Now the sounds of forks and knives clacking against the plates made Hazel even more aware of the quiet.

Hazel thought about what to say to break the silence. She could feel her words start to rise but she would pore over each syllable in her mind until they sounded too lame to say aloud. So she returned her gaze to her plate and pressed her food around it.

The absence of words was so heavy in the air. The tension in the room only increased as everyone waited for someone else to say something. It was like being at home all over again. She desperately wanted it to go back to how it was when they'd first arrived.

A feeling crept up from deep within her that this whole thing was so stupid. That, of course, it wasn't going to work. That, of course, these people wouldn't like her. That, of course, there was no new family to be created. No new love in her future. But she wanted it, so bad. She needed it. So she pushed that feeling way, way down and willed it to turn itself around.

Hazel observed Eve's every move as much as she could so that Hazel wouldn't let herself be discovered. Hazel didn't have to watch long to realize that Eve's expression was growing increasingly sour. She shifted her body position every few seconds, each movement accompanied by an indiscreet groan or sigh and a periodic eye roll so that she could make her displeasure known. She had left her utensils crossed on top of her plate and folded her arms across her chest implacably. She checked her phone a few times in her lap with apparent disappointment. Silas was sitting with one boot up on the seat of the chair next to him. One arm lay heavy on the table and the other he used to pull down on his black curls emerging from behind his ear.

"Should we make a fire later?" Hazel blurted out. Eve flinched like glass had shattered.

The silence on the other end of her question was thick and viscous.

The feeling crept up again. The terror that it wouldn't

work out. But again she willed it so far down that she hoped it would never see the light of day again.

"I think I'm going to hit the hay early tonight, Hazel," Silas responded and lifted his arm to give Hazel a characteristic rub of her hair.

"Same," Eve said and pushed her plate farther out in front of her, barely having eaten a morsel.

Silas started clearing dishes and Eve slunk upstairs, leaving Hazel alone at the table.

"I can help clean up," Hazel chimed in.

"Don't worry about it, kiddo," Silas said with a half smile. "Don't tell anyone but I kind of like cleaning. Keeps my hands busy while I clear my thoughts." He winked and turned on the water of the sink to drown out any potential for a response. He seemed almost dejected. But about what?

Hazel pushed the question down and skulked away.

When Hazel got upstairs to the bedroom, Eve was already tucked into her bed in the dark with the glow of her cell phone emanating near her face. Hazel thought better than to turn the lights on and slipped into bed.

She checked her own phone in some part to find herself on the same page as Eve in any capacity and in some part to distract herself from the weight of even more silence.

There was a text from her mother. A simple but still loaded How are you, honey? that Hazel still didn't feel compelled to respond to. She didn't know how to answer anymore. She didn't know whether she should say nothing or everything.

It occurred to Hazel that she used to find comfort in the solitude of her own bedroom at home, tucked under the covers with the door propped just open enough for her to hear the murmurs of the rest of the house. But now, the silence felt harsh and pressing. Hazel turned her attention from the room to any noise coming from the kitchen. She at least expected to hear the clamoring of pots and pans getting returned to their drawers or the rush of water from the sink. But the kitchen sounded hollow and empty like before. She feared this could be the new version of reality. And she was no longer a fan of the quiet.

Hazel was desperate for connection. Desperate.

She tucked her phone underneath her pillow where she couldn't see the glow of the screen.

"Eve," she blurted out into the darkness. "Are you awake?"

"Yeah, why?" Eve responded without turning around.

"How did you find out about me?" Hazel asked. She could see Eve stirring a bit now.

"What do you mean?" Eve responded lacklusterly.

"I mean how did you know we were sisters?"

"Oh, this is a good one," Eve replied with much more energy. She sat straight up and turned her lamp on.

The glow lit her face up, and Hazel could sense a maniacal twinge in her eye.

"Well," Eve began, slamming her palms onto the sheets next to her, causing them to ripple.

"As you know, I am always one to have all the information. Some people call it gossip but I really prefer to call it information. And there was no way I was going to not find every bit of information about my own *father*."

Hazel nodded along. The feeling resonated.

"And in this case the information wasn't just going to come find me. My mother gave up his name pretty easily."

Eve smiled proudly and flipped her messy bun from one side of her head to the other.

"I told her I was sick of her secrets and she just blurted it right out. So, one day after school, I googled his name. Silasbox.com was the first search result. I literally could not believe it would be this easy and I clicked on the page. The first page was boring. Just a bunch of shitty tables and stuff. But then I found the About Me page."

Hazel felt the room get a bit colder and the light of the lamp against Eve's cheek get more dramatic as the story continued.

"Silas's picture popped up right away and there was no doubt that this was him. His green eyes. His black hair. If it's not creepy to say, his good looks. And right there beneath the picture was a whole set of contact information. Email, phone number, address."

Eve paused and Hazel felt a pulse of energy run through her.

"I thought calling him would be the easiest first step so I did. The phone rang a few times and I thought he might not pick up but then I heard his voice on the other end."

Hazel was enraptured now. "Well, what did you say?"

"I said, 'I think I'm your daughter.'"

"Just like that?!" Hazel asked with true shock at Eve's straightforwardness.

"Yup, just like that. It was quiet on the other end of the line for a moment and then… Want to know what he said?"

Eve was giggling now, her shoulders bouncing up and down.

"He cleared his throat and he sounded a bit flustered. 'Uh, right. The other daughter.'"

Eve guffawed as the words left her lips and Hazel's tummy clenched into one big knot. Silas knew about her the whole time? Her father knew about her the whole time? It was almost as if it were all happening all over again. That kick in the stomach, those hot tears pressing behind the eyes, the constriction of the throat that came with learning that the things you thought you knew were not wholly true. She wasn't sure whether to interpret this as a betrayal or not. But Hazel wanted to stay far, far away from that idea. She wanted to push it way, way away. She wanted so badly for this new life to be her permanent one now.

Hazel had barely caught her breath again when Eve continued.

"Now this truly shocked me into a moment of confusion and silence, so he went on. 'Jane is your mother?' he asked, now sounding a bit nervous. 'No, I'm Eve,' I explained. And I could tell this one was a real kick in the nuts for him because all he could say was 'Oh, shit. I didn't know there was another one.'"

Eve rubbed her hands together like some kind of movie villain, but there was something in the slump of her shoulders and the downturned edges of her mouth that suggested this wasn't the outcome she'd hoped for or expected.

"As soon as we hung up the phone, I went on to Wassup? and I typed in your name; Hazel Box. It didn't really occur to me that you might have a different last name now like I did, but hey, lucky me. Your weird mom gave you his last name. The first image in the results was a close-up of a girl with one green eye and one hazel eye looking straight into the camera and black messy hair that could have used some help from a blow-dryer in my opinion. You looked a little chubby—sorry—and a little less cool, but definitely like we could be sisters. And that, my friend, my *sister*, is how I found out about you. It took me a while before I reached out to you. I wanted to get to know Silas first. You know, see how this new family thing would go. Silas and I didn't talk much about you last summer but I felt like messaging you anyway before this summer. That's the deal."

Eve pressed her mouth into a smile, raised her eyebrows and then clicked the lamp off. She tucked herself back under her comforter and then turned on her side and faced away from Hazel again.

"Why didn't you tell me then?"

Hazel felt short of breath again. Her lungs and tummy were in a pretzel.

"I decided I wanted to keep Silas to myself for a bit," Eve replied nonchalantly without turning back around. "Only one new family member at a time, you know? Plus, it allowed me to have yet another thing to hang over my stupid parents' conscience."

Hazel suddenly and vigorously wanted to be out of that room. She wanted to be anywhere where the silence wasn't weighing on her like lead. She felt her chest and lungs tighten and Hazel opened her mouth to swallow a big gulp of air to bring everything in her body back to harmony. But it didn't work. A tingly anxiety started creeping over her skin and that big green wall flashed in her mind's eye again.

Hazel lifted the covers, zipped down the stairs, pushed the

screen door open, and finally found relief when she sprawled her arms and legs out on the open grass and breathed in the evening air. The stars were bright and sparkling in the otherwise black, velvety sky. Silas's cabin appeared a big sturdy shadow in the night with the single exception of one window aglow. With the lights on, the one room became a great illuminated stage. She could clearly make out Silas seated in a chair rocking back and forth. She watched him for a few moments swaying back and forth rhythmically, just blankly staring out into the rest of the room.

It occurred to Hazel, though, that Silas's room faced the other side of the house. She counted the widows from the edge of the cabin. This was surely the window of the locked room. What was he doing in there, she wondered.

She thought about going inside and asking. She thought about pressing open that door she had been so curious about since she and Eve arrived. But Silas, rocking back and forth alone, looked like he didn't want to be disturbed. There were walls in this home, too, now. Big ones.

Hazel made her way back inside and down the hallway toward her bedroom. There was a glow around the edge of the locked door. She knew Silas was in there. She wanted to knock and ask why but walls were walls and sometimes even doors were walls. So she slunk back into her bedroom, tucked herself under her covers again, placed one ear against her pillow and drifted to sleep.

31

The next morning, Hazel woke up and made her way downstairs to the kitchen. Silas was leaning his hip against the cabinets and staring into his coffee. Eve had a half-eaten piece of toast on her plate and her knees up on the table and was waving her phone around in the air, presumably looking for service.

"Morning," Hazel said as she sat down. But no one answered.

Hazel took a piece of toast from the middle of the table and spread the huckleberry jam slowly over the surface. Her mother's favorite, Hazel thought, and smiled. She brought the toast to her mouth and bit down. The sound of the crunch echoed in the quiet room as crumbs sprinkled down her chin. The faint sound of her chewing only amplified the prior silence.

She looked up at Eve again and began to study her face,

looking for vibrations just under the surface of the skin that would give Hazel any hint about what she was thinking.

"What?" Eve said sharply as she looked up from her phone and straight into Hazel's eyes.

Hazel sat quiet and still. Eve must have seen the blatant longing in Hazel's face because she jutted her chin forward and raised her eyebrows, looking for a response from Hazel. But when Hazel didn't give it, she shook her head and returned to her phone. There was nothing there. Just disinterest.

Hazel took another bite of her toast and turned her gaze toward Silas. His shoulders were slumped but still. His thigh was pressing into the drawers casually. He was still just standing calmly, looking at nothing. Doing nothing. Saying nothing.

Hazel began to trace the quiet on Eve's face to Silas's face and back. She felt everyone's divergence. She could taste it. Everybody in this room was numb to their reality.

She wanted to yell and laugh and return to joy together, but now all of those moments seemed a distant illusion.

"I'm going to head down to the waterfront if anyone wants to come," Hazel said into the room, hoping it would jolt everyone back to life. But it was still quiet.

She took another bite of her toast and waited. But still nothing.

She couldn't not go now, so she slipped out the back door without another word. Hazel took a few steps across the grass and then turned back to watch the scene through the screen door. Neither Silas nor Eve had moved. She decided she would go down to the lake and at least put her feet in the water. She ended up spending time there, quietly thinking.

On her way back up to the house, Silas's workshop caught her attention.

Hazel made her way toward it and slowly turned her neck to look behind her before sliding the large barn door open. She had to push it with both arms with all her weight behind it to set the heavy weight of it into motion.

Hazel immediately felt an awareness of geometry and creativity and presence upon entering.

The space seemed to be governed by a specific but entropic rule. A purposeful disorder. The room felt smaller from the inside but Hazel was well aware that the perceived capacity was diminished by the precarious stacks of worn notebooks of varying stages of deterioration lining the walls and the color on the walls. The bound notebooks of varying thickness stretched entirely from one side of the space to the other, creating a rocklike strata along an entire wall. Above the wall of books, sketches of tables and chairs and benches were nailed into the wood. An assortment of dinged-up wooden surfaces of different heights and thicknesses and widths created a maze through the center of the space.

To the right was the workbench, where everything was kept in meticulous order. Each hammer and screwdriver and saw hung from its designated peg in an apparent order. The different nails and screws were stacked in transparent, scratched plastic drawers, arranged according to size.

Hazel imagined Silas standing in front of the workbench reaching up for a tool conveniently selected for the task in front of him. She imagined him hunched over one of the tables, sawing a thick piece of wood, and wearing a mask covering his mouth and nose as a storm of sawdust enveloped him.

Each thing in the workshop carried such specific purpose. Hazel could understand the call to a craft like this. The combination of human hand and instrument to create an object. An object that could be touched and used and interacted with. She imagined the power Silas would feel in changing the physical form of a thing. Cutting a raw slab of wood into a beautiful, usable form.

There was something divine in the ability to create like that. To make something more out of something less.

Hazel walked slowly and gingerly around the perimeter of the workshop, inhaling the scent of freshly cut wood and must. It all felt rugged and masculine. It was a place Silas belonged.

Hazel felt a surge of spirituality flow through her. The space felt simultaneously grand but heavy. Sacred but utilitarian. Illicit but inviting.

The competing forces made her feel a certain reverence for Silas's craft.

And this was no doubt his church, if anything was.

Hazel reached out to let her fingertips brush against the sketched-on paper. She liked the slightly ribbed texture and the grooves of the pencil markings. She pulled her hand away from the wall and looked down at her finger, which was now covered in black charcoal that had sunk into her skin, revealing her fingerprint. She pushed her pointer finger back into a piece of paper on the wall, leaving a black oval print.

Right next to where Hazel had left the mark, she noticed a photo nailed into the wall. The image of a person seemed to violate the impression of the space as something solely and wholly belonging to Silas.

It was a picture of a very beautiful woman with an arresting shock of long, straight golden hair. Hazel was immediately drawn into her smoky eyes. The woman couldn't have been much older than she was, but she seemed to carry more wisdom in her face. She was turned to the side with her head tilted toward the camera. Her lips formed almost a pout. Her crisp white and flowing tank top contrasted sharply with tanned and rich skin.

She wondered who this woman was. And who she was to Silas. The photo was intimate, and surely taken without fair warning to its subject during an intimate moment somewhere, sometime.

Hazel wanted to know more about this woman, her story, her relation to Silas. She couldn't remove the picture from the wall without tearing it, so she lifted it up to check the back for any hints of anything. Any annotations or scribbles. But there was nothing but a neon orange date—April 11, 1995—in blocky numbers like those on a digital clock.

Lifting the photo revealed two other images. Two sonograms. Each was taped to the wall haphazardly, strips of silver duct tape cutting across the top of each in no particular angle. Hazel wondered why one would preserve something on a wall, without more careful attention to how it was displayed. But alas, there they were. Two eerily grainy images of babies in their wombs.

Hazel pulled them off the wall instinctively and held them next to each other. She felt overcome with a sense of knowing and connection. Without thinking much about it, Hazel assumed that these two images were of Hazel and Eve in the womb. She knew it so deeply in her bones. On the basis of no evidence at all, she felt so sure of it. Who else could they have been? Two teeny-tiny little girls growing big enough and strong enough. Two teeny-tiny little girls getting ready to join the world.

Hazel could feel Silas's desire for fatherhood. His love for his girls, even though he wouldn't meet them.

She turned the sonograms over looking for evidence but there was nothing. Just blank images. No dates. No names. No inscriptions. No nothing.

She imagined Silas, her father, proudly taping these two images next to one another. She imagined him placing two girls permanently side by side on the wall of his workshop, knowing that they would not be side by side in their own lives.

She imagined Silas peeking at these photos every day when he came to work on his furniture. She imagined him thinking about his two girls, now no longer little, as he worked. Hazel imagined her father thinking about his girls growing up and wondering whether they'd inherited his hair or his eyes or his comfort with tools. She imagined him wondering whether they would come together in any place or at any time that wasn't on this wall.

Hazel imagined how he must have felt to have his girls here by his lake. In his home.

For the first time, Hazel felt confident that Silas may have wanted this summer to come. *Yes*, she thought and may have even murmured out loud. He probably longed for it. She was sure of it now, holding those sonograms in her hand.

Hazel held the images against her heart. She was too distracted by her fantasy of Silas to notice the faintly printed date in the corner of one image. It would have revealed her answer, even if she didn't want it revealed. But she was too distracted by her fantasy to seek reality.

Hazel just returned them to their position on the wall and left the workshop with a buzz in her veins.

She had everything she was looking for in coming up to Grandor. She had everything she needed. She could make this her home. She would make this her home.

Hazel pulled her phone out of her pocket and dialed her mother's number. The phone crackled as it rang, given the spotty cell service. Her heart was still racing from what she had found. The phone rang choppily again. Hazel strode toward the house as she held the phone at her ear.

"Hello?" her mother's voice rang through.

"Mom," Hazel said firmly.

"Hello?" her mother said again, presumably unable to hear her.

Hazel was close to the house now and the smell of dinner wafted toward her nose. *This was it*, Hazel thought to herself. The place where all of her meals would happen.

"I'm staying here," Hazel said into the phone and then hung up.

Hazel ran into the house and straight toward her seat at the dinner table. She was still swollen with imagined love.

PART IV

Homecoming

32

HAZEL

Hazel's insides were still rushing and pulsing and surging and glowing with her discovery in the workshop earlier in the day and her plans for a new life. A new family. A new happiness.

She had stayed at the lake…

She slipped her knees under the table and pulled her chair in tight. Silas walked over with a big bowl of pasta mixed with coarsely chopped vegetables scattered throughout and placed it at the center of the table. Hazel watched as his strong thick fingers set the bowl down. She watched as a single black curl slipped out from behind his ear and across his forehead. As Silas tucked his rogue lock back behind his ear with the side of his finger, Hazel caught his green, emerald eye in hers. She felt her cheeks get hot as she was met with the full force of his smoky, intense eyes. She smiled back warmly. Lovingly. Her father.

Silas returned her smile with a quick twitch of the eyebrow and returned to the refrigerator to finish putting together the meal. Hazel watched as his big heavy boots clopped against the hardwood floor. The old planks of wood surrendered just the slightest bit to Silas's weight as he crossed over them. She felt another rush of heat fill her cheeks. How these floors must have known the feeling of his feet. How Silas must have known the give of the floor. This was his home. And soon to be her home, too. Hazel closed her eyes and slowly took in the scent of the meal. It was rich and full of love. She presumed it now more than she ever had before.

When she opened her eyes, Eve was already seated in the chair across from her. Her arms were crossed and her legs were pretzeled between the chair and the edge of the table.

"Hey," Hazel said, trying not to let too much of her joy spill out with a single breath.

Eve rolled her eyes and tilted her head back. The messy pile of her hair flopped from one side of her head to the other. Hazel glided over the response and smiled back at her. Surely this was a thing that all sisters did.

Silas returned to the table with a plate of dark brown, perfectly sliced steak. The juice from the meat pooled below it and sloshed a bit as Silas set it onto the table. He took a seat and unlatched the cap from his beer. A gentle whoosh emerged from the bottle before Silas tilted his head backward and poured the beer into his mouth. Hazel watched the black stubble of sprouting hair on his neck undulate as the liquid moved down his throat. He slammed the bottle down against the table, perhaps a little too firmly.

"Dig in," Silas said, without looking up at either of the

girls. He lifted the plate of steak, served himself three pieces and returned the bowl to its place in the middle of the table.

By now, only Eve hadn't spoken. Her expression had grown sourer and sourer since Hazel sat down. Eve was making her annoyance known by one indiscreet groan after another. By folding her arms and shaking her head at every move. But it wasn't like Eve to stay quiet for long.

"I decided to become a vegetarian," Eve said, head still dangling unnaturally to one side as gravity tugged on the bun.

If it weren't for the subtle nod Hazel observed, she would have thought Silas didn't acknowledge it at all. He just served himself several large spoonfuls of pasta and then slammed his fork into the pile and thrust whatever noodles had been caught by the tines into his mouth. He chewed vigorously.

Hazel waited for someone to fill the space of the quiet. But once again, there was only the sound of forks against plates echoing between them. She looked at Eve, who was limp on her chair and looking at the floor. She looked at Silas, who was alternating between shoveling his pasta and pouring his beer into his mouth.

Suddenly, she couldn't take the anonymity of Eve's gaze. The directionlessness of Silas's silence. The distractedness from each other. The hollowness of the room. Something molten and volcanic surged around inside of Hazel. And then it erupted. Detonated. She needed it all to be different. She needed these people to save her.

"What is with you people?!" Hazel spewed.

Now, Silas and Eve looked up from their plates with wide eyes.

"Seriously. Can't we even talk to each other over dinner?" Hazel demanded and slammed her fists, still curled around her fork and knife, into the table. "We are a family!" Bits of food flung from the silverware. "We are sisters and you are our father and this is our family dinner!"

She looked at Eve and then at Silas. They were both erect in their chairs now, eyebrows pressed up toward their hair like exclamation marks.

Hazel took her fork to the pile of pasta and tried to continue eating. She jammed a few noodles into her mouth and chewed. Her heart was racing and her throat was too tight to swallow without great effort. And then she thought she heard Eve mumble something.

"What was that?" Hazel asked with a threatening energy she had never experienced in herself before.

Eve wiggled her shoulders, sat up straighter and appeared to have found her own reactive energy.

"I said, you guys are losers." Her chest rose and fell with feigned calmness. "And I'm sick of it here."

Hazel tried to slow her breathing to get her food down and to let the sharpness of Eve's words subside.

"And I told my mom to come and get me," Eve added matter-of-factly. "I think she's on her way right now. God, I hope she is." The cadence of the rising and falling of her chest picked up speed now. "It is time to get the fuck out of here."

Everything in Hazel's insides sank down and melted into a pool of sadness and betrayal and anger and heartache. But then she stopped the feeling. She needed to salvage this situation. She could still salvage it! She was lost for words but looked up at Silas in such a way that she hoped might urge him to do it.

Silas fumbled with his utensils and coughed and then looked up at Eve, obviously entirely clueless about what to do.

"That's not the way to share that update," Silas said in a dejected but unsurprised manner that in no way made up for the gravity of what had just happened. "And, Hazel, I just want you to know that..." Silas said and placed his palm on Hazel's forearm. The end of his sentence dangled in his mouth. She could tell he had more to say.

But before he could say it, Eve chimed in. "Oh, this is going to be good," she chuckled. From the corner of her eye, Hazel could see that Eve had recrossed her arms but took a new, more participatory pose.

Hazel yanked her arm out from Silas's grip. "Oh yes. It *is* going to be good," she said, eyes still down on her plate but with a fierceness in her voice. "It's going to be more than good. We're all going to live here together, and it's going to be better than good. It's going to be *great*."

As her words spilled out of her, she felt the hot prickling of tears forming behind her eyes. Her throat constricted again. She didn't know if she was telling or begging anymore. Her truest, deepest desire was now lying out in front of everyone on the table.

33
JANE

Jane grabbed the keys to the car and pressed the front door open. Cam and the twins were right outside, on their way in. Jane burst into tears at the sight of them all and fell into Cam's shoulder.

"I have to go get Hazel back," she said as she sobbed. "I'm losing her, Cam."

Jane's tears formed a wet puddle on Cam's shirt.

"I've been losing her for a long time. I've—"

And just as she prepared to head further down the tunnel of her guilt, the phone in her hand buzzed. Before she even picked up the phone to see who was calling, she hoped and hoped that it was Hazel. Jane bumbled the phone in her hand, her fingers still frantic and shaking. It was Hazel! She wiped her tears with the back of her hand and pinned the phone to her ear.

"Hazel," she said as calmly as she could muster.

But the other end of the line was quiet and empty.

"Hello?" Jane said again, the anxiety building in her throat again. But still, there was nothing but quiet on the other end of the line.

Jane pressed her forehead again into Cam's shoulder as another wave of tears erupted.

Cam's hand arrived gently on Jane's back. He rubbed it up and down calmly as Jane's back rose with choppy inhales and fell with choppy exhales.

Cam brought his lips to Jane's wet cheek and kissed it.

"Well, let's go get her, then," he said with his mouth still at her ear. "None of us wants to lose her."

Jane pulled her head up from Cam's shoulder, her tears curiously subsiding at the thought of all her family in one place. She crouched down to the twins, who were seated in their car seats. At the sight of their mother, gummy smiles spread across their faces. Their eyes were clear and bright. They knew nothing but love.

Jane looked up at Cam. His face and eyes were so kind as he nodded, urging Jane along.

Jane picked up the car seats and she stood up. Cam's face lit up with a smile and he took one of the car seats from her.

They both buckled them in tightly in the back seat and got in the front seats themselves. Jane put the keys in the ignition and the cadence of her breath finally slowed. Before she put the car in Drive, she picked up her phone to make one more phone call. She dialed the number of a woman whose number she had kept in her heart for sixteen years despite never having dialed it. A woman whose past was part of her past. Whose present was about to be part of her present.

"It's Jane," she said calmly into the phone. "Silas's ex.

From that summer. Meet me at Silas's. I know it's a been a long time since you've been to that house but I promise you, you won't regret it. I'm going, too, for the first time in a long, long time."

Jane took a deep breath. She had Susie's words in her mind. *All mothers' stories are the same. All mothers' stories are the same.*

"It's about time we all find our way there," she said to the woman, the should-have-been mother, on the other end of the line. And for no reason at all, without any signal from the woman on the other end of the phone, Jane felt confident that her instructions would be abided by.

"Who was that?" Cam asked with one eyebrow raised.

"You'll see," she responded cryptically with a smirk.

"Well, okay, then," Cam replied and placed his palm on his wife's thigh.

Jane put the car in Drive and took off.

She had certainly made a mess of things in her life, and others had made a mess of theirs, but it was nothing that love couldn't overcome. She got on the highway, headed for Grandor, Maine, in the dark, with a feeling of peace in her heart she hadn't felt in a long time.

34

HAZEL

Hazel was still seething when Eve jumped in in a calm and steady voice that didn't match the thick tension filling the rest of the room. "I only came to this shithole to piss my parents off." Eve flipped her bun from one side of her head to the other.

"Eve!" Silas yelled, his voice deep and serious, urging her to stop. "That's enough!"

"What? It's true," Eve replied in a tone that was now de-escalated. As if what she'd said meant nothing at all. And perhaps it didn't.

Hazel wanted to have words, she wanted to know. She wanted to hear. And she wanted them all to wiggle right out of it.

"For most of my life, my parents neglected to tell me what a little slut my mom was after she and my dad couldn't get pregnant. Yup, she fucked that guy and made me." Eve pointed at Silas with a fire in her eyes that could have burned a hole in both of them.

Silas was steaming, his teeth gritted and shoulders tense. But he didn't try to stop her again.

"And I wanted to punish them for waiting so long. There, I said it. You think I give a shit about either of you?"

Eve turned her eyes back down to her plate and without a trace of anxiety or emotion, dealt another blow.

"If you did, that's pathetic and I feel sorry for you."

Hazel's head felt light and heavy and frantic and still, all at the same time. She didn't know how to stop it. She didn't know how to grab it back. So Eve continued.

"But I think my mom and dad have got the message by now. And I'm going back to a life I actually like, and when I do, I'll probably never think of either one of you again. They are on their way to come and get me right now so I don't have to spend another second with you losers."

Eve turned her phone over, began to type, but then slammed it back on the table.

"No fucking service. But they are coming. I know they are coming."

As Eve crossed her arms, Hazel erupted again. Her mind went to the sonograms immediately. *Every single person on this planet wants nothing more than love*, she thought. Every single person. Even Eve. Hazel knew it. She could show her that she'd been loved. That she was still loved. By the people in this very room. It was her only chance.

"You pretend you don't care. But I know you do! And he does, too! I'll show you," Hazel said forcefully. And without another breath, Hazel pushed her chair out from the table, burst through the back and ran toward the workshop. The outside air felt crisp in her lungs and she felt a happiness fall over her upon seeing those two sonograms taped to the wall. With a gentle tug, Hazel pulled the pictures from the wall. She held them tight between her thumb and her index finger as she sprinted back through the screen door and to the dinner table where Silas and Eve were sitting in silence, eyes down on their plates, without a word between them.

Hazel slammed the two sonograms down on the table between Eve and Silas. She looked up at Silas.

"He's been looking at these sonograms of us all these years. They are taped up in his workshop right near his bench."

Silas's spine straightened and his eyes got wide.

"He thought of us every day until we got here, Eve."

It wasn't until now that Hazel realized she was out of breath. From the running and also the energy of it all.

"Every day."

Silas's head tilted forward and he rolled his chin across the top of his chest before looking back up.

"Do you understand what this means, Eve? This is your father. Your real one. And I am your sister. Your real one. We are the people that care about you. We are your family. Your real family. Not those people at home. It's us. It's us!"

Hazel turned to look at Silas, her voice now quivering. Silas's green eyes met Hazel's and they were full of tears. He swallowed harshly even though there was nothing in his mouth.

He placed one palm over Hazel's hand and one over Eve's shoulder.

"Listen, kiddos," he said, with peacefulness. But a somber one. "I do like knowing you both. I really do. And, in a way, yes, we are a family."

Eve was looking straight back at Silas as he spoke, her indifference overpowered by his earnestness. Hazel felt a tear start rolling down her cheek. Eve tried to roll her eyes but couldn't.

"But those sonograms are not of you," Silas explained, in a calm and sobering tone. "Both of those sonograms are images of a little baby named Ruby who never made it into the world." He painstakingly surmounted each word as it rolled up through his throat and across his tongue. Hazel could tell each word was harder than the last to get out. Her heart sank and sank and sank. A bit for Silas, but more so for herself. It sank so deep she wasn't sure it could ever be retrieved.

"Before either of you were even a twinkle in my eye—" he smirked a little now "—I was married and in love with my high school sweetheart. Her name was—well, is—Torrey, and she is perfect. We were meant to have a baby together."

Hazel started piecing together all the things she had sensed and observed. The garden. The baskets. The locked door. Silas in that room in the middle of the night. The sonograms.

Her whole image, her whole future, shattered before her very eyes.

"We were meant to have that baby together."

Silas brought his thick fingertips over the image.

"But the baby didn't make it."

Silas's voice remained steady but full tears were now falling down his face. Hazel brought her hand to her own face, which was wet and salty now. Even Eve appeared stricken as she held her hands to her heart.

"Well, what happened to Torrey?" Eve asked, with more curiosity than care.

"It was too hard, so we split." Silas brought his hands up to his head and then let his head fall into them. His dark curls fell through the spaces between his fingers and swayed as he rocked his head back and forth.

"But I miss her like crazy, girls."

No one said anything.

"I miss her so much." It wasn't clear now who he was talking to.

His words turned to a mumble that Hazel could barely make out. She could make out very few words—something about a car and a note and a crib, perhaps.

Hazel's mind blurred. And surprisingly, the image that emerged in her mind's eye was the twins. Those precious little boys. She wondered what the world, her world, would be like without them. She didn't want to know. And she felt for Silas. But she was broken. Into tiny little pieces that could never be put together. She'd abandoned her family for Silas and Eve, and they had abandoned her. She was alone. And broken. She was alone.

"I think we all need some space," Silas eked out with a tear in his eye. "Let's all get to bed and talk about it all in the morning, okay?"

"Works for me!" Eve said somewhat sarcastically, but with a fake enthusiasm. She pushed her chair out with a huff and stormed up the stairs. "I'll probably be out of here by the time you wake up anyway."

Hazel was still left at the table and Silas had yet to move. He seemed catatonic. "I'm sorry that happened, Silas," Hazel said in a whisper. And then she, too, pushed her chair out from the table and got up. "I'm sorry this all happened."

When Hazel got to the bedroom, the lights were off and Eve was already tucked into her bed, facing away from Hazel. Hazel thought she could make out the glow of Eve's phone from under the comforters. Hazel slipped underneath her comforter and pulled out her phone, too. She wanted to call her mother. She wanted to hear her voice. She wanted to feel the comfort of her hugs. She wanted to be giving the twins a bath. She even wanted to see Cam. But she had thrown it all away. She had thrown everything away.

She pressed her eyelids together and inhaled, trying to hold the tears back. But they found their way out at the corners and streamed down her cheeks. She could taste the salt on her lips. Her purposeful breath turned choppy and her heart ached. Oh, her heart ached.

And before she knew she fell asleep, she was woken by the sound of a loud knock at the front door.

Silas, Eve and Hazel all convened in the foyer and then Silas walked over, slowly, to the door. There was a second set of knocks and Eve perked up at the sound of it. Certainly, Eve's parents were here to take her back home. Her back was zipped up straight and her eyes widened, as if someone had come and breathed life into her body.

Silas pressed his feet into the wood purposefully as he walked toward the door. The floor creaked with each step and then he took his hand to the doorknob. There was a trepidation to his movements. What was it? Was it so unusual to have visitors? Or was he unprepared for the beginning of the end of their summer?

Silas opened the door slowly at first, but then with a velocity Hazel had not yet seen him move with. Silas stood frozen in the doorway. The woman on the other side of the door was not Eve's mother at all. Hazel looked over at Eve, whose shoulders had gone limp and face had gone white. The woman at the door appeared to be full of spirit despite a nervousness in her eyes. She had tanned skin and almond-shaped eyes. Her hair was over one shoulder. She was wearing a long flowing skirt that rippled in the same way as her hair.

Suddenly, the woman burst out for him. Her arms stretched in front of her with nothing but yearning in them as she crossed what might have been perceived as an impenetrable shield between them in the doorway. She wrapped her long arms around Silas's back and pulled him in tight. Her thin arms and slight frame should have been no match for Silas's wide shoulders and thick chest, but the way they held each other looked right and comfortable. They swayed a bit to the right and to the left.

It was at that very moment that Hazel realized exactly who this woman was. It was the woman in the picture in Silas's workshop. This must be Torrey. This was what Silas's love looked like when it was deep and true and real.

Silas's entire body slumped and he let his head fall right into the crease of the woman's neck and shoulder. His curls fell gently over her clavicle.

"What are you doing here? What are you doing here?"

Silas repeated over and over and over and over in varying degrees of surprise and anxiety and relief and happiness.

Hazel thought to turn away. She felt she wasn't meant to be bearing witness to this kind of intimacy. This depth of feeling. But she couldn't keep from staring. It was so simultaneously shocking and enlightening and heartwarming.

"I'm so sorry," Silas tried to whisper into her ear, but his voice was too hysterical.

"I'm so happy I'm here," the woman said calmly and she rubbed her hand across his back in warm, concentric circles.

"I'm so happy you're here, Torrey," Silas said back to her, this time with more of a grip on the quiver in his voice.

"How did this happen? How did you get here?" he asked, with his arms stretched out and his palms on her shoulders.

"A wise woman told me to get here," Torrey replied and then looked over Silas's shoulder at Hazel. Hazel thought she detected a wink but just recoiled into her own ball of confusion and loss.

Hazel looked down and noticed that Eve was squeezing onto her hand and staring out toward the doorway. Hazel, confused at the sudden gesture of solidarity, traced the line of her eyesight. To her surprise, she was looking past Silas and the woman's embrace into the space behind them.

There was the crackling sound of tires against gravel and Eve took a few steps toward it. Hazel followed closely behind her to get a view of what she was looking at. A sleek black car with no business up north in Maine was rounding the bend of the driveway. The car had barely come to a stop when two legs peeked out from the driver's-side door and then two legs swung out the passenger-side door. Eve barreled toward them, interrupting Silas and Torrey as she whooshed by him.

Just as Susie had managed to stand all the way up, Eve threw her whole body around her mother, knocking her back into the seat. They both fell over into the car into a ball of laughter and hugs and kisses. Parker slowly made his way over to the pile, as well, and embraced his two girls.

"I guess she really did call her," Silas said, looking over toward Hazel with one arm still slumped over Torrey's shoulder.

Tears welled up in Hazel's eyes. She was really alone now. For the first time to Hazel, Eve seemed a whole person instead of just a sketch of a high school girl and the outline of a sister. She had seemed someone that almost stood for the concept of those things without embodying any of them. But now, standing with her arms around her mother, vulnerable and loose with her body and heart, Eve appeared to be more filled in. More real. More human. There was a density to Eve that Hazel hadn't seen before.

"I'm here," Susie said over and over, stroking Eve's back and hair. "I'm here."

Eve looked over to Silas and Torrey, who had their arms slung around one another. They were both smiling and giddy, holding each other tight and watching Eve do the same.

Silas caught Hazel's eye and gestured for her to come over.

"This is Torrey," he said. "This is the woman I was telling you about. This is Ruby's mother."

The corners of Torrey's mouth turned up into a smile.

"It's nice to meet you," Hazel said, with an unexpected constriction in her throat. Hazel recognized Torrey's lips and the hair and her smooth skin from the photo.

Hazel was now missing her mother and Cam and the twins more than ever. Her mistakes in love had suddenly caught up with her. Her aloneness was now fully apparent.

"Look, kiddo. I'm going to take Torrey down to the garden," Silas said while interlacing his fingers with Torrey's. "Is that okay with you, to hang here solo for a few minutes? And maybe it'd be a good time to, uh, call your mom, too? Only if you want, though."

"Mmm, I don't think she has to worry about that phone call," Torrey chimed in.

The churning in Hazel's stomach and the tears pressing up behind her eyes distracted her from really, really hearing what Torrey had said. There was no mistaking it now. She was actually, actually alone.

"Yeah, don't worry about me," Hazel replied and took a seat on the steps.

Silas smiled, glowed even, and then pressed his strong hand into the small of Torrey's back so gently as they walked down toward the garden.

Hazel watched Silas and Torrey until they disappeared down into the woods next to the house. And then she turned her attention back to Eve, who was still locked up in her mother's arms. They were swaying back and forth in one rhythm.

Hazel wondered to herself whether she should call her mom now. Whether she could. Whether it would be easy to undo everything she had done and said. And even if she called, how long would she sit and wait there alone? A tension rose in her body. Her muscles tightened and her tears pressed harder and her throat constricted. With each second that went by, those feelings only became more intense. She wanted something to happen. For someone to save her. But the absence of it was so palpable. Her reality was so heavy on her. She was alone. She had been for so long. But this aloneness hurt more than ever before.

Hazel wished she had said no when Silas asked if he could leave her alone. She wished she had told him that the whole reason she came up to this place was so that she wouldn't have to hang solo anymore. She thought about shouting it out so it rippled through the air and the trees for Silas to hear. She thought about running toward Eve in her mother's car and begging her to save her from her place on the steps.

Hazel let time pass, sitting with those feelings stirring around inside, until she needed to release them. She couldn't tell how much time had passed, but it wasn't enough to alleviate her need to be part of something the rest of them were a part of.

She tried to open her mouth to yell out. She tried picking up her legs to spring forward. But she couldn't. Hazel realized that she couldn't yell or thrust her way into Silas's or Eve's lives. Into their families. They had their families.

And so did Hazel. They were just back home.

The weight in her body turned into a panicky numbness. The green wall came into her mind's eye again. Pulsing and breathing. Luring her in. Hazel pulled her eyelids together and placed her hands over her temples until the vision passed. She needed to get her mother here. She needed to get out, out, out of this place. She needed to go back home. Her real home.

Just as she prepared to reach for her phone, Hazel heard

the familiar sound of the crackling of gravel below tires. The nose of her mother's old green Subaru, dinged up on all sides, rounded into sight and Hazel sprung to her feet. Hazel ran toward it and slammed her palms into the glass of the windows as the car came to a slowdown.

Her mother popped out of the car and rushed to her. Before wrapping her up in a hug, Jane placed her hands on top of Hazel's shoulders.

"How did you know to come up here?" Hazel asked through a smile.

"I just knew, my love." Hazel's mother pulled her in close and stroked the side of her head. "I just knew."

As Hazel's head rested on her mother's shoulder, she heard the sound of a car window going down.

"Hi, Hazel!" a voice said, in a slightly jumbled and staccato manner. She hadn't heard either of the twins utter these words before, but she was sure it was Trevor's voice. "Hi, Hazel!" a second voice added. This one, she was sure, was Griffin's.

Hazel's heart felt light and she unraveled herself from her mother's arms to peek into the back of the car. The twins were in there waving and bouncing their legs up and down in their car seats.

"They missed you," Cam chimed in from the front seat with a smile.

"It looks like it!" Hazel chuckled and gave Trevor's thigh a squeeze.

She looked up at Cam. He seemed as gentle and kind and calm as he always seemed. Hazel looked right into his eyes and said, "Well, I missed you guys."

35

JANE

When Hazel pulled her head out of the car window, Silas and Torrey were arm in arm on one side of the driveway, having just emerged back from their walk to the garden, and Eve and Susie and Parker were arm in arm on the other side of the driveway, having just emerged from their circle of hugging and talking.

"Hey, Jane. Hey, Susie," Silas said with a shaky voice. "I, uh, can't believe everyone made it up here."

There was a moment of thick quiet. Of everyone trading stares. There was a mixing of past and present and future.

"A mother's instinct, I guess," Jane said with a smirk.

"I'd say so," Susie chimed in.

Torrey smiled, too, and squeezed Silas's side.

They had all embarked upon journeys of love once upon a time. It was the greatest story of each of their lives and all the characters were right there in Silas's driveway. Where did the stories start? Where did they end? What did they learn?

It was a mess. How couldn't it have been? But it was finally becoming untangled.

It couldn't be said for certain who was squeezing whom more, but Jane squeezed Hazel and Hazel squeezed Jane. And Silas squeezed Torrey and Torrey squeezed Silas. And Eve squeezed Susie and Susie squeezed Eve.

"I think it's time we all head home, wouldn't you say?" Jane said into the quiet between them all. "Well, except for you two," Jane said with a smile in the direction of Silas and Torrey.

"Yes, I'd say we're already home," Torrey said and then kissed Silas's cheek. Silas wrapped his arms around Torrey as if he would never get enough of it. With her chin on Silas's shoulder, she mouthed toward Jane, "Thank you."

Jane stood there stoically even though her heart was simultaneously full and melting. She nodded and then turned her attention back toward the Warringtons and her own daughter.

"Why don't you go and get your stuff, girls?" Susie added. She swallowed and then pressed her chin into the air a bit.

She saw Hazel glance at Eve, who was already looking over at her, and then they disappeared up into the house.

With Silas and Torrey out of sight, the girls up in their rooms packing, and husbands and twins in their cars, Jane was left with just Susie. Where there might have been tension, there was a warmth between them. At the same time, the two women turned toward each other.

"I read your letters," Jane said. And Susie said at precisely the same time, "Did you read my letters?" The two women laughed. They understood each other. They shared something meaningful.

"They helped," Jane shared earnestly. "They really did."

"Oh, I'm so glad to hear that," Susie replied with obvious relief.

"I wrote my own, too," Jane continued. "It felt good to get it all out there. And to know I wasn't alone."

Susie moved closer toward Jane and curled her slender fingers over Jane's shoulder.

"Think you'll ever share them with Eve?" Jane asked.

Susie shook her head from side to side. "No, I don't think so. After writing them, I realized they were more for me." She pulled her hand down off Jane's shoulder and smiled. "And after meeting you, I realized they could be for you."

Jane smiled back. "Hold on one second." Jane dashed off to the car and pulled the two heavy notebooks from the car.

"What are those?" Cam asked from the passenger's seat, but Jane just bolted off with them tucked in her arms. When Jane reached Susie, she extended the notebook out in front of her. "I figured you probably want this back?"

"Is that other one yours?" Susie asked, pointing to the other notebook pressed between Jane's arm and side. "How would you feel if I said that I think I'd rather have yours?"

Jane pulled Susie's notebook back and swapped it for hers.

"I'd feel pretty good about that. One mother's mess is another mother's treasure."

They chuckled again. And as they did they could hear the patter of the girls making their way back down the stairs. Eve emerged first with a pep in her step and hair swaying from side to side.

"Let's get out of here already!" Eve yelped, dragging her suitcase dramatically behind her. Hazel emerged next, looking a bit weary and older. Her eyes shone brighter. She even appeared taller. More adult. Hazel looked straight at Jane, right into her eyes. She felt them both soften again. Jane motioned to go hug her daughter again but there was Eve to break the mood.

"What are those fat notebooks you're both holding? What are you, freakin' pen pals now?"

"Nothing," both Susie and Jane said simultaneously and made eye contact.

"Go put your bag in the car," Susie said to Eve. And Eve abided. Hazel had already started doing the same.

Just as everyone had piled into their cars and started leaving, Silas and Torrey emerged back in front of the house, their fingers intertwined like they would never let go. And perhaps they wouldn't.

"Hey!" he shouted and motioned with his other hand for them to roll down the windows.

"Thank you, daughters. And thank you, mothers."

And then the cars drove off.

36

HAZEL

Hazel was surprised with how light she felt in the car. It felt okay to want things in a way you couldn't help. It felt okay to go after those things. And she had.

Hazel looked out the window at the great and moody lake and watched it disappear into the distance. Hazel's path to this moment had started how everything always started—with mothers and fathers and sons and daughters and sisters and wanting love. Mostly, wanting love. And it had ended with everyone holding those people a little bit tighter. It had ended up with a little more understanding of each other and a lot more love in the right places.

She thought of how quiet it had been in the room as she and Eve packed their bags, both as quickly as they could without seeming as desperate to leave as they both knew they were. For the first time, Hazel didn't feel self-conscious about the things she wanted. Whether Eve could detect the vibrations of effort under her skin. For the first time, she didn't feel Eve or her mother or Cam or the twins was in control of her. She was her own girl, her own woman, and she knew where to find her love and security.

Hazel felt warm and safe in the car, in the seat between her brothers and behind her mother and Cam. This was the kind of love she was seeking. The kind of love that took time. The kind of love that built through experience. Through knowing all the parts of each other. A kind of love that finally allowed her to see how grasping her love for Eve and Silas was.

Hazel felt her phone buzz in her lap.

Hey, Eve had texted. Sorry about all that.

Hazel tucked the phone between her legs so that she wouldn't respond. What was there to say? But then she felt the phone buzz again.

Check your backpack. Another text message flashed onto the screen.

I left you a note.

Hazel dug around in her backpack until she felt a folded piece of lined paper. She pulled it out and opened it.

Dear Hazel,

I've been writing this note in my head for a long time but finally feel like I could put it on paper. The first thing I want to say is that I'm sorry I brought you into this mess, but I'm also glad I got to know you.

It's probably no surprise that I didn't come all the way up to Maine for the old walls and rickety floors and bugs and humidity. To be honest, I barely even came to meet Silas. I came because I was mad and I was sad that my parents lied to me. You're lucky that yours didn't. I wanted to punish them. I wanted them to feel scared that they would lose me. I wanted them to feel scared that things would change. Because that's how I felt.

Last summer when I came up here, I was filled with anger and fear. This summer, it was different.

I didn't feel mad or scared anymore. I felt like I understood them. The more time I spent up here, and the more time I spent with you and Silas, the more I understood why they would want to pretend like it never happened. The more I understood that they would want to live happily-ever-after, just the three of us.

I realized this summer that I felt like that, too. I still feel like that. I want to pretend like none of it ever happened. I want to go back to my life before this all happened.

Genes don't tell the whole story of family. I know you know that, too.

I hope you understand. I hope you're happy.

I'm sorry if I made a mess of things for you.

Your (kind of) sister,

Eve

After reading the note, Hazel understood not only Eve, but also herself.

Genes *didn't* tell the whole story of family. It would never be enough. It was true for her relationship with Eve and it was true for her relationship with Silas. Her family was not up in Grandor. It was back home where there were reels upon reels of memories and boxes upon boxes of photos that proved what family was. There was a home and thousands of meals and thousands of good-night kisses and thousands of welcome-home-from-school hugs that proved this to be true. There were bikes that wouldn't have been ridden, kites that wouldn't have been flown, raspberry jam that wouldn't have been eaten, bath toys that wouldn't have been played with, movies that wouldn't have been watched, books that wouldn't have been read and grass that wouldn't have been run upon if this family had not been a family.

Hazel felt a fierce magnetic pull toward her mom and Cam and the twins. She understood them. She understood the life they had built with her. For her.

She couldn't be mad or sad about her parents' choices. Not at all. They had wanted this family so bad and they'd got it.

Family was the most important thing. Love was the most important thing.

And this family, this love, was the life that they worked for. This was what they wanted to wake up with. This was what they wanted to go to sleep to. This was the air they wanted to breathe. And who was Hazel to say that wanting this family and this love was wrong?

She could never say that. This family, this love, was perfect.

Hazel pressed her eyelids together and inhaled, trying to hold tears back. But they found their way out at the corners and streamed down her cheeks. She could taste the salt on her lips. Her purposeful breath turned choppy and her heart ached. Oh, her heart ached. But she knew that this was the feeling of it healing.

A flood of relief coursed through her. It was time to go home. And this, the people in this car, was home.

Hazel looked at her mom in the front seat, Cam's hand on

her thigh. She looked at the twins on either side of her, kicking and cooing. Hazel felt a new confidence, a self-assuredness, strength flow through her, and just placed the phone next to her without an answer.

The car ride was full of the best kind of quiet. Hours next to one another in silence without a single drop of tension. The world felt right again.

This was what it meant to be a sister, a daughter, a stepdaughter, a husband, a wife, Hazel thought to herself. It was the feeling of unexpected, boundless, soaring, unconditional tenderness for someone, when all circumstances might predict otherwise. The knot that had lived in her stomach for so many years untangled. She looked into the rearview mirror and caught her mother's eye. Hazel couldn't see her mouth in the mirror, but she could tell by the squint of Jane's eyes that she was smiling. And then, her mother's voice rang out through the car.

"Sleep little baby," Jane said. And Hazel replied.
"Clean as a nut."
"Your fingers uncurl," Jane continued.
"And your eyes are shut," Hazel continued some more.

And they recited the entire poem, leapfrogging each other's words, re-intertwining their stories. Reminding themselves that they were connected in ways that could only be felt. She knew that Silas and Eve, and even Susie and Torrey, had found that, too. And she was grateful for it all. Mothers and daughters and fathers and sons and lovers were all home. They were all finally home.

★ ★ ★ ★ ★

THAT SUMMER IN MAINE

BRIANNA WOLFSON

READER'S GUIDE

1. Which character do you identify with most? Why?

2. Does this book have an uplifting or tragic ending? Do some characters have a happier ending than others?

3. What do you think about Jane's decision to let Hazel go visit Silas? Susie's?

4. If the book were told from Silas's perspective, what more do you think we would have learned? Eve's?

5. In what ways are Hazel's and Eve's stories the same? Different?

6. How would this story look different if Hazel and Eve were five years younger?

7. Do you or anyone in your life have experience discovering a biological sibling they hadn't known about? What was that like?

8. Hazel wants so badly to be more connected to those around her. Do you think she was running away from something or running toward something? How do you know?

9. Silas's house is almost like another character in the book. How does the setting enhance the book?

10. Do you like or dislike Silas? Is he a good or bad father figure?

11. What role do you think the twins play in Hazel's story?

12. How would you characterize Eve's relationship to Silas? To Hazel? To her mother? How are Eve's relationships different than Hazel's relationships?

13. What is the significance of the notebook for Jane and Susie?

14. What does this book suggest about the nature and trajectory of motherhood? Daughterhood? Fatherhood?

15. If there were a sequel to this book, what would the plot be?

16. Hazel finds herself at one of her lowest points while at the market. What do you think was really going on there?

17. What are the important symbols in the book? What do they represent?

What inspired you to write this novel?

I think, write and talk to others a lot about family dynamics. (This is the center of my debut novel, Rosie Colored Glasses, too.) The topic of meeting biological parents is one that comes up again and again. This is especially true lately with the availability of genetic testing and online communities that connect genetic relatives. So many people I know and have talked to are using these genetic tools and finding new family members, and I'm always interested in how these stories go. I'm specifically interested in how others weigh nature versus nurture in these relationships. I have some nonbiological family members of my own (stepsiblings and stepparents) whom I deeply adore, so it's a topic near to my own story, as well.

How would you describe your writing process?

I do my best to write every day! I think of writing like I think of exercising: it's much easier once it's a habit. And once I've gotten out the door and in front of my laptop or into the gym, I may surprise myself with what I can do!

What are you working on now?

I'm always working on projects related to family dynamics, some narrative nonfiction based on my experiences and some fiction. What family stories are you interested in seeing? Get in touch at briannawolfson.com.